SHADOWS OF A TUSCAN MOON

A Novel

SANDRA CARRINGTON-SMITH
&
GIOVANNI LOGLI

This book is dedicated to men and women in our community who suffer in silence.

We would like to thank everyone who has supported the conception and creation of this book. Our friends, families, and everyone in the community who has come to our aid with information, feedback, and support – we thank you from the bottom of our hearts.

PROLOGUE

I wish I could say my brain is in a fog, because it would mean that ghosts from my elusive world are still dancing beyond the soupy thickness. Instead, I see nothing and I feel nothing, as if the hard drive of my mind was wiped clean, with only emptiness left behind. I have been awake for a while, though I don't know if it has been minutes or hours. My eyelids feel heavy, and I crave the memory of something familiar to help me make sense of this void, but thoughts slip away before I can catch them, as grains of sand spilling through dry fingers. I have been listening for sounds outside my door since I woke up, but I hear none. Is anybody even out there? The blind on the window is drawn, but sunlight filters through, and I wonder what I will see if I look outside. I push off the covers and sit for a moment at the edge of the bed, delighted to feel the cool floor beneath my feet. I wiggle my toes and run my fingers over the sheets, as I look around and take in the whole of the room. My bed is one of three pieces of furniture. The other two are a small white nightstand, and a small table with a matching chair. There are no pictures hanging on the white walls, nor is any medical equipment tucked away behind faux decorations, strategically placed to give patients the illusion they are in a hotel room instead of a medical setting. Is this a hospital room? What is this place? I stand up and walk toward the window, determined to see if I recognize anything outside of these walls, eager to find something I know, and terrified that I will be disappointed if I look. I see a folder laid out on the table, and my heart skips a beat. Is that my medical chart? Maybe if I see my name, memories of my life will come back to me. My legs tremble a bit as I reach for the folder with shaky hands, but

5

when I open it all I see are three clean pieces of white paper. I feel anger rising from the pit of my stomach and tears burning my eyes. As though impelled, I grab the folder, crumple it between my hands, and fling it across the room…just as the door opens, and a woman walks in.

"Good morning, you are up finally." A plump woman dressed in powder blue scrubs enters the room and closes the door. "You have slept for several days, dear. How are you feeling?"

I scan the details of her appearance, hoping for memories, but I am sure this is the first time I have ever seen this woman. Her eyes are the color of amber and set far apart, and her facial structure is round, framed by a cascade of soft, caramel curls that make her look like a middle-aged doll. I sigh deeply, and as I inhale, I detect a faint scent of gardenia emanating from the woman and hovering around her like an aura. "Where am I? Is this a hospital?"

"Yes, dear," she says, as she strolls briskly toward the window and opens the blind. A wave of sunlight washes into the room, bringing to life tiny specks of dust floating in the air.

"Why can't I remember anything?" I ask impatiently. "I don't even know what my name is."

"I wish I could help you remember, but unfortunately, I don't know what your name is—none of us does. The doctor will come to see you shortly; maybe he can help."

"Well, what is your name, then?"

"My name is Elena, and I am one of the aides here."

"Elena. I like that. It fits you."

Elena smiles, still standing by the window. "Well, come on, then. Let's get you dressed. There is a change of clothes in the cabinet in the bathroom."

I follow her into the bathroom, and watch her produce a set of clothing from a folded bag tucked into the cabinet. "Are those my clothes?" I ask, hopeful.

Elena just smiles sweetly. "They are now, dear. I am quite sure they are your size."

"Yes, but are they *my* clothes? Is this what I was wearing when I got to this place?"

"I don't know, sweetheart. I was instructed to give these to you, but I was not told where they came from, or what you wore when you arrived. As I said, hopefully the doctor can provide some answers to your questions. I will step outside while you change. Let me know if you need any help." With those words, Elena exits the bathroom, leaving me once again alone with my thoughts. I look forward to meeting this doctor and getting some answers, as — apparently — he is the keeper of knowledge in this place. I strip off my gown and slip into the blue sweat suit Elena left on top of the cabinet. I can't remember if these clothes were ever mine, but at least I like the color. I wonder if I have access to a brush and maybe a toothbrush. I open the bathroom door and call out for Elena.

"Elena, do you know where I can find a toothbrush and some toothpaste? And, if I am not asking for too much, a brush or a comb for my hair?"

Elena is changing my bed, but she lifts her head immediately when she hears my voice and turns in my direction. "Yes, dear. Open the top drawer of the cabinet. Everything you need is in there. There is also a pair of shoes, in the small compartment underneath the drawers."

I find the items I need and, within minutes, am ready to meet the doctor, so I step out of the bathroom and march resolutely toward the table by the window, to sit on the chair and wait for him. I don't have to wait long. As soon as I sit, I hear a knock on the door and a tall, slim man walks in. His hair is thin on the top, and he wears a white shirt with no tie and a pair of black pants. I can't really see his eyes too clearly behind the dark-framed glasses resting on the bridge of his nose, but I think they are blue. He strolls towards me with a smile pasted on his face and his right hand extended, ready to shake my own.

"Hello. It is very nice to finally see you awake. My name is Dr. Castelli and I have been following you since you arrived."

I shake his hand, and I am ready to fire questions. "I am glad to meet you, doctor. Elena has been very helpful but she doesn't have any answers for me, and I am hoping that maybe you can help me remember. What is my name, and why am I here?"

Dr. Castelli flashes a fatherly smile. "I wish I could help you with that, my dear. Unfortunately, you came to us in a state of confusion, and we were unable to determine what led you here."

I could feel frustration edging up again. "But who brought me here? And what is this place?" I am close to tears.

"I suppose you could say we are a retreat of sorts. People come to us when they need to heal and figure out where they are going next. You came in on your own; nobody brought you here."

"So, this is like a mental hospital?"

"Not quite, but it is okay if you see it that way. You will meet other patients who are also struggling to remember, and others who are trying to develop different types of coping skills. Some of our patients have lived through extremely traumatic experiences and they are working through them, but you will hear their stories directly from them, during group therapy. Maybe listening to what they say will help you remember your own events. You see, when a person experiences something extremely traumatic, their mind sometimes chooses to hide those memories, to avoid going through the same pain again. I believe that's what happened to you. Whatever happened was bad enough for your mind to shut itself down."

"Will I ever remember again?" I am almost in a panic.

"It depends on what you will allow yourself to accept. You might gradually come to remember everything, you might only remember parts of it, or you might choose to remember none of it. Only time will tell." Dr. Castelli's tone is calm and matter-of-fact.

"How can I choose that?"

"You don't. You can only become stronger and learn to accept that certain things happen. When you reach that point, your subconscious will probably send out a sample, to see how you deal with it. If you can handle it, then it will send out increasingly larger amounts of information." Dr. Castelli looks directly into my eyes. "Part of becoming stronger is to understand that you oversee how things will work out from any given moment on. Once you have a plan, events will take place and your choices will dictate the direction things will be moving. You always have a choice, even when you think you don't."

I nod at the doctor's words, but not a single syllable escapes my lips. I wish I knew what happened, I wish I knew if I have a family, parents, a husband, children, friends. I feel alone; displaced. Apparently, I am a prisoner of my own making.

Dr. Castelli sighs deeply. "Well, I must be off to see some other patients. Will you join us in the meeting room in ten minutes? We will have coffee and pastries, and then we will start our daily group therapy."

"Of course. How will I find the meeting room?"

"Take a right outside your door and come to the end of the hallway. It is the last door on your left."

With that he was gone, leaving me alone with even more questions than I had before.

CHAPTER ONE

"Please come in." Dr. Castelli's voice is calm and welcoming when I enter the room. Six women are mingling and talking with each other, all standing near a table at the far end of the room, and they automatically turn to look at me when they hear the doctor speak. I feel a little self-conscious about introducing myself, since I don't even have a name, but I take a deep breath and make my way toward the gathering.

"Hi! Thank you for joining us," one woman chimes in. "Don't be nervous. I was unnerved myself, the first day I came to a group meeting, but we are all friends here. It won't take you long to get to know everybody."

I nod with a smile, and study her for a moment. She has long, black hair, and her olive complexion is blemish-free. She is probably just a little over five feet tall, with a medium build, and her smile appears sincere. She extends her hand and waits for me to shake it. "My name is Giulia. It's great to meet you."

"Hi, Giulia. I don't know my name, but it is nice to meet you, too," I reply a bit awkwardly.

Giulia smiles knowingly. A shadow of sadness darts across her eyes, but vanishes as quickly as it had appeared. "Yes, I struggled with my own identity, too, when I first arrived. But, they prefer that we choose a new name here, anyway. It helps with recovery. Dr. Castelli explained that assuming a new persona creates a distance between ourselves and the pain we have experienced, and it makes it safe to remember. I really liked the name Giulia, so that's the one I picked, and I think it fits me. Is there a name you like particularly?"

"I am not sure…"

Giulia reassures me as soon as she feels my hesitation. "Don't worry about it now, you'll think of something. Let me introduce you to Rita, Gina, Arianna, Romina, and Olivia. We all came here looking for answers. As you will hear from our stories, once we begin our group meeting, we all share similar situations, and we find strength in identifying our past suffering with one another. The worst feeling one can experience is to be alone, to feel like no one understands. Knowing that other women have gone through similar ordeals really helped me put things into perspective."

The first woman steps forward and, rather than shaking my hand, she hugs me tightly. I am not sure what her name is, since Giulia mentioned all their names at once, but it feels good to hold someone, and for a second I don't want to let go.

"I am glad you could join us" she says. "Giulia is right. I, for one, came here with a very dark outlook on things, and I gather now that I was just really scared, but once I realized it wasn't just me — that other women know what I went through because they also lived through similar events — I was suddenly able to look at my own situation without shame. I have come a long way since I arrived."

"How long have you been here?" I am a little hesitant to ask, but I am fishing for something to say.

The woman laughs heartily. "I am not sure. I once asked Dr. Castelli why we don't have clocks or calendars anywhere in the facility. He told me that keeping track of time adds stress, because one feels pressured to achieve certain milestones within time frames, and it is best to just focus on healing instead of keeping logs. But, if I had to guess, I would say that I have probably been here a few weeks. It feels that way, at least. And my name is Romina, by the way. I am sure that hearing all our names at once made it a little confusing for you."

I suddenly like this woman, and I am grateful she told me her name before I had to ask. There is something about her appearance that puts me at ease. She looks unpretentious, with shoulder-length brown hair, brown eyes framed by glasses, and a slightly chubby build. I am unsure of how old I am, but at first look, we appear to be about the same age: mid-thirties, early forties at most. Her smile is friendly and contagious, and I find myself smiling back at her, exhilarated by the instant connection.

One of the other women smiles timidly and approaches to hug me as well, but just as her hand touches my arm, Dr. Castelli's voice preempts her greeting, and she retreats gracefully. "If you ladies are ready, we might as well begin."

I follow the other women to a circle of chairs in the middle of the room, and sit beside Romina. The others take a seat and wait quietly for the doctor to start.

"Good morning, ladies. I hope you are all doing well this morning. We have a new member in our group, who arrived here in a state of confusion. She doesn't remember who she is or what happened to her, and she can benefit from these sessions to regain a sense of identity. Have you thought of a name you would like yet?" The doctor's question suddenly turns the spotlight on me, and I shift nervously in my seat.

"I haven't really given it much thought. In all honesty, all of this is still a bit surreal. I feel like a child who was just born, and now I must pick a name to write on the birth certificate. Will I be able to change my name back once I remember my real one?"

Dr. Castelli nods softly. "It will be up to you. You are the only person in charge of your own life."

"Okay…let's see…I feel like I should open up. Flowers open when the light of the sun warms them, and they know the time is right to unfold. I will call myself Rosa. Hopefully it will prove a good omen.

The circle of women nod, welcoming my suggestion. "I like that! Roses are beautiful," says the woman two chairs to my right. She has short, light blond hair, dark eyes, a beautiful smile and, somehow, the impish gleam in her eyes reminds me of a mischievous tomboy. She appears to be around 45 or 50 years of age, dressed in a pink sweatshirt and jeans.

As I scan the faces around me, all I see is kindness. I don't know what led these women here yet. Whatever it was, though, they all seem to be at peace now, connected by a common thread of soul survival, and — although they are perfect strangers — I feel linked to them. I want to pick their brains, see if anything they have seen or done can trigger a memory of my own; but I know I must be patient and, as Dr. Castelli explained, give myself time to recall my life gradually. I will be happy when I can at least remember something. Anything.

"I really like Rosa, also." Dr. Castelli says. with his usual fatherly smile. "Well, let's get started by introducing ourselves. Giulia, I noticed that you took the lead in welcoming Rosa when she first came into the room. Would you like to start?"

"Certainly." Giulia places her notebook and pen on the floor and crosses her legs, as she relaxes against the chair. "Let's see, where should I start?" She purses her lips as if absorbed in deep thought for a moment. "Yes…my name, as I said, is Giulia. I have decided I am not going to use my old name any longer, because doing so would only bring me back to my old reality. I used to be married to a man I thought was the epitome of masculinity and charm. He was strong and imposing, and he always made me feel like he was in charge. I didn't really have a problem with that—my family is from the south, and historically, men are the dominating figure in a family structure. I don't even know when my husband's assertiveness morphed into abuse; it was such a gradual shift that I was taken completely unawares. Lots happened, and eventually things got worse, but I will tell you more in detail later. Regardless, I am here now, and I am at peace." Giulia pauses and smiles, then looks at the woman beside her. "Gina, would you like to take it from here?"

Gina nods and tucks a lock of blond, shoulder-length hair behind her ear. When she looks at me, I notice a hint of sadness in her soft blue eyes. She is wearing an olive green, short-sleeved shirt and a white skirt to her knee; the only jewelry she sports is a pair of tiny diamond studs on her lobes. Gina looks a bit older than the rest of the crowd, and her demeanor and appearance make me think of a teacher.

"My name is Gina; my story is different from the others, but the common denominator is that I allowed another person to crush my body and my soul. I believe now that the reason I didn't see it coming is because I, like many others, had come to think it was normal to be treated like an object. I felt uneasy about the attention I was receiving, but I hid those feelings from everyone: my family, my close friends, my students."

Students?! So, she really is a teacher?

"I wanted everyone to believe I had a good life and a handle on things. I couldn't stand the thought of being pitied by anyone, or for any of my friends to see me as weak or vulnerable. Now I think I should have handled things differently, but unfortunately what happened cannot be undone." Gina touches the corner of her left eye as if to stop a tear from escaping. Whatever she went through is obviously still affecting her emotionally. She is quiet after that, and for a moment, the pain she is experiencing impregnates the air.

One of the other women takes the cue, breaking the wall of silence. She is petite and blond, with her hair cut short. Her hazel eyes are warm, and she smiles frequently. "Hi, Rosa. My name is Arianna, and I believe I am one of the veteran residents here. I came a long time ago, and although I feel completely healed, I have decided to stay and help others on their path of recovery. The life I had before is gone — one can never go back to trusting blindly again — so I accepted my new identity and asked the doctors if I could just continue living here, as a support to other women who have undergone similar experiences."

From the corner of my eye, I notice one of the other women nodding while Arianna speaks, and I wonder if her story is similar to the one I am about to hear. I nod as well, silently encouraging Arianna to continue.

"As I was saying," Arianna continues softly, "I arrived here unsure of what to do, and almost literally eating myself up with anger and fear. My life was quite ordinary and, in its own way, happy, until my world came crashing down when I began to suspect my husband might have a lover. I dismissed the thought at first, unwilling to accept that the person I slept beside every night, the man who fathered my son and had promised to be true to me until death did us part, would be choosing to destroy everything we had. I pretended not to see; I forced myself to stay busy, and not think about the times he was late coming home from work. But at night, when I lay there in the darkness unable to find sleep, my mind worked overtime. By then, no matter how hard I tried to fight the little green monster, the seed of jealousy was planted and being fertilized by my husband's dismissive attitude. Sometimes we would argue more intensely, and he would become defensive, but then he would tell me that it was all in my head and that he loved me. We would go a few days with barely a few words exchanged between us, then he would approach me saying something nice or bringing me a bouquet of flowers, and we would kiss and make up. At times, I even believed he might be right, that my mind was constructing scenarios that didn't take place. I wanted to believe him — for myself and for my son — so I would accept his excuses and life would go on, until one day when I couldn't resist going through the log on his cellular phone. There I found a number for someone whom he called — and who called him — regularly, but I was sure that number didn't belong to anyone we both knew. I asked my son's girlfriend to call the number from her phone, confiding in her my worry. She called the number and a woman answered, so she hung up. All the fear and all the doubts that I had kept locked in my heart erupted into a stream of raw anger. I started checking his phone regularly. As I suspected, the calls from the mysterious number continued, usually followed by his absence from home with one excuse or another. My jealousy continued to grow until it almost blinded me, and I became increasingly unsettled. Suddenly, I could see the man I had known for all those years and that I still, unbelievably, loved, with clear vision. I confronted him several times, always hoping that he would hug me tightly and tell me it wasn't true, but I soon realized I was holding onto a fantasy that would never manifest. His betrayal left me scarred and bitter, and I tried everything I could to change how the future would unfold. I contacted his lover, and begged her to leave him alone, but instead of saving my marriage, that decision proved to be a catalyst for disaster."

I am so enthralled by Arianna's story that I hadn't even realized I was holding my breath while she spoke. My heart aches for her, and I instinctively wipe a tear that has run down my cheek. I turn to look at the woman who was nodding before, and see that she, too, appears shaken. She stares ahead without focusing, apparently reliving painful images of her own. Her deep blue eyes are laden with fresh pain, and I wonder how recent her story is. Dr. Castelli seems to have read my mind, and he addresses her softly, just as the woman sitting beside her picks up her hand and holds it in her own. "Olivia," he says gently, "try to breathe. Remember, what you are seeing is a ghost of Christmas past."

Olivia shakes her head and closes her eyes for a moment, as if to ward off the memories that seized her. "Yes, doctor, I am sorry. It is just that Arianna and I have lived such parallel lives that when I hear her story, I am suddenly plunged into facing my own. There are still a lot of holes in my memory, and sometimes I think it would be easier if I never fully find out what happened."

"We have talked about this, Olivia. Covering up painful memories is a temporary coping skill, but to fully heal you must gradually face every shadow." The doctor's voice is soothing but firm, and I watch Olivia's face relax a little.

"I know," Olivia responds, her attention once again in the present moment. "It's just that oblivion is kinder sometimes. It's hard to think back about those I love, and know they are hurting because of me. I feel somehow responsible for their pain."

"You shouldn't!" We all turn toward the woman who nearly screamed, and she clears her throat in embarrassment. I noticed her earlier, when I first entered the room, and now I am taken aback by the passion she pours into reassuring her friend. Anger has infused her cheeks with a reddish tinge, and her dark eyes appear like two pools of melted tar, their dark color a stark contrast to the near-white blond hair. She no longer looks like a mischievous young boy, but rather like a tigress ready to pounce on the demons still lurking in the back of Olivia's mind.

"I am sorry for interrupting, Olivia," she says, with a much more controlled voice and a motherly tone, "I certainly didn't mean to yell at you. It's just that I have felt what you feel, and I know how easy it is to assume responsibility for those who were hurt indirectly by the actions that made us victims. You did not hurt those you love: Someone else hurt you, and them."

Olivia smiles at her, not necessarily surprised but surely comforted by her friend's passionate support. "I understand, Rita. Sometimes it is easy to forget I was the victim. I heard for so long how I was the one causing the turmoil that I guess, after a while, I came to believe it. Rationally, I know I am not responsible…but my soul is still wounded, and I am still holding onto the pain."

I just want to cry. I don't know if the reason stems from the sadness I feel for these women and the horror of what happened to them, or if I am just overwhelmed by the raw love I can sense flowing between them. I want to stand up and give them all a hug, I want to tell them they will be okay, and even if I am lost right now, I still believe love overcomes everything, and we can all heal together.

We can all heal together…where is this thought coming from? I feel something tugging at the edge of my soul, like a small child pulling his mother's shirt to get her attention. I try to focus on the feeling, but it's already gone.

"Would you like to share your story with Rosa, Olivia?" Dr. Castelli urges gently.

"I think I need a little more time, Dr. Castelli. Rosa is new, and my story is little different from Arianna's. The only difference is the number of children we have. I have a fifteen-year-old boy and a ten-year-old girl." Olivia's face softens as images of her children's faces flood her mind, and she closes her eyes to hold onto them for a moment. My heart breaks for her. I don't know if I have any children of my own, or what happened to hers, but I know there is a powerful bond between a mother and her offspring, one that neither time nor man can break.

Dr. Castelli smiles reassuringly. "Of course. You know there is no rush, and no pre-set timetable. You can share your story with Rosa when you feel comfortable."

I can see the anxiety on Olivia's face melt away as the doctor's words settle in. "I will. I promise" she says, her eyes clear again and set directly on me. "I am glad you are here with us, Rosa. If I can help in any way, please let me know."

Rita jumps in again. "I haven't really shared my story yet either, but we are nearing the end of our session, and I know Romina hasn't spoken yet. All I will say is that I, too, experienced domestic abuse, both physical and emotional. The physical scars healed, while the emotional ones still linger in my soul. I have one daughter whom I love dearly, and a great deal of pain was caused to her, but I have come to understand I wasn't the one who should feel guilty for hurting my daughter. The weight of that responsibility belongs to my ex-husband, though I doubt he will ever be man enough to own it. You see, there is another thing I have learned: We are all victims of victims. A whole individual thrives on making others happy; it is the broken ones who become selfish enough to steal another person's happiness. I have forgiven and, like Gina, I am here mostly to offer support. Someday, when we have more time, I will share details of my story. Until then, please know you are among friends who understand."

Dr. Castelli thanks Rita and turns to face Romina. "Would you like to add anything to today's conversation, Romina?"

"We are out of time, doctor. Rosa and I met when she first came in, and I am sure we will have plenty of time to talk and share."

"Very well, then," the doctor says. "I guess we are done for today. Rosa, I will have one of the aides bring a copy of the schedule to your room. Rest for a while, and maybe a little later one of the other girls can show you our recreation room. It's quite fun."

I feel a knot in my throat and can only nod. As the group begins to disassemble, I stand and head toward the door without saying anything. I can feel them staring at me, and it makes me feel self-conscious, so I straighten my back and inhale deeply to maintain my composure. I have just turned the corner and headed down the hallway back to my room, when I hear the whisper of a child. I look around but I don't see anyone. And then I hear it again. *Mommy, mommy! Make him stop!*

CHAPTER TWO

My lungs feel like they are going to explode, but I can't stop running or he will catch up with me. Where is he? Is he getting closer? The wheezing in my chest sounds like a bicycle tire losing air, my ears are ringing over the pounding of my heart, and I wonder how long it will be before I pass out or die. Maybe dying would be the easy way out, maybe I should let him catch up with me and give up the fight. What caused his anger to flare this time? What did I say or do that set him off? I don't hear him anymore, but that doesn't mean he isn't still behind me. It's daytime, but the sky is overcast, so I don't even know what time it is. I can hear the voice of a television host in the distance and, in my mind, I see a family sitting together in the living room, enjoying a program. Why can't I be part of that family? Why me? What have I done to deserve this — the violence, the menacing words, the fear? The wind is picking up, the cold air slicing through the thin fabric of my shirt, and I shake uncontrollably, unable to determine if it is the temperature or fear that causes me to shiver. I instinctively wrap my arms around myself and draw a deep breath to calm down. I can't be out here for long without proper clothing or food, and I understand I will, at some point, need to go back home and face his wrath. Maybe I can give him a little time to settle down, maybe he will have some time to think things over and realize his reaction was over the top, and whatever I did, maybe he will forgive me and all will be well. I need to stay away for just a little longer, and then I will be safe. For now I will just stay here and think of what I will say to him when I get back.

I hear a loud banging and a wave of panic erupts from the depths of my soul to flood my mind.

"Rosa, are you awake?"

I open my eyes…and it takes me a moment to figure out I am in my room at the clinic. Someone is knocking on the door. "Rosa? It's Romina. Are you in here?"

I jump out of bed, my muscles loose from the deep sleep, and, still unsettled by the dream, I hurry to open the door.

"Oh, you are here. I thought maybe you had gone for a walk. I have knocked a couple of times and you didn't answer, so I was about to leave."

"Sorry about that, Romina. I must have fallen asleep when I got back from the group meeting. I don't even know why I was tired, since, apparently, I have slept away the last few days." I grin, hoping that Romina will not detect the anxiety I feel.

"Well," she says gingerly, "I would like to show you the recreation room, in case you get bored and you need something to do to pass time."

"Sure, why not? I can't spend my entire life sleeping, can I?" I respond too quickly and too eagerly, and for a moment I wonder if it is obvious that I am nervous, but Romina doesn't seem to notice and strolls toward the chair by the window to take a seat.

"So, what did you think of the group therapy session?" She inquires nonchalantly.

I shrug. "I'm not sure yet. It was nice to meet everyone, and it was kind of sad to hear the stories, but it was also inspiring to witness the spirit of communion among all. It was nearly overwhelming to feel how much you care about one another. I just wish I could remember some of my own story."

Romina smiles. "Yes, it feels like a warm blanket, doesn't it? It will take a few days for you to feel comfortable around us, and to begin your own healing process. Have you remembered anything at all yet? From hearing our stories, I mean."

"No, not really. When I left the therapy room I thought I heard the voice of a child, but of course, there was no child there. I didn't see anything in my mind that could give me a clue, so I am assuming it was, maybe, just an auditory illusion?"

Romina lifts her left brow in surprise. "A child? We definitely don't have any children as residents here, so it could be, as you say, an auditory illusion, or maybe it is a memory that's surfacing."

"I'm not sure."

"What did the child say?"

"He said…" Panic suddenly grips my stomach like a talon, and I suck in my breath. "I don't know. I couldn't make out any words, it was just a whisper." I turn my back to Romina and inhale as silently as I can to regain my composure. What just happened? Why did I lie?

"Are you okay, Rosa?" Romina inquires when I continue to stare away from her.

"Yes…yes, of course. I am ready when you are."

Romina stands gingerly and heads toward the door. "We will go through the garden to get to the recreation room. The mimosa is just blooming and it is spectacular."

We take the elevator down two floors, and I am amazed to see what appears to be a hotel lobby when the doors open. The light coming through the glass door reflects on the marble floor and rests on a large plant by the desk. Hunting scenes dominate the theme of most of the pictures hanging on the wall, aside from one that depicts a face. Half of the face is shielded by a grill, perceiving reality from the window of a prison cell, while the other half is free to view things as they are. I find this picture quite intriguing, and I pause in front of it to inspect it further, wondering about my own perspective when I look at the world. Do I see things as they are, or is my perception changed by the confines of my experiences?

"It's an interesting concept, isn't it?" Romina asks, suddenly by my side. I hadn't heard her walking up behind me.

"Yes. It's disturbing in some ways. It makes one wonder if what we see is really how things are, or if what we perceive is somehow altered by what we live through."

"That's a concept we have discussed at length with Dr. Castelli. According to him, fear makes us prisoners of ourselves, and it changes how we process what we see. He told us of a study that was done on rats, not too long ago. A group of rats was placed in jars filled halfway with water, and scientists timed how long it would take for the rats to drown. Most rats only fought for about fifteen minutes before succumbing to their fate, but if, after scrambling for safety for nearly that long, they were pulled out to safety and then placed in water again at a later time, they were able to survive several hours. The researchers understood that the first time we are exposed to a scary situation, we instantly panic and focus on getting away, but the next time we are exposed to it, we use information we have learned from the previous experience to increase our likelihood of survival. The first time around, fear incapacitates us, and it makes it nearly impossible to think rationally and get out. I guess it would be equal to seeing the world around us from a self-imposed prison we cannot escape. The second time, we know that we have the skills to survive for a brief period of time, so rather than cowering and surrendering, we rely on what we know to avoid panicking, and to increase our chances of survival. I suppose, in that case, we could identify with the side of the face that sees danger for what it is, but is not being kept captive by fear."

I take in what Romina is saying and nod, though I don't really agree with her. I think the face means something different altogether, and so does the study Dr. Castelli related, but I don't really have the time to reflect on it right now, and I prefer to not delve into a philosophical discussion at a time when I can't really think straight.

We pass the desk and I notice the man behind it nodding in our direction, so I smile at him before we reach the door. The man appears to be in his late fifties, with short, curly, salt-and-pepper hair, and a tanned complexion. He has warm brown eyes, the shade of milk chocolate, and he looks distinct in his blue uniform, even if he is not very tall. I wonder if he is a security guard, or maybe a concierge, and I make a mental note to ask someone.

We don't exit through the front entrance, instead going through a smaller door on its right. We follow a breezeway, which spills into a garden that is fenced in by a six-foot wall, and I catch my breath at the beauty that suddenly ambushes us. There are rows of fruit trees symmetrically planted, their vibrant leaves swaying gently in the afternoon breeze, and on the left I see a pathway, edged by bright flowers, leading to a maze.

A faded image takes shape in my mind, and I see myself approaching the entrance of a corn maze. My heart suddenly jumps as I stop and try hard to focus, but the image is gone as quickly as it had appeared. "Do you ever walk the maze?" I ask Romina.

"I have. Dr. Castelli says that walking the maze helps us figure out things by expanding the pathways in our minds," she replies.

"Well, does it work?" I ask, genuinely curious.

"I think so. I am still looking for new paths."

"To remember?"

"To forgive."

I raise my eyebrow at her answer, but I don't know if I should ask who or what she needs to forgive. We have literally just met, and from the little information about these women that I gathered at the meeting, they all have been through some serious ordeals. I don't want to pry unless necessary, so I decide to spin the conversation in a different direction.

"Do you have any children, Romina?"

I watch quietly, as a shadow of pain scurries over Romina's face, quickly replaced by a loving smile.

"Yes, I have one girl and three boys. My girl is the oldest, and she makes me very proud. She is not like other teenagers, you know? She has a good heart, and she is a good role model for her younger brothers."

"How old are your boys?"

"They are six, nine, and eleven. They are good kids, too. Boys will be boys, but like their sister, they have good hearts and stand by the truth."

"Do they ever visit you here?"

"No, children aren't allowed here, but I go visit them from time to time."

Her reply surprises me a little, and although I don't want to pressure her, curiosity gets the best of me. "When do you think you will leave this place?"

Romina stops a moment to reflect. She kneels to pick up a sprig of rosemary, brings it up to her nose, and inhales deeply. "I'm not sure yet. As I said, there are things I still need to work on, but I keep tabs on the kids, and go visit them sometimes, to make sure they are doing well." She hands the sprig of rosemary to me, and I bring it up to my own nose to breathe in the scent.

"Do you know that rosemary is said to aid in strengthening the memory? One of my teachers told me once that I should keep rosemary nearby when I study, because it would lock in what I was learning."

"Really? I didn't know that but I am extremely interested, given that I have no memory of anything and I would gladly eat an entire bush of it, if it could help."

"That's what my teacher said, at least. I never really tried."

We walk toward a small line of olive trees and I am suddenly reminded of something I read somewhere, of a man walking through an olive garden, but I can't really remember anything else from that story, so I am about to dismiss it when I suddenly remember it is a scene from the Bible. I am pleased to remember *something*, though I doubt that remembering a religious passage will help me remember anything about my actual life.

"Here we are. The recreation room is inside that building." She points to a square construction with cream-colored stucco walls. The windows are covered by green venetian blinds that open externally, and I notice a small balcony directly above the front entrance. *Romeo and Juliet*...I smile, excited by my progress. Remembering the books I have read might not be a lot, but it is still something, and I hope that, as Dr. Castelli says, I will soon recall more.

We enter the building and turn right beyond the foyer, into a hallway bejeweled with doors on each side. Most of the doors are closed, but I follow Romina past them, and we come to a room with open double doors. This room stands out from among the rest, with bright yellow walls and large windows ushering in a great amount of natural light. I notice four or five stations set up for different activities, and I am immediately attracted by the painting corner, where blank canvas and a multitude of painting supplies are stacked neatly on a table adjacent to an easel.

"Do you like art?" Romina asks as she leans on the supply table.

"I do. I don't know if I have ever painted, but I would like to try."

"We also have a reading area, a quilting corner, and a movie theater." She says proudly.

"Do we have access to the Internet?"

"No, I'm afraid not. Do you see those hills out there in the distance?" she points at the mountains in the distance that are visible through the window. "Our clinic is tucked in the middle of a handful of hills, and we can't get a good signal. Also, Dr. Castelli says that we need to focus on healing, not on worrying over the craziness that takes place in the outside world. He thinks that it is human nature to concern ourselves with things we have no control over, and believes we don't need to expose our minds to anything negative while we are here." Romina explains quickly.

"It makes sense, I guess. What is your favorite activity here?"

"I really like quilting. I love matching patches of material into a pattern and working them together into something pretty. I think that's therapeutic in its own way."

Romina's words make me think of a Kintsugi vase I have seen before, crafted from broken pieces held together by gold. Kintsugi is a form of Japanese art symbolizing that beauty can be found in broken things. "Yes, I can certainly see how quilting would be therapeutic. "Where do the scraps of material come from?"

"They are cut from the clothes we come in here with. It's part of the healing process."

I look at Romina questioningly — our clothes are used for quilting? Are they donated willingly, or are they taken without our permission after we arrive?

"That's odd. Are my clothes in there, too?" I ask.

"I don't know. What were you wearing when you arrived?"

"I honestly don't remember. I don't remember coming here at all."

Romina dismisses my uncertainty, and leads the way to the quilting area. There are three other women sitting at the table, talking among themselves, but they are not part of our group and I don't believe I have seen them before.

"Who are those women?"

"They are residents in a different department, but we all share the same recreation room. They don't have any trouble with their memory; they had different types of accidents."

"What sort of accidents? I ask, my attention piqued.

"I'm not really sure," Romina replies, as she opens a large tub filled with patches of material and starts sorting through it. She picks out a few of the patches and lays them out on the table to show me. "What do you think of this pattern?"

I inspect the pieces of material and shrug. "It looks nice, I guess."

"I can show you how to quilt, if you want."

"Sure." Quilting does not sound like my cup of tea, but Romina seems so excited about it that I don't want to ruin her moment.

She lays a large piece of satin material on the table and pulls out a sizeable amount of stuffing from a bag. "You place the fluff between two layers of satin and sew them together. The product we use is cotton, but I know my grandmother used to use wool as well, because it retains more heat, and makes for a better quilt to use in the winter. Once you have prepared the base, you sew the patches in a pattern of your choice."

"That's great. I have never tried, but I am pretty sure I wouldn't have the patience for it. I am more in tune with technology, I think, and that's why I was asking about the Internet."

"Technology is half the reason why I am here," Romina says, softly. This time, sadness lingers on her face.

"What happened?" I ask without thinking, regretting my words as soon as they escape my lips.

"I used the Internet to meet friends," she replies without looking at me, seemingly busy aligning the second piece of satin over the stuffing material.

"What's wrong with meeting friends?" I nudge timidly.

"Nothing, unless you are married to my former husband."

"Was he jealous of the people you met?"

"You could say that. He wasn't completely wrong, you know? I wasn't always faithful to him, even when we were just engaged. It was a stupid fling I had, and no more incidents until much later in the marriage." Romina's eyes are fixed on the fabric in front of her.

"It takes two people to make a marriage work, Romina. You seem like a sensible woman, so I am sure you had your reasons if you cheated on your husband."

"Oh, I had reasons..." she interjects with a sneer. "The biggest reason of all was the level of control my husband was trying to impose on me. He literally smothered me. I couldn't even pay for purchases because he had to have complete monopoly of the family money. He would tell me to go to our neighborhood shop to buy groceries and tell them that my husband would stop by to pay."

"You couldn't buy groceries on your own?"

"No. He watched everything I did, and he decided whom I could talk to."

I try to remain impassive but I am seriously stunned by what Romina is telling me. Men still act like that? "How did you meet friends online if he would not even allow you to pay for purchases?"

"I used my daughter's computer when she was at school. I connected with some friends from the past — some were men. It's not that I needed the attention, but it was nice to know someone who talked to me respectfully, who liked to have fun with me. I was so used to being talked to like I was stupid, that it genuinely surprised me to hear a man talk to me like I had a brain."

"Wow...no offense, but your ex-husband sounds like a prick."

"Yes. He is also a liar, but I guess I could have put up with that side of him if he was at least nice to me. He was nice in the beginning of our marriage; he told me sweet things and even brought me flowers. Things didn't really get bad until after I had children. It started with small things — a word here and a complaint there — and progressed gradually. The seed of abuse insinuated itself into our marriage with such stealth that I didn't even notice how oppressive my life was until I started talking to other people."

"How did your husband react when he found out?"

Romina sits back and draws a deep breath. "He was awful. The fear of losing control over me nearly drove him mad. He called me some of the worst names I have ever heard."

"That's sad," I reply, not really knowing what to say. "Did he do that in front of the children?"

"Oh yes, he didn't care at all. In fact, he probably felt justified in scaring them, so he would at least have them under his control." Romina's face is a mask of anguish and anger.

"How did the children deal with it? You said your daughter is a teenager; surely she had an opinion of her own."

Romina laughs bitterly. "Women didn't have opinions in my house, Rosa. My husband was supreme emperor of the family and his word was the only one that mattered. The children grew up with his attitude and didn't dare to challenge him."

"That's terribly unfortunate," I say, feeling sorry for Romina and wanting to end that conversation at the same time. I am not sure why her story is making me uncomfortable, and I shift nervously on my chair. "Well, I am going to inspect the painting station a little closer. That's definitely something I wouldn't mind trying." I walk away before Romina has the chance to respond, and hurry toward the table with the painting supplies. I pick up a canvas and place it on the easel, then I look through the stacks of paint to select the type I want to use.

As I pick up a bottle of red oil paint, a sharp pain slices through the front of my head like a blade, blinding me. I bring my hands to my head and drop to my knees, just as the canvas hits the floor with a muffled thump. I can hear people running toward me but the pain is too intense for me to open my eyes. I feel someone lifting me up and placing something soft under my head, then I hear a woman's voice telling someone else to stand back and let me breathe. And then, I hear the child's voice again, this time much closer and clearer. *Wake up, mommy! Please wake up! Why isn't she waking up, Grandma?* Then, all goes black.

CHAPTER THREE

"I can't tell you how much I appreciate your inviting me to join you, Olivia."

"You looked like you needed a day out," Olivia replies with a grin. "As peaceful as our center is, one can go crazy staring at those walls, and at the same people, all the time. We are free to come and go, as long as we feel comfortable about not getting lost, and we can always go with a friend."

A friend. I love the sound of this word. For someone who feels as alone as I do, the mere concept of having a friend feels foreign and exhilarating at the same time. I love being able to walk around and see the outside world, and I wonder if this is the town I lived in before I lost my memory. "What did you say the name of this town is?"

"San Gabriele," Olivia replies.

The name of the town does not trigger any memories — but then, nothing really does yet, so I am not surprised.

I pick up a strong aroma of coffee wafting from the bar across the street, and my senses are on full alert. Coffee is exactly what I need right now, but I hesitate to ask Olivia if we can go buy a cup. There are people everywhere, some walking in and out of shops carrying grocery bags, and others riding their bikes or talking to each other. They remind me of a colony of ants: each following a different path, but all undeniably connected by the same passion for gathering provisions and absorbing sunshine. The fragrant smell of freshly-baked bread permeates the air, and I find myself fantasizing about sinking my teeth into a crunchy, warm loaf. I scan the street for a bakery, trying to identify the source. The culprit appears to be a nondescript, single-door shop directly across the street. Once again, I want to ask Olivia if she would like to grab some lunch, but I am too timid to speak up. Thankfully — and, as if she could read my mind — she suddenly asks if I am hungry.

"Yes, as a matter of fact, I am famished!" I say, a little embarrassed. "I barely ate anything last night. I think Dr. Castelli gave orders to keep me on a light diet after I recovered from my fainting episode. I still can't understand what happened to me, exactly. I felt this horrible pain in my head, heard the voice of a small child…and then woke up in my room."

Olivia shrugged. "It was probably a cluster of memories that came to the surface too fast. Maybe you saw something that triggered some sort of recollection. Did you say that you heard a child? That's odd."

"I know. There are no children at the center, and it is not the first time I have heard it either. I heard the same voice yesterday morning when I left the therapy group, and I thought it was only an auditory illusion."

Olivia raised her brow. "Does this child say anything to you?"

"The first time, he wanted me to make someone stop. Yesterday afternoon, I heard him ask why I wasn't waking up."

Olivia's face darkens for a moment, then she smiles at me. "Well, you will figure it out, eventually. Let's go find something to eat. I know a great place just across this plaza."

We set off across the town square, and I am nearly running to keep pace with Olivia's long strides. We finally approach a small bar with a "Closed" sign on the door, and I wonder whether, like most businesses, this place is also closed during lunchtime hours.

"We might need to find a different lunch spot," I say, a little disappointed — my secret hope of a dreamy lunch quickly vanishing like a shadow in a sun-bathed room. "This place doesn't look like it is open for business."

"Maybe not," Olivia responds, "but it is open for us. The guy who runs this place is a friend of mine." She knocks lightly on the door, and then we both wait until a middle-aged fellow comes to let us in. He is a huge man, tall and bulky, with blue-black hair and a five o'clock shadow that is approaching ten o'clock. His eyes make me think of charcoal, and they look even darker in contrast with the pristine white of his shirt, open in the front to display a hairy chest and a thick gold chain. "Well, well…what good wind brings you, Olivia? Long time no see."

Olivia hugs him quickly before she introduces me. "This is Rosa. She lives at the center. Rosa, this is Claudio."

"Nice to meet you," I say timidly.

"Likewise," Claudio replies politely. "Are you ladies hungry? I was just preparing everything for this afternoon."

"Yes," Olivia says for both of us. She has probably realized that I am painfully shy.

Claudio leads us to the counter. "What can I serve you?"

Given the modest appearance of the building, I didn't expect the fancy layout of focaccine filled with anything one might desire, laid out beside tiny butter Panini filled with Prosciutto, and Tramezzini two inches high. Olivia selects a focaccia with tomato and mozzarella cheese; as Claudio arranges Olivia's choice on a plate lined with a white doily, my eyes rest longingly on the glass display that houses the pastries. As if they are a specter in a diabetic's nightmare, succulent round pastries, filled with fresh whipped cream, are laid out beside others shaped like mushrooms, filled with chocolate and custard; and, as if that was not tantalizing enough, an array of cookies and fruit-topped tarts are only inches away. I don't know what to choose, so I diplomatically opt for one of each pastry and one focaccia with mortadella. The focaccia is delicious, but the pastries are downright sinful; as I sink my teeth into the delicate layers of the cream filled "Ciambellina," I blissfully close my eyes in a revelry of flavor and texture.

"So, how do you know Claudio?" I ask Olivia after we take our selections to one of the small round tables by the window.

"I used to come here with my family to have dessert sometimes. I still occasionally visit."

"That's cool," I reply automatically, then I shrug and change the subject. "I really like this town. I was looking around for something familiar before, but nothing triggers any memories. I wonder if I lived here, too."

"You might have."

"Tell me a little about this place."

"I will do better than that," she replies with a grin and hands me one of the bar menus. "I can hand you a menu, and you can read about San Gabriele all on your own." She indicates a small paragraph on the front.

"San Gabriele is a small community tucked in the folds of the Chianti Hills near the outskirts of Florence, almost isolated from the hustle and bustle of larger towns. We are wedged between the Apennines Mountains and the Tyrrhenian Sea, and our region is world-renowned for its artistic and historic wealth, delectable food and wines, friendly atmosphere and unpredictable weather."

"No kidding about the weather," Olivia interjects. "This year is no exception, with the warmest March on record following polar temperatures in the month of February. Did you see the mimosa blooming out there? It's gorgeous!"

I nod in agreement, picking up the napkin laid out on the table to wipe my lips.

"Well, are you almost done with your lunch?" Olivia asks as she pushes her plate toward the middle of the table, her sandwich barely touched.

"Yes, but you didn't eat anything. Are you not hungry?" I reply, a bit surprised. I was starving when we walked in here.

"No, not really. I ate before we left, and I try to watch my weight," she whispers with a wink.

"You look beautiful," I say with sincerity. Olivia's blue eyes look like deep oceans, and they contrast sharply with her dark hair. "You don't need to worry about your weight."

"Oh, but I do. I have gained more weight than I would like in the last few years, even working out regularly to keep it off. I miss going to the gym."

"Why did you stop?"

"I didn't have time for it anymore."

"Do we have a workout facility at the center?"

"We do, but it is being updated right now, and we can't use it. So, are you ready to go? There is a park nearby, we can go stroll around for a while, if you want."

"Sure." I get up and stretch lazily, suddenly feeling full and lazy from the heavy lunch. Claudio is busying himself behind the counter when we bring the dishes back. The awareness that I have no money to pay for the meal hits me like a sack of bricks. I panic and look at Olivia. "I don't have any money with me!"

Olivia laughs. "It's not a problem," she says with a hint of amusement in her voice, "Claudio never lets me pay, anyway."

I stare from her to the burly man who's now laughing as well. Apparently, my embarrassment is entertaining to both.

"Olivia is right. I couldn't accept money from her, or from you for that matter, since you are her friend." He bites his lower lip to keep himself from laughing. "Hey, would you like to meet my friend while you are here?" He asks us as he opens a cabinet and pulls out a can of sardines.

"A friend?" Olivia asks surprised. "I thought we were alone."

"Not in here; he is outside waiting for me."

Olivia looks at me and shrugs. "Sure," she says, and we both follow Claudio as he leads the way out of the bar and closes the door behind him.

"Buddha! Where are you, buddy? I have a snack for you!" Claudio asks with a high- pitched voice.

Olivia and I look at each other. *Buddha?*

Before we can wonder any further, Buddha, a small black cat with a snow-white patch on his chest, materializes from the claustrophobic alley adjacent to the bar, meowing loudly.

"Here you are!" Claudio exclaims excitedly. "Ladies, this is my friend Buddha. Buddha, meet my friends, Olivia and Rosa."

Claudio opens the can he is holding in his hand, and the piercing aroma of sardines rises through the air like a genie. Buddha rubs against Claudio's legs, his tail straight up in the air to signal his approval, as Claudio runs his large hand over the cat's back and places the open can on the ground. "Here you go, little buddy."

There is something so sweet about seeing a large man being so gentle to an animal that I automatically find myself smiling. "It looks like Buddha is enjoying his lunch," I say, feeling now completely at ease around this gentle giant.

"He loves sardines," Claudio replies matter-of-factly, his eyes fixed lovingly on the small creature at his feet.

"Well, we'd better be going," Olivia says, breaking the spell. "It was great to see you, as always, Claudio."

"Don't be a stranger, Olivia," he replies softly. "Come back soon. It was great to meet you, Rosa." With that, he stoops to stroke Buddha once more, picks up the empty can and goes quickly back inside the bar, waving at us before he locks the door.

We retreat across the town square, but, rather than taking the same street we arrived from, Olivia turns right onto a different road.

"So, are you still up for a walk to the park?" she asks.

"Sure. I would love to remain outside in the sunshine a bit longer."

We walk slowly, and I take deep breaths as I go. Each of my senses is in overdrive. I hear scooters buzzing in the distance, mixed with the occasional beep of a car horn. I detect the scent of mimosa from nearby gardens and, for the first time in days, I feel truly alive. Before I realize it, we come to the entrance of a park. An open gate welcomes visitors and, as we step through, we find ourselves surrounded by majestic oaks and tall pine trees. The park is mostly shaded; I notice a few small structures nearly covered in vegetation, and mostly in disrepair. One of the buildings has a restroom sign, though it, too, appears old and abandoned from the outside. The voices of small children filter through the trees — giggles mixed with an occasional squeal — and I am confident that we are walking toward a playground.

Olivia selects a bench somewhat removed from the play structures; we sit down and catch our breath for a moment. "I love this park. The stately trees and the old buildings give it a feel of immortality," she says, drawing a deep breath as if to inhale the antiquity of the place.

A little boy with long brown hair and sprinkles of dried mud on his shirt approaches our bench, driven by a level of curiosity with which only toddlers are blessed.

"Andrea, come back here!" A young woman runs toward us, to retrieve the pint-size adventurer. I expect her to say something apologetic, but I am wrong — she quickly retrieves the little guy and leads him back to the playground, without even acknowledging us.

"My daughter looks like that young girl," Olivia says softly. "She comes here often — I think she is the boy's baby-sitter — and she is one of the reasons I like to come here."

"She is beautiful," I whisper, as I take a better look at the girl: tall — as I would, in fact, expect Olivia's daughter to be — with long, strawberry-blond hair. "Where is your daughter now?"

"She lives with my family. She is a sweet girl, focused on school and dance."

"Do you ever see her?" I ask.

"Occasionally. Sometimes I go by at night, when she has already gone to bed, and I watch her sleep. I have spent hours caressing her hair while she is asleep, but I leave before she wakes up."

"Why don't you want her to see you?"

"She is young and she wouldn't understand why I am not back at home. She was told that I had to go away for a while to get better, and she has made peace with that concept. I don't want to upset things and undermine her stability. Out of sight, out of mind, you know?"

I listen to Olivia and I wonder if I could do what she is doing. Would I have the strength to sneak into my own home and not awaken my son? *My son??* Where did that thought come from? And suddenly here he is: The image of a little boy explodes in my mind, and I gasp for breath.

"Rosa, are you okay?" Olivia asks, alarmed by my sudden reaction. She turns toward me and places her hands on my arms. "Breathe deeply. I'm right here."

I am crying uncontrollably now. As I continue to stare at my son's face looking back at me from the corner of my mind where he waited patiently for me to acknowledge him, I feel a wave of pain rush through my entire being. His name edges into the confines of my consciousness and I finally grab it, before it slips off into darkness again. "Matteo!!" I scream, emotions erupting like spewing lava, and burning everything they touch.

"Rosa!" Olivia is screaming at me now." Her fingers dig into my shoulders but I barely feel them. As I continue to spin into a vortex of memories, I can see other images, and I hold my breath as they overlap each other and demand my attention. I see a man, a wave of blond hair swept across his handsome face. He smiles, and I feel a loving connection with him. In the next image, he appears angry, and I am suddenly shaking with fear. I open my eyes, and for a moment I see Olivia's face, her pupils dilated with alarm, then I see the trees over us spinning out of control. I know I am going to be sick, so I push Olivia off and run blindly toward the trees opposite the playground, until I feel my legs buckle under me and I fall. I remain there in a fetal position, digging my nails into the hard clay under me. I don't understand the images I just saw, but they terrify me. I am sure that child is my own, but I don't know who the man was. Is he my husband?

"Rosa!" Olivia kneels beside me and caresses my hair.

"It's okay, Rosa," she says softly. "You are just remembering. Come on, let me help you up."

I don't want her to help me; I don't want her or anyone else to touch me. "Get away from me!"

The raw edge in my voice makes Olivia wince, and she immediately retreats. She sits quietly beside me until my breathing returns to normal. I want to see the little boy again; I want to inhale his scent, and hold him in my arms. And then I see the man again. He is in the driver's seat of a car, half undressed. His pants are unzipped and his shirt open in the front to reveal a muscular, hairless chest; beside him, in the passenger seat, is a woman, also half undressed. I look at both with disdain but, most of all, with pain. He betrayed me. She betrayed me. Anna, my friend and confidante, and this man whose name still eludes my awareness. Anna's mouth opens and closes as she hones in on me, but no words escape her guilty lips. At least, she has the decency to not make any lame excuses for her behavior. The man leaps out of his seat and pushes me off the car door. "I told you to stay home tonight, you stupid bitch! Look at what you've done now!"

I feel his hands on me, and I hear Anna scream. She tries to pull him back and he yells at her to back off. His grip on my arm is burning; I can't get away from it, and then I hear the little boy's voice again: "Make him stop, mommy, make him stop!" And I don't see the man anymore. Then all the images stop, and I am left with only tears, bubbling up from the hard knot in my stomach. I cry for a long time. When the sobs finally lessen, I feel Olivia's hand again, softly pushing my hair away from my face, wet from tears and profuse perspiration. She doesn't say anything, but continues to caress my hair with the gentle touch of a mother whose mission is to comfort her child.

"That child is my son, Olivia," I say as my voice cracks again. "I saw him. He is little, maybe five or six years old, and his name is Matteo. I also think I saw my husband and…and…"

"And…?" Olivia encourages gently.

"And his lover. I can't recall his name yet, but I know hers: Anna, a woman who was supposed to be my friend."

Olivia shakes her head, continuing to smooth my hair and, in a moment of lucidity, I wonder what people around us are thinking. Olivia doesn't seem to care. "I know all too well what you lived in that moment, Rosa. Sadly, I, too, have experienced the harsh blow of betrayal, not only from my husband, but also from someone I thought was a friend…someone I knew for many years."

She has my attention. I sit up and look directly at her, as she shares her own tale of deception.

"I thought I had it all, you know? From the time I was a young girl, I had big dreams. I wasn't like many girls my age: I didn't like smoking, drinking, or doing any of the things other kids thought were fun. I was focused on school, and I knew I wanted a family. Maybe that desire stemmed from the fact that I was an only child, I am not sure. I met my husband when we were quite young — I was barely 20 years old, and he was 25 — and we both fell head-over-heels in love. We got married after a short engagement; that day, I felt like a princess. I still remember floating up the aisle toward my handsome groom, and thinking that I was the luckiest girl in the world. He was so striking in his tuxedo! And when our eyes met, I saw nothing other than a bright future. The wedding was beautiful — everything a young girl could dream of — and after a short honeymoon, we settled into our new life together. The first couple of years were wonderful: I took care of the house and helped run a clothing store his mother owned. Although he could have worked at one of the many family-owned activities, he chose to work as an independent contractor for a construction business. He worked long hours, but I understood. I tried to keep myself busy around the house, and picked up a hobby or two to fill time. Then, our daughter, Isabella, was born. She was beautiful and she filled my life, and I soon started to get her involved in activities I would have liked to participate in myself. Ultimately, I lived my childhood dreams through her. I enjoyed cooking and baking, and I also started quilting a little. By the time my daughter was four, I got pregnant again, and this time I had a little boy, Emanuele. Emanuele was a little devil on wheels and he kept me busy in ways his sister never did! Isabella was also experiencing some issues with anger management, and we visited many doctors before finding one who succeeded in managing her outbursts. My days were so filled with appointments, activities, and other responsibilities, I hadn't taken time to notice how little my husband was home. By then, though, I was so busy I didn't even care. The honeymoon was over, and we were both exhausted from being pulled in different directions. There were times when I complained about his lack of presence at home, and, during one argument, I spat at him that he was likely responsible for our daughter's mental instability. That was the first time I saw a much uglier side of him than I had ever seen before. He loomed up so near that I could feel his hot breath on my face. "Don't you ever dare to blame me for your inability to raise our children," he hissed. "It is your job as a mother to control these kids. Look at all you have! Is that not enough for you, princess? You live in a golden palace, with everything any woman could possibly want, and you dare to complain? The reason I am gone so much is to give you all this! Without me and my hard work, you would be nothing!" With those last hateful words, he stormed out of the room and left the house. He didn't come home until much later that night —two or three in the morning, if I remember correctly. It didn't get better. As days turned into weeks, and weeks into months, he was always gone. A dinner here, a meeting there. He always had an excuse, and as much as I missed his presence, I resented the way he treated me when he was home. There was little intimacy left between us. Oh, we still had relations, but I feel that for him it was more of a chore than something he really wanted. Our bond was broken. I began to obsess over it, and I knew instinctively that something, or someone, was responsible for our fall. I still had family, but my pride kept me from sharing how I felt with them, and I let them believe that I was happy. I did not have many friends, aside from a few childhood connections that I maintained into adulthood. We were close, but not close enough to share my deep insecurities. I was slowly becoming a prisoner of my own self, and I chose isolation as my jail keeper."

Olivia's tale held me in a spell. "So, did you and your husband stay together?"

Olivia smiles bitterly. "I really didn't have much of a choice. I allowed my husband to take over my entire being and to be in control of all the finances in the family, including assets that were initially only my own. Thanks to his advice, I poured my heart, soul, and money into a vacuum that would, ultimately, suck out my very soul. I had nothing left; only my children."

"That's really sad..." I say, shaking my head.

"Yes, it was. To the eyes of the world, I had everything: A beautiful home, my own transportation, two beautiful children, and all the money I wished to spend. I lived in a golden cage, indirectly controlled by outside forces, and I knew that there was no way out for me. I didn't know for sure who his mistress was, but I was sure he had one. I had some suspicions, of course, but I couldn't bring myself to face the storm that a direct confrontation would bring upon us, for multiple reasons."

"Was the woman you suspected the one who turned out to be his mistress?"

Olivia pauses, her mind retracing the painful steps of her marital demise. "Unfortunately, yes."

"So, did you leave him after you confirmed that he had another relationship?" I ask, holding my breath. *What about me? Did I leave my own husband after I caught him with Anna?*

"I couldn't. There was more at stake than meets the eye, but that's a story for another day," Olivia replies calmly. "Come, Rosa. It's getting late, and Dr. Castelli is probably wondering why we aren't back yet."

I don't pressure her. I know that, as my own memories continue to surface, she will share more details of her own story with me, and hopefully, someday, we will both be healed from our past and able to embrace a brighter future.

CHAPTER FOUR

I don't have much of an appetite this morning, nor do I have any interest in the small talk Olivia and Rita are engaged in — but I try to be involved, just to avoid being asked any questions. I still can't fully understand the images that have surfaced in my mind, and being unable to place them in context is genuinely unnerving. I remember Olivia's words during the first group discussion, when she claimed it is sometimes easier to *not* know, to let oblivion keep us safe, but I know it is not an option for me. Seeing my husband — is he even my husband? — with another woman was painful, even though I recall no detail of our relationship. Matteo's face, however, has filled me with hope and strength, and I am determined to walk through the pits of Hell and confront the devil himself, if doing so will buy me a ticket back to hold my sweet boy.

Something else that Olivia said haunts me: She goes to visit her daughter sometimes, and watches her sleep. I can't even do that, as I don't know where Matteo lives, or even what our last name is. If my memory doesn't come back, I will never see Matteo again.

I am so absorbed in my thoughts that I haven't seen Dr. Castelli approaching our table, and I am unaware of his presence until he speaks directly to me.

"Good morning, Rosa," he says with his usual kind smile. "How are you feeling this morning?"

I tilt my head to one side and consider a response. How *am* I? "Confused" would be the closest description of how I truly feel, but for the sake of conversation, I smile back and produce a polite reply that won't darken the mood for everyone else. "I am feeling much better. Thank you for asking."

"I understand that you and Olivia went out for a while yesterday," he continues. If I had hoped my vague reply would get me off the hook, I was wrong.

"Yes, it was great to get out and feel sunshine on my skin."

Dr. Castelli is not the least bit fooled by my cheerful tone. "That's wonderful. Would you like to come by my office and talk with me about how you felt?"

I shrug. "Sure. I can come by as soon as I am done eating breakfast," I add, hoping he won't look at my plate and notice that my food is barely touched. It is hard enough trying to arrange the few puzzle pieces I have uncovered so far; I don't need any added pressure.

"Very well," Dr. Castelli replies as he nods his head in agreement. "I will see you shortly, then."

The instant he walks away, I turn to face Olivia. "Did you tell him that I totally freaked out yesterday?"

Olivia swallows a bite of food and thoughtfully wipes her mouth before replying. "No, not really. I crossed paths with him in the hallway last night, and told him you are beginning to remember a few things. I am sure he knows how hard it is to accept some of the memories. Don't hold back your feelings, Rosa. Dr. Castelli is here to help. He is not your enemy."

I wonder why Olivia said that…I certainly don't consider Dr. Castelli an enemy! If anything, I see him as a kind, fatherly figure, supporting our efforts to make peace with our individual demons. I notice that, although saying nothing, Romina and Rita are nearly gaping with curiosity. As soon as I lock eyes with them, though, they resume their small talk, with barely a glance at one another while staring at their plates. "I don't think Dr. Castelli is my enemy...frankly, I'm not sure I can tell the difference between friends and enemies just now. I don't even know who *I* am, yet!" Despite my effort to control my voice, a jagged edge of frustration sneaks in.

"Well…I should go and see what he wants to talk about." Standing, I pick up my still-full plate from the table, then head toward the trash can to dump the uneaten contents. I leave the dining room without looking back, though I am sure my table companions are watching me as I walk out. I didn't mean to snap at them; I certainly didn't mean to give the impression that I resent Dr. Castelli, or that I was trying to run for the hills. But I *do* feel abrasive this morning, and I don't even understand what is making me feel this way.

I detour through the garden on the way to Dr. Castelli's office, so I have a moment to organize my thoughts before seeing him. What, exactly, have I remembered so far? I know I was probably married and, if the man I saw was my husband, he was a two-timing bastard. I know I have a little boy named Matteo — of that, I have no doubt: My heart *knows* he is my life and joy. I remember I had a friend named Anna, though if what I remember took place, she wasn't really my friend. What else? I am sure I am strong enough to deal with the knowledge that my husband was a piece of lowlife scum, and that my friend was my enemy instead — injustices of that sort are a part of life — so, what is it that my mind can't accept?

My thought-gathering attempt is illusory; reality is that I don't remember anything beyond those two moments, and I must come to terms with the fact that I need help to retrieve the threads of my life as I knew it. Deep down, I think I am afraid of the memories. What if I was a bad person? What if my husband betrayed me because I was a poor excuse for a wife and mother? Will I be able to accept myself, if I discover that I caused my own downfall?

I am so absorbed by my thoughts that I don't even realize I am already in front of Dr. Castelli's office until I have nearly passed it by. I knock lightly and wait for him to respond.

"Come in, please." Dr. Castelli's voice is even and gentle, as always. Something about this man sets me at ease, even if I don't really know him, and I wonder once again why Olivia said not to think of him as my enemy.

I open the door slowly and enter, immediately drawn to the simple décor. As much as I have felt from the first that Dr. Castelli is a humble man, I am pleased to confirm that initial impression. His desk and chair are unpretentious and comfortable — and, aside from one three-drawer filing cabinet, the only other furnishings are a full-size couch upholstered in a cheerful, flowered fabric, and an additional chair in front of the desk. None of the furniture appears new or expensive; the ambience is welcoming and not in the least intimidating. "You wanted to see me, Doctor?"

"Yes, yes, Rosa. Come in, please, and make yourself comfortable."

I take the chair across the desk from him, and wait for him to say something.

"So…" Dr. Castelli wastes no time getting to the point. "Olivia vaguely mentioned that you remembered some things during your outing. Would you like to talk about what you saw?"

"Honestly, Doctor, I don't know what I saw, exactly. I had a mental image of a man whom I felt connected to, but then that image shifted and I saw him in the car with a friend of mine. Well…I can't say she was really a friend. With friends like that, who needs enemies? At any rate, the two were having a secret rendezvous, and, apparently, I caught them."

"How did you feel when you saw them?"

I reflect for a moment, reaching back in my mind. "I think I was hurt, but mostly, I remember being scared — especially when he leaped out of the seat to push me away from the door. The woman — Anna — screamed and told him to stop, but he grabbed my forearm so tightly that, even now, I can still feel his grip." I study Dr. Castelli's face for a reaction, but he remains impassive.

"Did you see anything else?"

"No. The only vivid memory I have is of a little boy. I know his name is Matteo, and I know he is my son. He appears to be about five or six years old. I can't say for sure, but I think it is Matteo whose voice I keep hearing."

This time, Dr. Castelli's brow arcs in surprise. "You've heard him speak? Since you've been here?"

"Yes. The first time, I heard him when I left the group meeting, and he told me to *make him stop.* I am assuming now that he was talking about his father, though I can't say for sure. The second time, I heard him before I fainted in the recreation room. He was asking me to wake up."

"Why didn't you tell me this before, Rosa?"

"I'm not sure. I only first told Olivia about it yesterday. Bottom line, doctor, I remember very little. The few memories that have surfaced so far make little sense, until I can place them into context. Is there anything I can do to speed up the process?"

Dr. Castelli is deep in thought. I can imagine the gears in his brain spinning to formulate an answer to my question. "There is a way, Rosa, but it can be dangerous. We can use hypnosis to retrieve memories from your subconscious, but you need to understand that your mind buried those images for a reason. If they surface too fast, you might not be ready for them, and your brain will shut them down again — this time more permanently. The alternative is, you will remember, and be so overwhelmed that you won't be able to cope with what you're seeing."

I straighten myself on the chair, steel determination pumping through my veins. "I can deal with them, doctor. What I can't deal with is not knowing. What I can't live with is being sure that I have a child out there who needs me, and I not even recalling his full name, or where he is. As for the rest…I am sure I can find a way to make peace with it."

Dr. Castelli remains silent for a moment, as if weighing my words. "How about if what you find out is irreversible, Rosa? Would you be able to deal with the acceptance of something that's completely out of your control?"

"The only thing out of my control is death, doctor. I am pretty sure I can work with anything else."

Doctor Castelli nods, then draws a deep breath before speaking again. "Very well, then. Would you like to come tomorrow morning? Around ten, maybe? I am busy this afternoon, and this is likely going to take a while."

Even a slight chance of retrieving my memory is exhilarating, and I have to focus, to keep from jumping out of my seat. "Really? Do you think it will work?"

"I hope so. One never knows when the human mind is involved, but hypnosis can accomplish good things, if you are ready to journey deep down within yourself."

"Oh, I am ready! Thank you, doctor, I look forward to trying. Do I need to do anything to prepare?"

"No, not necessarily, but you must trust me."

"I trust you. At this point, you are my only hope."

"I will see you in the morning, then," Dr. Castelli says as he stands. He extends his hand to shake mine, and I grab it eagerly.

"Thank you again, doctor! I can't wait! Before I leave, though, I have another question for you…" I pause for a few seconds, hoping to find the right words. "You told me that this place is like a mental facility, but it is not really a hospital. So, what is it, exactly?"

"This is a shelter for women who have been abused. The center is in a secret location, and the section you are in is, in a way, like a hospital. During their stay, our patients revisit their lives, and learn to make better choices. They also learn the power of acceptance and forgiveness, as skills that will help them ease into a new, more satisfying reality."

"Does that mean I was abused, doctor?"

"I don't know, Rosa. We will find out when you remember."

"But, if this place is in a secret location, how did I find it? Did someone bring me here?"

"You have a lot to figure out, dear. You will remember everything in due time. Don't worry yourself with it right now. It's a beautiful day; why don't you go sit in the garden for a while?"

The kindly but dismissive tone I detect in the doctor's voice tells me with certainty that I am not going to squeeze any more information out of him — not yet, at least. I have too much energy right now to go sit on a bench. Instead, I decide to go by the recreation room, to see whether any of my friends are there — knowing full well that I will drive myself crazy without the benefit of company.

I don't recognize anyone I know in the recreation room when I peer inside, but I go in, anyway. Two women are at the quilting table, but I am not in the mood to talk to strangers, so I stride over to the painting corner. I select a 10-by-13-inch canvas and some water colors, and place the canvas on the easel, ready to work. *What does one paint when their memory of anything they have witnessed fails them miserably?* For a moment, I consider painting a portrait of Buddha, the little cat I met yesterday — but Matteo's face flashes through my mind, and I feel my heart squeeze. I decide to paint my son's portrait instead. Art is supposed to evoke emotions, and Matteo awakens powerful feelings within me. I trace an oval on the canvas, then close my eyes, to contemplate the details of his cherubic face. His hazel eyes sparkle like stars, so intense that I feel myself being pulled into them — and into a vortex of memories — by a force I can't fight.

I am standing by the stove in the kitchen, stirring soup in a large pot on the back burner. I look repeatedly at the clock on the wall while I cook, because Matteo's school bus is going to arrive shortly. I wish I could alternate hands as I stir, because my right hand is getting tired, but my left arm is too sore to use: I have no choice. I should go get this arm checked — it hurts too much to be simply bruised — but the doctor would ask questions that I can't answer, and all I can do is pray it is not broken. I am grateful that Matteo was asleep when Marco got home last night. He was late, as always, and in a terrible mood. It didn't take much to anger him — again, nothing new — and he didn't think twice about pushing me against the door when I asked if he had worked late again. In my mind, I can still hear Marco's threatening voice thunder through the room.

"What? You have a problem with me *working* now? Who else is going to provide for this family, if not me?" He nearly spat in my face, the venom in his voice deadlier than acid.

"Of course not," I replied quickly, hoping to defuse the anger that escalated without warning. "It was just a question, Marco. I didn't mean to be disrespectful."

"You aren't disrespectful, Iliana, you are just plain stupid! A stupid, pathetic woman, who would be on the streets if it wasn't for me."

"You are right, Marco. Please, don't be angry," I whispered, my voice broken by fear.

"How can I not be angry when you ask such stupid questions? You nag at me all the time, and you never appreciate anything!"

I hardly heard the last word, as he slapped my face so hard it made my ears ring. I was crying softly now, too scared to sob or make any other sound. Marco took one step back, then grabbed my arm and pinned me against the door frame. His fingers dug into the flesh of my arm, painfully enough that I would have cried out, if my mind was not already numbed by sheer terror. I prayed silently that Matteo would stay blissfully asleep.

And, thankfully, my prayers were answered. Matteo didn't wake up, and after reminding me a few more times what a useless, ungrateful, and ugly human being I was, Marco went to bed. Matteo woke up early this morning; thankfully, Marco had already left for work, allegedly headed for Bologna to meet some clients. His job as a sales representative for a clothing firm keeps him on the road a few days each week, for which I am grateful. Matteo was too sleepy for small talk as he got ready for school, so he inhaled his milk and cookies, and bounded out the door for the school bus.

I am still upset from last night's outburst, but I need to wipe the pain from my face before my sweet boy comes charging through the door. After taking one more look at the clock on the wall, I run to the bathroom to check my appearance. I still have five minutes before Matteo arrives—enough time to wash the tears from my face, and freshen the foundation I applied this morning to cover the finger marks that are — thankfully — only red and no longer swollen. I am grateful for the chill in the air today: I can wear a roomy sweater that will adequately cover the bruises. As always, the physical bruises will heal in a few days; the emotional ones, however, are here to stay. I stare at the image looking back at me from the mirror. Marco is right: There is nothing attractive about me. I am lucky to have him in my life, and I know many women out there wish they could be in my place. Is he right about me being ungrateful, too? Maybe he is. Our house is beautiful and comfortable, and we never lack anything we need. Matteo has all the clothes and toys a little boy dreams of, and he is happy — though I wish he could have a brother or sister to grow up with. But, as Marco says, we only need one child, and arguing that point will lead nowhere. Marco knows numbers; he keeps our budget, and if he says we can't afford another child, he must have his reasons.

The school bus honks its horn, and I rush outside to meet Matteo. As the doors swing open, he bursts out with such impetus that I fear, for a moment, he will tumble down the three stairs of the bus. He flies into my arms and kisses me on the cheek — the same cheek that was struck by Marco's open hand — and I nearly recoil. But I wince and don't move as my son's lips touch the burning flesh.

"Come, Mommy," Matteo says with the enthusiasm only a little boy can possess. "I have to show you something."

We walk inside, hand in hand. As soon as we cross the threshold, Matteo drops to his knees, rummaging in his backpack. He pulls out a card he has drawn at school and hands it to me. Glancing at it, my eyes fill with tears. My hands shake so hard that I nearly drop the card my son made for me. "You saw this? I thought you were asleep…" The pain I feel tightens around my chest like a vise, and I can barely breathe.

Matteo looks down, his eyes focused on the open laces of his tennis shoes. "I couldn't sleep, I was thirsty. I didn't mean to look. I swear!" And with that, his tiny body is shaken by powerful sobs.

I don't know what to do, what to say. I simply kneel and hug him tightly, as I start crying, too. Matteo pulls himself back and looks at me with eyes full of tears, anger twisting his beautiful face into a mask of pain. "Why is Daddy mad, Mommy? What did you do?"

"I don't know, love. I don't know."

A hand on my shoulder makes me jump out of my skin. *Is Marco back from his trip?*

I open my eyes, and Romina's face is there, flooding me with sudden relief. I raise my hand in a futile attempt to wipe the tears streaming down my face, and it takes me a moment to catch my breath.

Romina apologizes immediately. "I am so sorry, Rosa, I didn't mean to startle you! You appeared to be a hundred miles away, lost in your thoughts, but I was curious about the picture you were painting.

I stare in disbelief at the image: It is Matteo's card, desperately — and subconsciously, it seems — reproduced by my own hand in a near-manic attempt to reconnect with a painful moment. I don't remember painting this. I see myself, cornered against a door frame, helpless against my husband's fury. There is blood on the floor; the face of a little boy looks on sadly, from a distance.

Despair erupts from the deepest recesses of my soul, invading every cell of my being. The pain I feel is raw and overwhelming, and I begin to hyperventilate.

"Easy, easy!" Romina grabs me by the shoulders, supporting me when my legs threaten to buckle. She threads an arm around my waist and leads me to a chair in the corner. "Here, Rosa, sit down for a moment and catch your breath." She breathes with me, slowly and evenly, until I can finally catch a lungful of air. "There…you are okay. You are safe here. Continue to breathe."

My head is hurting and I feel nauseous. Tears seem imminent — and would be welcome, if they could only wash away this coat of suffocating anguish. Romina is kneeling in front of me, taking both my hands into her own. "You are remembering, Rosa, and reliving emotional experiences. It's okay to be scared, and it is okay for you to remember. You are safe here."

Iliana…Marco…the names spin in my head like numbered balls in a Bingo cage. The man in the vision is the same man I saw in the car, and I lived in the same house with him, so I assume we were married. His name is Marco — this much I know about him, and I remember that he is a salesman, but the rest is still hidden. I need to know his last name, at least, so I have some hope of finding him, and making sure my son is safe. Is he hurting Matteo, too? Is he redirecting his anger at Matteo, now that I am not there?

"My name is Iliana. I just remembered." I say to Romina, still feeling the sound of my name vibrating on my trembling lips.

"Do you want me to call Doctor Castelli?"

I shake my head vigorously. "No! I can't talk about this yet."

Romina disagrees gently. "Quite the opposite, Rosa — I mean, Iliana — you do need to talk about it, to sort out the memories and seal them in this reality, so they don't slip away again."

"My heart is still pounding, Romina. I was terrified of him. I thought he was going to kill me! All along, though, my greatest fear was that Matteo would see what was happening, and that Marco would turn his anger on my son."

"I understand all too well, unfortunately," Romina replies, a trace of sadness tingeing her voice. "I had four children, and my husband never worried about the way his behavior affected them. They were present many times, when he yelled at me and called me names, and they have witnessed a few incidents in which he beat me."

A single tear escapes Romina's eye, trickling down her face before she has a chance to wipe it off and conceal it from me. "My daughter was already a young woman; I hope she didn't see that sort of treatment as acceptable. My boys were little; my greatest fear is that they will grow up to be like their father. He was in control of every aspect of my life. It was as though I couldn't even *breathe* without his permission."

"Have you ever pressed charges against him?"

"No...I should have, but I never did. It would have made things worse. Our laws aren't powerful enough to deter abuse — they only buy time until the next beating — and angering the abuser only results in further abuse. I could have left, of course, but I didn't think I could take care of myself and four children. Over time, my self-confidence was reduced to shreds, and I didn't even trust myself to make small decisions involving the children without first consulting him."

"Did you have any friends you could talk to?" I inquire, already knowing in my heart what she will say.

"I didn't, in the beginning. I made some friends online, but I never told them what was happening at home. The worst part is that people thought I was happy and well cared for." She sneers. "What a joke!"

I nod, remembering how I felt in my memory. I believed I was ugly and incapable. Marco led me to believe I would be nothing without him, and like a cancer eating at an organ over time, his words slowly eroded my self-esteem. I saw myself as human garbage, an imperfect reject whom only he had the kindness to tolerate. "Did your husband ever abuse the children?"

Romina shakes her head. "Not directly, and not physically, at least. He disciplined them, of course, but he never went overboard — probably because they were too scared to do anything that would anger him to begin with. Witnessing abuse is a scarring experience, and I suppose it can be likened to emotional abuse. Seeing someone you love being mistreated weakens your own strength, and it makes you think twice before you misbehave."

I feel my heart aching for my son, Matteo. How many times did he witness his father being abusive? Was he also abused?

"I am supposed to undergo hypnosis tomorrow morning. Now I am scared," I say, with a nervous laugh that betrays my deep-seated fear.

Romina smiles sweetly. "Don't be afraid, Ro...I mean, Iliana. How do you want me to call you?"

"I don't know...I like Rosa; it feels safe. But, Iliana is my real name, and someday I must learn to use it again."

"You might want to discuss this with Doctor Castelli. No matter how painful the memories, you are safe now. That awareness should help you process what comes up."

"Doctor Castelli worries that if I remember too quickly, my brain might shut down again, and this time it might be for good. That's the only deterrent I see in this whole thing."

Romina weighs the information. "That *is* a huge risk. If you shut down, you might never see Matteo again."

Those words hit me like a thousand icicles. "I can't take that chance."

Romina stands and brushes invisible dust particles from her clothes. "Sleep on what has surfaced today, and tell the doctor what you saw. If I were you, I would defer to his expertise before you take another step."

"I will," I reply, with a smile that dies the instant I glance back at the canvas. "What should I do with this?" I feel suddenly helpless.

Romina shrugs. "It's the depiction of a memory. As painful a reminder as it is, it is also a powerful testament of the love your son has for you. That alone should be enough motivation to remember…and go back to him."

I agree. I lift the canvas gently off the easel, following Romina out of the recreation room. I am going to take the painting to my room, and hang it on the wall as a reminder of my son's love for me. Matteo needs me, and no matter what demons I must slay to get there, I will find my way back to him.

CHAPTER FIVE

"I know I insisted on being hypnotized, doctor. After what happened yesterday, though, I have a few questions to ask before we proceed." My voice is firm, and I am determined to clear away any lingering doubts.

Doctor Castelli's face registers a bit of surprise, but he listens attentively without interrupting me.

"I remembered my real name, yesterday, and that of my husband. My real name is Iliana; I was abused by my husband, Marco. All I can recall is one incident at my house. Apparently, I asked Marco why he was late coming home, and my words triggered his anger. He pushed me against a doorway and slapped me. He also grabbed my arm hard enough to bruise it. I clearly remember him talking down to me, telling me that I am nothing. He called me stupid several times — just during that one episode — so I think it is safe to assume that he did so regularly. The part that disturbs me most, about what I remembered, is that *I believed him.* I believed that I deserved the way he was treating me." It's strange to hear myself talking about this, and for a moment I hope my mind is simply making it up.

"It's very common for victims of abuse to reach a point at which they believe what the abuser tells them. Look at it this way: If water drips over a rock, you don't see any immediate damage — no one does — but, over time, the constant drip carves a hole into the rock. The same thing happens with abusers and their victims, although the process is not as slow. The way abusers talk to their victims erodes the victims' self-esteem so insidiously that it is not even detected. In many interviews recorded during case studies, survivors have reported that their partners began the cycle of abuse by isolating their victims from family and friends. Initially, many victims thought there was somehow something romantic in the exclusive attention their partners demanded, but most soon discovered it was not love that motivated the isolation. It wasn't until much later that many of the women realized they were being manipulated into cutting everyone out of their lives; by then, the relationships with people who cared about them were so compromised, they felt they had no chance to reconnect. At that point, many of the abusers began to belittle their victims — especially when they were around company — which led to further isolation, out of embarrassment. By the time they were hit for the first time, many of the women were so tightly wrapped up in the web of lies their abusers had woven, they believed they deserved to be treated that way. Many of them had also come to believe themselves unattractive and overweight, which was not the case. Because of the isolation they were subjected to, they had nobody around who could help them see the truth."

"I thought that, too, doctor. When I looked at myself in the mirror to cover the mark he left on my face the night before, I did not like the woman looking back at me from the mirror. What I find strange, is that I didn't have those thoughts when I looked at myself the first day I arrived here. I felt like I was looking at a stranger, but I never thought of her as ugly. Oh, I know I don't look anything like a Marilyn Monroe, or a Cindy Crawford, but I am not as unattractive as I felt when I looked in the mirror on the morning I recalled in yesterday's memory."

Doctor Castelli nods, apparently pleased. "That's good. As your brain shut off the memories of the abuse, it also removed the scars. Hopefully they will remain gone after your memory comes back further."

"Does that usually happen?" I ask with apprehension.

"No, not usually. Emotional scars are usually the hardest to remove, and it takes years to regain the self-worth one loses in the battle."

"Why did it not happen to me?"

"I don't have an answer for that, Rosa. Let's hope it stays that way, even after your memory returns completely."

I nod in agreement. "Do you think it is wise to move forward with the plan to hypnotize me?"

Doctor Castelli sighs, then he clears his throat. "Again, it all depends on you. A lot has surfaced already, and you seem to be dealing with it as you should, but it is hard to know how much is too much. Are you sleeping okay?"

"I believe so. I wake up a few times in the middle of the night, but I am usually able to go back to sleep without medication."

"That's good. You need the rest, for your brain to 'reset' whenever a new memory surfaces. It takes a great deal of energy for your subconscious to release the memories, and for them to have clearance to reach cellular level."

"There's another thing…the women who live here, the other residents…will they ever go home?" I ask, just out of curiosity.

"You are here to heal yourself, Rosa, not to develop concerns for other people. I know it sounds cold and uncaring, but each of you is here on an individual journey. You are helping each other out, but where things go from this point forward depends entirely on the choices of the people involved."

"Do you mean that I could leave here today, doctor?"

"Of course. You are not obligated to remain, but it is in your interest to stay and continue your healing process."

I nod, humbled. I wouldn't know where to go from here, anyway — at least, not yet. I don't even know what my full name is. "I plan to stay until I remember what happened, doctor. After that, I need to go back and take care of my son."

"I understand, Rosa. But please be aware that you can't help your son until you have learned to help yourself."

"My son is in the hands of a man who can't control his anger! How can it be better for him if I stay away?"

"Because your husband's goal is to control you. He is not going to leave bruises on a child that would alert a teacher or another figure of authority to dig deeper."

What the doctor is saying makes sense. "If that's the case, I would like to be hypnotized. I am no good to anyone, including myself, if I continue to invest time and energy in fighting shadows. I can handle whatever comes up. I know I can." I lock eyes with the doctor, and challenge him to help me.

"Very well, then. Let's go over there, so you can lie down on the sofa." He stands and leads the way, then waits for me to lie down.

"Get comfortable. Would you like a blanket? I usually find that a blanket helps make patients feel more secure."

"Sure," I reply, though it doesn't matter to me, one way or another. I am ready to get aboard this ship and sail away; I don't care about the details.

Doctor Castelli produces a throw-blanket from the top drawer of the filing cabinet and brings it over. The blanket is soft, and a pleasant shade of forest green. I wrap it around myself and stretch my legs, appreciating the fact that the sofa is more comfortable than I initially thought.

"Do you see this black dot on the wall, Rosa?"

I nod. The dot is small, but it stands out on the white wall.

"Very well. Look at the dot…don't take your eyes off it. I will start reading from a script, and I need you to breathe, deeply and evenly. Breathe in to the count of three, hold it to the count of three, and then release it to the count of five. Continue doing that as I read, and keep your eyes fixed on the dot."

As he begins to read, the doctor's voice loses any expression. It is a flat monotone that makes it quite challenging for me to keep my eyes open and focused on the dot. I hear numbers, and then a new suggestion to breathe deeply…then more numbers…and then, I no longer hear anything.

I am in a church, waiting in line to enter the confessional. The church is small, and it feels comfortable being here. A few elderly women are kneeling on the pews at the far end; an altar boy is busily re-stocking the candle supply, beneath the altar of the Virgin Mary.

I have always enjoyed coming to church. Well, maybe I didn't when I was a little girl and was forced by my parents and my grandmother to attend, but over time I came to appreciate the haven this church represents for me. Our priest, Don Carmelo, always talks about issues that resonate with me and feel right in my soul, and I enjoy listening to him. Marco hates coming to church; he makes fun of me for attending. He will not let me take Matteo, because he thinks religion is a form of brainwashing, and he prefers to keep his son shielded from all the "nonsense" discussed within the church walls. Marco is out of town today, and with Matteo in school, I took advantage of the fact that I was home alone, to come here and go to confession. There is only one more person ahead of me, so I examine my conscience to figure out what I will say when I go in. How long has it been since I have set foot in a confessional? Six months, maybe? A lot of sins pile up in such a long period, and I don't know if I remember them all.

The last woman before me exits the small chamber, and I enter. I kneel and wait for Don Carmelo to speak.

"How long has it been since your last confession, child?"

"It has been about six months, Father. I have sinned."

"What would you like to confess today?"

"I have disobeyed my husband on multiple occasions. I have lied, and I have used the name of God in vain. And then, I...I..."

"You can tell me, child. God forgives our sins."

"I have had impure thoughts, Father, and I have allowed my husband to do things that are impure."

"God forgives all, child, don't be afraid."

"Do I have to obey him, even when I know what I am doing is a sin?"

"The Bible teaches that a woman should do as her husband says, but if you know that you are committing sin, maybe you should resist."

"I can't resist, Father. He won't allow me."

"Is he forcing himself on you?"

"Yes. And he likes to hurt me. I don't like that, but when I have said so to him, he gets very angry. He thinks he should be able to do anything he wants, because we are married."

"God unites a man and a woman in marriage, and no man can dissolve that bond. And yet, if what your husband asks of you is a sin, child, you must resist and respect our Lord."

I am filled with shame, and I wish I could disappear. I can't tell Don Carmelo that I have no option to resist. If I even attempt that, I get an even worse beating than I would if I suffer silently. How do I tell my childhood priest that my husband takes pleasure in hurting me when we have sexual relations? How do I explain to him the type of physical pain I must endure every time? And then, the mental anguish I am obligated to live with, knowing I have done something completely unnatural? Why won't God deliver me from this cross I am forced to carry?

"Is there anything else you would like to confess, child?"

"No…"

"Then by the power invested in me, you are absolved in the name of the Father, the Son, and the Holy Spirit. Go in peace, and say three "Hail Mary"'s and three "Our Father"'s. May God be with you."

"And always with you."

I leave the confessional as quickly as possible, keeping my face low and hoping that Don Carmelo did not recognize me. I don't feel absolved. I don't feel forgiven, maybe because I can't forgive myself. I am still in pain from the night before, when Marco woke up and groped for me. I cringed when he touched me, but I didn't reject him. He made me undress completely and then got out of bed to get his "toys," as he calls them. I begged him mentally not to do this again, not to hurt me like he always does, but I was too scared to say anything that would make him angry. He made me turn on my stomach and he penetrated me with something cold and hard. The pain was lacerating, and I couldn't help screaming. He placed his hand over my mouth, then, and he bit down on my earlobe before smacking my bottom with a full hand, over and over. It lasted for only a few minutes, but those minutes felt like hours. As my insides were being ripped open, he masturbated over me. Then he got up and went outside to smoke a cigarette, leaving me like that: dirty and used, like an old shoe that has no value…the heel almost gone, the sole worn through and flapping, cast into a gutter.

Just thinking about last night makes me feel unworthy to be in this sacred place. I feel unclean and unwanted; I just want to run away and not think about anything. Matteo is the only thing that keeps me grounded, and Marco has made it clear many times that he will never allow me to leave and take Matteo with me.

The voice of Doctor Castelli filters through my consciousness. "You can come back now, Rosa…slowly. Just breathe, and at the count of three you can open your eyes. You are safe."

I open my eyes, and I breathe in relief when I realize I am inside the doctor's office. It takes me a few moments to regain my composure, and I am grateful that he is not pressuring me.

"He sexually abuses me. That son of a bitch sexually abuses me!" My anger is so raw that I feel I am going to auto-combust from the fire roaring through every inch of my being. I stand up from the sofa, pacing in large circles. "Why? Why? That sick son of a bitch is beating me and sexually assaulting me!"

"These experiences are probably the reason why your brain shut down, Rosa. Especially if you have a strong religious conviction, engaging in those behaviors is deeply troubling to you, even if you felt you didn't really have any choice. Deep down, you still feel like you are sinning."

"How much more is there to uncover, doctor? How much worse can it get?"

"I don't know. Honestly." Doctor Castelli's voice is even and void of any emotion.

"I don't even know how to wrap my mind around all of this!" My frustration with the revelation I just experienced is so intense that I can't keep my voice steady. "I was married to a real jerk, and because of the love I have for my son, I couldn't leave."

"Let it sink, Rosa. Don't think about it too much. Those memories are inside you, but you need time to work them out, one at a time. I could have kept you in longer, but I feel it is best if you don't have too much to deal with at once. The emotional load could prove too heavy to handle."

I nod silently. As the burning anger subsides, I feel like crying, and I don't think I can say a single word without bursting into tears. Doctor Castelli seems to understand what I am going through; he simply stands and walks over to open the door.

I try to avoid everyone on the way to my room, but unfortunately, I run into Giulia. She glances briefly at my face and her smile fades away. "Are you okay, Rosa?"

The dam breaks at that very moment, and a torrent of tears gushes over my face. "No, I am not okay. I just remembered that my husband Marco used to sexually assault me and beat me."

Giulia hugs me. "I am so sorry, honey. I know first-hand how that feels. My own husband thought he could have sex with me whenever he wanted, whether I agreed to it or no."

I look up and stare into Giulia's eyes. "Really?"

Giulia simply nods. "Yes, unfortunately. As I said before, men in the south are raised to believe they own their women, and therefore they think that it is okay to force them to engage in sexual activity if they get aroused, even if their wives don't want to. Not all southern men think that way, of course, but my husband did."

"Did you ever reject him?" I ask, suddenly feeling connected with Giulia through the tragedy of our experiences.

"Not usually, but I did one day." She replies without averting her eyes.

"What did he do? Did he get mad?"

"Yes, you could say that. He got *really* mad."

"My husband did unnatural things to me." I hesitate to go on, as embarrassment begins to settle in. "I don't really want to go into details of what he did, but it was bad. It made me feel dirty. I just had a memory of being at church and confessing to my priest that I had sinned."

"It wasn't your sin, Rosa," Giulia interjects, "It was his. It took me a while to understand that, but I finally did. I grew up in church, too, and I felt that sex between a man and a woman should be something beautiful, but it never really felt that way. I also think my husband felt he was getting the short end of the bargain, so he began seeing other women."

"I know Marco did, as well. For one, he was seeing someone I used to consider a friend."

"That's terrible," Giulia agrees. "At least, Ettore had the decency to have an affair with someone I didn't know."

"Well, I should be going," I say, moving to give her another hug. "I feel exhausted. I think I am going to take a nap. The doctor said that I need to rest after each memory surfaces."

"That's a good idea. You need to give yourself time to absorb the shock."

73

"See you at dinner, then." I leave hurriedly, hoping that everyone else is busy elsewhere, out of my path. I wasn't lying when I said I feel exhausted.

I turn left at the end of the hallway, speeding up to get to my room, when I notice two men carrying an old furnace. When I lay eyes on the younger one, my breath crystallizes in my chest and I gasp. Standing in front of me is a man who could be Marco's twin. My first impulse is to run and hide. *How did he find me?*

I put my head down and hammer past the two men with such strength I nearly topple the furnace they are carrying.

"Hey!" One of them — the older man — calls out. "Watch it, lady!"

I can barely hear him over the pounding of my heart. Is Marco here? Is he pretending to be a maintenance guy to come after me? I turn the handle of my door with force and enter, slamming the door behind me. I look for a lock, but I don't see one. I lean on the door, my back practically glued to it, trying to catch my breath. Could it really be him? I don't remember all the details, but I know Marco is a salesman, not a handyman. I crack the door open and peek outside, just as Elena walks by.

"Do you need something, Rosa?" She asks with a smile.

I can barely speak. "Those two men that just went by. Do you know what their names are?"

Elena scans the empty hallway. "What men?"

"I don't know. They were carrying a furnace, I think. I almost ran into them on my way to my room."

"I am really not sure, Rosa. I didn't see anyone, but from time to time we have contractors who come in to maintain the place. Why do you ask?"

"One of those men looks just like my husband!"

My words seem to strike a chord, but Elena's composure remains intact. "Are you sure, dear? It's unlikely. Should I call Doctor Castelli?"

"Can you find out if there were two men here, fixing a furnace? I think it was a furnace, at least."

"I will," Elena replies quickly, her tone of voice concerned and infused with genuine kindness. "Why don't you stay in your room while I find out?"

"Can I go with you? I don't want to be alone."

"Certainly, if it makes you feel better."

We charge down the hallway looking for the two men, or at least to find someone who can confirm the two individuals were even in the building. After checking every room and utility closet, we ride the elevator to the lobby and inquire of the doorman.

"Pino?" Elena asks, as we approach the counter. "Have you seen two men coming through here?"

Pino appears surprised. "Two men? No, I can't say I have. What did they look like?"

Elena turns her attention to me. "Rosa? What did they look like? The two men."

"One of them was young — mid-30s to early 40s, maybe — with blond hair, longer on the top than on the sides. Maybe around six feet tall, medium build. He is the one that looks just like my husband. The other one is older and, honestly, I didn't take as good a look at him, once my defenses went on overdrive. But I think he was shorter than the younger man, with gray hair, and slightly overweight."

Pino looked at us with a bewildered expression on his face. "I have been here all day, and I haven't seen any men coming through."

"Are there any other entrances to the building?" I ask, desperate to prove my own sanity.

"There is a service door in the back, but it stays locked. And anyone who uses it would need to come by here first, to have us unlock it. It's normally used only for deliveries."

"I know where that door is," Elena says, grabbing me by the hand and leading me down a hallway to the right, toward the dining area. "Thank you for your help, Pino."

"I swear I saw them, Elena." An edge of desperation bleeds into my voice.

"I believe you, dear. Let's go find out who they are."

The service entrance is at the end of the hallway, adjacent to the staff doorway for the kitchen. I can feel my heart pounding in my throat as we approach it.

"As Pino said, it is locked," Elena states as she tries the handle. "It locks with a key, even on the inside, so only a key-holder would be able to open it."

"Who has the authority to carry keys around here?" I ask, jiggling the handle myself to confirm what Elena said.

"Only Pino, and maybe Doctor Castelli, but I saw him leaving about thirty minutes ago, so he couldn't have opened this door," Elena replies. I can't make out what she feels right now, but I am hoping she still believes what I told her.

"And Pino doesn't remember letting the men in," I reflect out loud. "Do we keep a visitor's log, I wonder?"

"No, I don't think so. There are not many people who visit us, and Doctor Castelli never felt the need to document deliveries, especially since anyone coming into the building has to check in with the front desk before they are granted access."

"I don't know what to think, Elena. I *know* I saw those two men. I even hit my hand on the furnace as I ran. I almost knocked it over." I say, the knot in my throat threatening to dissolve into bitter tears. I raise my left hand to illustrate what happened, and notice a small cut still bleeding on the side. "Look! This is where my hand hit the furnace! It is still bleeding!"

Elena examines my hand. It's hard to read the emotions parading across her face, but I am sure I see a shadow of concern.

"Let's retrace your steps, back to your room. At what point did you see the men?"

We head back to the second floor and I take the lead, as we begin to tread the hallway. "I was standing right here when I saw them. They were carrying a heavy piece of equipment that looked like a furnace, or some other appliance. I became agitated when I saw the face of the younger man, and I ran toward the safety of my room. I was so distraught that I wasn't paying attention to where I was going, and I remember brushing against one of them. I think it was the older man who told me to be more careful. After that I bolted into my room and stood against the door for a moment to catch my breath, before I peered outside to see if they were still there, and that's when you saw me."

"Hmm..." Elena absorbs my words and allows them to sink in before speaking. "So, you'd say that you had just seen the men a minute or two before I saw you looking out?"

"Yes. I don't know how many minutes went by, exactly, but it couldn't have been more than a couple. I wanted to know which direction they were heading."

Elena examines the door carefully. "There is a spatter of blood here, on the door." She points out a blood smear on the door frame, near the handle. "You might have hurt your hand on this protruding nail, as you were frantically trying to open the door."

I look at the tiny head of the nail, and then back at Elena, disbelief seeping into my voice — quickly replaced by frustration. "You don't believe me, do you?"

"I do. All I am saying is that you could have hurt your hand on the nail, Rosa."

"Do we have cameras in the hallways?" I ask, clinging to the last shred of hope.

"We don't have cameras up here. They are only on the first floor, by the entrance."

I nod, and open the door to my room. I need to be alone to gather my thoughts. Elena says nothing. She watches me go inside and she retreats, so that I can close the door. I know I saw the two men…I know I am not crazy. Or am I?

CHAPTER SIX

"Hurry up, Rosa," Olivia says before taking a full bite of toast, "Francesca is waiting outside with the van. We shouldn't let her wait too long."

After a day like yesterday, rushing is the last thing I feel like doing this morning! And who the hell is Francesca, anyway? My head is reeling from all I learned about my past, my chest still constricted by the fear I felt when I saw the man who looked like Marco. No trace of him was found. Nobody at the center is aware of anyone coming to fix an appliance, and the doorman is absolutely convinced that he did not see two men coming in through either of the two entrances. I could barely sleep last night, thinking about it. Is Doctor Castelli right? Am I retrieving too much information at once, maybe, and that's causing me to go insane? I don't feel crazy, but do crazy people know they have a problem? If I have any hope of conserving my sanity, I need to figure out a way to distract myself. Being locked up in here might be peaceful and safe, but as days turn into nights, and nights back into days, nothing ever changes…and it is hard to not become fixated on things. I need a distraction, at least for a day, to break the routine and rest my mind. As if they could read my thoughts, Giulia and Olivia asked me last night if I would like to join them on a day trip to Florence, and it felt like the perfect opportunity to change things up a bit. When they knocked on my door at 6:00 a.m., though, urging me to get up and get ready, my excitement for the trip had already fizzled out; I silently cursed myself for agreeing to go. Now, sitting at the breakfast table and feeling like a zombie with anorexia, I am barely able to touch my food. Deep down, I wish I could just tell everyone to leave without me.

"Come on, girls, it's time to go!" Giulia seems even more cheerful than Olivia, if that's possible. How can these people be so vibrant at this time of day? I get up from the table, making it a point to push my chair in as loudly as possible, in an effort to convey how grumpy I feel. I follow Giulia and Olivia outside, and we wait for the driver of the blue van that is parked directly in front of the main entrance.

It's a glorious morning with only a slight chill lingering in the air, and a sky devoid of clouds, tinged by the vibrant hues of the rising sun. I wrap my arms around myself, wishing I had chosen a heavier jacket than the denim one I am wearing…and I wish I could have brought along an extra cup of coffee.

"Here's Francesca. Ready to go, ladies?" Olivia's voice is entirely too enthusiastic for this early in the morning. I turn to see the driver barreling out of the building, and I come face to face with a tiny woman, no taller than five feet, maybe, with dark brown hair cut like a mushroom top, and sparkling brown eyes that remind me of milk chocolate. She is quite petite, and I wonder how old she is. At first glance, she appears to be around 25, but after a closer examination of her face, I am more inclined to think that she is probably a little over 30.

"Francesca, this is Rosa. Rosa, meet Francesca. Francesca used to be a resident here, but she occasionally still comes by to visit and drive us around."

I shake Francesca's hand and nod politely. "Nice to meet you, Francesca. It's nice of you to drive us to Florence today."

"My pleasure," she replies. "This center helped me a lot, when I felt stuck and I was left without hope. Sometimes you just have to pay it forward."

I instantly like her. She is warm and bubbly, and I feel good being around her. As much as I hate not remembering my previous life, I am grateful for the friendships I have forged in this place. These women are like war veterans: They might all have fought different battles in different eras, but we all understand the struggle each goes through, and we strive to support one another toward collective healing. I suddenly realize the depth, the significance, of what I just thought: *We.* I included myself in the group…now that my hidden past has begun to surface, I have become one of them. I feel a sense of camaraderie connecting all of us, and I immediately feel energized by it. The morning fog has lifted. I am ready to go to Florence.

The drive to the city is not too long — 30 minutes, or even a little less. We journey through soft hills, along roads barely wide enough for one car at a time, until we merge onto the highway. The Tuscan countryside is truly breathtaking and, since my memory is gone, I am savoring the view with the wonder of a child on her first trip to see the ocean.

Francesca lets us off in front of the train station while she goes to park the van, and all I can do is stand there and take in the beauty for a moment.

By eight in the morning, the sun is almost completely up, though strokes of pink and yellow still set the eastern sky on fire, with shadows barely darkening the exquisite details on Brunelleschi's *Duomo*. Giulia stands against the metal pole of a bus stop, her eyes fixed on the majestic beauty of the *Duomo*. She pulls a booklet from her purse, scanning the pages until she finds the right one.

"Listen to this, everybody," she says with her eyes riveted on the booklet. "The construction of the *Duomo* was started in 1426, and its breathtaking beauty was accredited to Filippo Brunelleschi and Giotto di Bondone, among several other artists of the time. The *Duomo* was a perfect example of how Gothic Revival architecture, Italian Gothic architecture, and Renaissance architecture, could all come together to create a masterpiece that was both stunning and timeless." She looks up from the book, and opens her eyes wider. "Isn't this an amazing sight to behold? It is absolutely majestic!"

Francesca is coming around the corner and waves at us. She is so small and light that her feet barely appear to be touching the ground when she walks.

"Are you ladies interested in fashion?" she asks, and looks at each of us to check our reaction. "The Salvatore Ferragamo Museum is not too far from here, or we could stroll down Via de' Tornabuoni, and have a chance to admire the latest creations of high couture."

"What about the Ponte Vecchio?" asks Giulia, still perusing her book.

"The Ponte Vecchio is definitely a must-see if you have never been to Florence before. The entire bridge houses the best jewelry artisans in the country — even, I daresay, in the world. Some of the jewels are perfectly breathtaking."

"Well, what is stopping us? Let's go!" Giulia chimes in, enthusiastically. "I love jewelry!"

It takes us about ten minutes to walk to the Ponte Vecchio and, as Francesca claimed, it is a must-see. The jewelry stores are encased within the ancient brick walls, adorned with windows featuring small green shutters, and my first impression is of an exceptionally long house suspended over the Arno River. Francesca was also right about the quality of the jewelry. Hand-crafted 18-karat gold necklaces, encrusted with emeralds, diamonds and rubies; stunning bracelets and rings on display along both sides of the small pathway, cast an enchanted glow over the entire bridge.

"I used to love jewelry, too," Olivia says, inclining her head to take a better look at a gold, snake-shaped necklace with eyes of amber. "Now I no longer find it as alluring. Maybe I am just getting old."

"Or maybe," Francesca suggests, "you have traded the glitter in for freedom. Luxuries often keep us imprisoned by our realities."

Olivia considers her friend's words. "I guess you are right. I lived in a golden cage while I was married, and it never occurred to me that the very same person who fed me every day also clipped my wings to prevent me from flying away. He never hit me physically, but he ignored me for so long that I became convinced I deserved to be pushed away, and I felt I was incapable of making it on my own. I honestly don't know why he wouldn't just divorce me. He didn't love me anymore — *that* he made extremely clear on multiple occasions! — but he still owned me. I was one of his many possessions, not even as important as his car, or his speedboat. Men like him don't necessarily play with their toys anymore, once they have had them for a while, but they can't accept that someone else might play with them, either."

None of us can really afford to buy anything from the stores on this bridge, so we cross over to the other side of the river, and head toward the Cathedral of Santa Maria del Fiore. After scanning through the pages of her booklet, Giulia also informs us that we should go visit the leather factory on Lungarno Acciaiuoli.

The Cathedral is stunning. It was built in 1412 on top of the second cathedral of Santa Reparata, another church that remained in activity for nine centuries, until orders were given to demolish it in 1375. We make a beeline toward it and, as we step inside, we are immediately welcomed by a shift in temperature of several degrees. The main artistic attraction is a fresco of *The Last Judgment*, painted by Giorgio Vasari over the course of seven years.

I am at a loss for words. I can't wrap my mind around the immensity of religious fervor by which one would need to be fueled, to create such a masterpiece.

We remain inside the cathedral for a short while longer and then spill back outside — all shielding our eyes from the sun's blinding brightness, in such a simultaneous movement that we might almost have been ordered to do so by the bark of a military command.

"Is anyone hungry?" I ask, hoping that someone other than me agrees it is a good idea to go somewhere for lunch.

"I am," Francesca says, raising her hand like a child in school. I knew I liked this girl for a reason!

"Should we pick a café somewhere? There are so many around here that we can just toss a coin and see where it lands."

"We can do better," Francesca replies. "I stopped by the kitchen this morning and picked up the lunch the staff prepared for us. That's why you had to wait for me to come back to the van." She pulls the backpack off her shoulder and opens it, displaying the goodies carefully packed inside. "There is a lovely park not far from here, where we can go eat lunch. It has a lot of shade trees, and beautiful pieces of artwork are scattered throughout the grounds."

"Sounds like a plan to me!" Giulia says with her usual enthusiasm.

Olivia nods in agreement, though I can't quite tell if she is happy about the picnic idea, or if she would have preferred to sit at a cheery café somewhere.

The walk to the park takes a little longer than I expect and, by the time we arrive, I am starving, and my feet hurt. Francesca finds a place for us to sit on a bench under a huge poplar — right beside an armless statue of Venus, its features softened by centuries and the elements. She kneels on the ground, carefully unpacking the contents of her backpack, and hands out small paper bags — filled with a sandwich, two pieces of fruit, and a small bottle of water — to each of us. As soon as I unwrap my sandwich, my stomach almost leaps with joy: The tantalizing aroma of mortadella that escapes the confines of the thin plastic wrap is more tempting than Satan himself. I dig my teeth into that tasty goodness, my eyes nearly rolling into the back of my head.

"I really needed this!" I exclaim, sheer pleasure oozing out through my words. "I barely ate any breakfast this morning."

"You should always eat in the morning," Giulia says, knowingly. "Eating early in the day speeds up your metabolism."

"I can't eat when I first wake up," I respond quickly. "But after a couple of hours of moving around, I usually get hungry." Laughing, I add, "Never mind that we've covered a few miles on foot today, and burned a considerable number of calories."

"I love walking around Florence," Francesca says, after she swallows a bite of her sandwich. "I think Florence is my favorite of all cities in Italy."

"It's beautiful, alright." Olivia chimes in.

"It's stunning." Giulia adds her two cents to the already unanimous opinion.

They all turn to look at me, and I feel pressured to say something. "It's definitely a beautiful city. I think we all take for granted the amazing artistic wealth we have in this country."

Everyone nods, leaving me free to go back to my lunch bag.

"So, Francesca," Giulia asks, "how long have you been gone from the center?"

Francesca pauses for a moment, seemingly intent in calculating the length of time.

"It has probably been about five years since I left. It is nice to come back and visit sometimes, and to help out as I can."

"Did you go back home after you left?" I ask with genuine curiosity.

Francesca smiles, and I can't detect a hint of sadness or bitterness in her at all. "No. I didn't really have any family left to go to. All I had was my fiancé, and it was thanks to him that I ended up in the center to begin with. Being an orphan, and with no siblings, he was all I had."

Francesca's words make me wonder about my own family. Do I have anyone, aside from Matteo, who's waiting for me to come back?

"At any rate," she continues, "I think my biggest mistake was to allow him to gradually control everything I did. It felt good at first, to be taken care of, but after a while, I felt suffocated."

Everyone nods at the same time. Control, sadly, is one of the building blocks of abuse.

"Did you have a job outside the house?" I ask gently.

"Oh, I did. And I really enjoyed it. That's how Marco and I met."

Marco?! Her fiancé's name is Marco? Jesus…

I shift uncomfortably on the bench, intent on not showing the anxiety that name has triggered inside me, but I see Olivia and Giulia immediately look in my direction, and I make an extra effort to appear cool.

Apparently unaware of the effect her words have had on me, Francesca continues her story. "As I was saying, that's how Marco and I met — through work. We both worked for the same company."

I am holding my breath as words fall from Francesca's lips. How odd is it that we both had partners named Marco?

"How long were you and Marco engaged?" Just uttering the name makes my throat dry up.

"For about two years. I was in a very dark place after our relationship ended, and it took me a while to come to terms with the fact that nobody aside from myself would save me from the demons that had been unleashed."

"Did you come straight to the center?" I ask, suddenly more interested in her story than I should be.

Francesca shakes her head, and a fleeting shadow scurries along her beautiful face. "No, unfortunately. I couldn't."

"Why not?" I ask, determined to put these puzzle pieces into place before this day trip is over.

"I was trapped inside my own pain, and I couldn't see a way out of it, so I needed to see clearly before I embarked on a healing journey."

"Wow…" I say, at a loss for anything better. "I am sorry you went through all that. I am glad you were able to find the strength to overcome the feelings that dragged you down."

"Thank you. What about you? I already know Olivia, and Giulia and I have met briefly once before, but you are new."

I sit back against the bench, folding my hands in my lap. "Well, I wish I could tell you more, but I am just now beginning to remember. I only recently discovered that my real name is Iliana, but I still like to be called Rosa. I was married to a psychopath named Marco — odd, isn't it, that my husband's name is the same as your fiancé's? — and we have a beautiful little boy named Matteo. So far, I have remembered that my husband beat me — physically and emotionally — and even forced me into sexual activity that made me uncomfortable and caused me pain. I can't remember anything else yet, but the severe abuse is probably why I lost my memory."

"Oh yes, it is quite possible. Are you planning to go back to your old life once you retrieve all your memories?"

Nobody has asked me that question yet. *Am I?*

"I honestly don't have an answer for that. There are still a lot of holes in my memory, so I guess it would depend on what else I remember. I imagine that whatever he put me through was bad enough to put me away for a while, but I still have a son to take care of. I don't even know who is taking care of him right now."

"Hopefully not his father," Francesca says with conviction, nodding her head to emphasize her statement.

"I hope not. I hope I have family somewhere, who is taking care of Matteo. I can't remember much about anyone else but the two of them."

"You will, you just have to give yourself time," Francesca reassures me, before picking up her backpack from the ground. "Well, are you ladies ready to get back? We can do a little more sight-seeing, or we can go back to the center."

"I don't want to go back yet," Giulia replies quickly. "It is so beautiful out here that I want to make the most of this day."

They all look at one another first, then at me. "What do you think, Rosa?"

I shrug, neutral to either decision. "It doesn't matter, really. I am thoroughly enjoying our time here, but I am okay with going back if everyone else is tired."

"Well, I vote for staying" Giulia interjects as soon as she has a chance. "There is one more place I would like to visit. Isn't there a famous museum around here? Not the fashion museum, an art museum. I remember reading about it."

"There are three, actually. The Uffizi Gallery, the Bargello National Museum, and the Galleria dell'Accademia. The one you have probably read about is the Uffizi Gallery. Aside from the building itself being amazing — it was built in the 1500s — the Uffizi Gallery houses a stunning collection of masterpieces by artists such as Giotto, Piero Della Francesca, Leonardo, Raffaello, and Michelangelo."

"Yes, I think that's the one!" Giulia exclaim excitedly.

"Well, what do you say, ladies? Should we make one more stop?" Francesca asks, and then waits for us to say something. Giulia has already expressed her opinion, so it is down to Olivia and me.

"I have no problem going to the Uffizi. It's a beautiful gallery to visit." Olivia says, then she passes the ball to my court.

"Sure," I reply timidly. "I don't know if I have ever been there, though I assume that, if I lived near here, I probably have. Maybe I will see something that will trigger a memory."

"It's settled, then." Francesca springs to a standing position and threads her now empty backpack over her shoulder. "Let's go!"

Walking through Florence is an experience. Unbelievable masterpieces of art are sprinkled throughout the city, buildings — perfectly maintained — date back centuries, and even the numerous cafés contribute to the magical atmosphere of the place. We finally arrive at the main entrance of the Uffizi Gallery, and we wait in line to go inside. Giulia pulls out her travel guide and reads to us while we wait.

"This is quite interesting. Listen," she says with excitement. "This building was initially not intended to be a museum at all. Instead, it was ordered by Cosimo I de' Medici in 1560 to house the judiciary and administrative offices of Florence. Cosimo I de' Medici was Grand Duke of Tuscany at the time. The artist who designed the U-shaped building, Giorgio Vasari, also created a secret passage that connected this building to the Pitti Palace. The Pitti Palace is an iconic hotspot for fashion now, and the passage — the Corridoio Vasariano — was built in less than five months, and inaugurated in 1565, in observance of Cosimo's son's wedding to Giovanna, a royal from Austria. Many of the masterpieces we enjoy today were part of a private collection from the Medici dynasty, and one of the reasons why they are still in Florence after so many centuries is because of the *Family Pact,* signed by Anna Maria Luisa de' Medici before her death in 1743. The pact ensured that all the artistic treasures collected by the Medici family over the course of three centuries would remain in the city. The private gallery opened to public viewing sixteen years after her death."

"Wow," I say, when Giulia pauses. "The historical value of this place — as of many others we have seen today — is humbling!"

"Yes," Giulia replies, awe permeating her voice. "I have always loved history and art. My husband never supported my passions; he thought women's only purposes were to cook and produce children, leaving their husbands free to philander at their whim."

"Marco liked art, I think," Francesca threw in. Just hearing the sound of that name feels like nails scraping a chalkboard, and I involuntarily shiver.

"Dino never had time for art," Olivia adds, a pained look on her beautiful face. "He thinks art is a waste of time. If it doesn't make him money, it has no value."

"And you didn't make him any money, did you?" I ask and, before the words even leave my mouth, I regret saying them. Why did I ask something so insensitive?

She replies before I can apologize. "No, I didn't. He cashed in on the little money I had when we were first married. I owned a house that had belonged to my grandmother, and he sold it, claiming it was just a money pit — old, and in need of constant repairs. He invested the money in stocks and, according to him, the stocks lost value when the economy crashed in 2009. I literally had nothing to my name; he controlled our finances completely." She doesn't seem upset by my inane question.

"Let's go, ladies," Francesca calls out, as we approach the main entrance to the gallery.

I am not prepared for the stunning beauty awaiting us inside. The checkered marble floors and priceless statues on each side of the corridor are absolutely breathtaking, but even they pale in comparison to the mind-blowing collections carefully arranged in individual halls. A quick peek into Hall 35, dedicated to Michelangelo and the Florentines, makes me literally gasp. The *Tondo Doni,* also known as *The Holy Family with the Infant and St. John the*

Baptist, is the main piece on display in this room, and also the only work of Michelangelo's that remains in Florence. This particular work has played a major role in influencing later artists, not just because of the serpentine composition of the bodies of the sacred family, and the bright colors of their clothes — but also because of the nude figures in the background, reminiscent of Christianity's struggle to stifle Paganism. The blood-red walls in the hall only seem to highlight the battle between good and evil, as depicted in this famous painting.

With our minds still reeling from the striking beauty of the Michelangelo display, we tag along with a group of tourists headed to explore Hall 15 — the room which contains the early works of Leonardo Da Vinci, painted before he relocated to Milan in 1482. What I find most striking about Leonardo is the scientific detail he applied to his artistic work, especially in the *Annunciation,* a beautiful painting in which the wings of the angel resemble the wings of a bird. We leave the tourist group and continue to explore the different halls, blown away by the works of Caravaggio, Andrea del Sarto, Raffaello, and Botticelli, but — as if my mind hadn't already reached the capacity of what it could absorb in one day — my heart skips a beat when I lay eyes on an elderly woman talking to a group of teenagers. There is something hauntingly familiar about the woman, and I pause to register her facial features. She has a mane of silver hair, framing an angular face that has only been slightly softened by the passing of time. She appears to be around 65: She is tall, and dressed smartly in a two-piece navy suit. I wonder if she is a teacher, or maybe a curator of the gallery. The group around her is listening attentively to her words; I feel inspired by her strength she exudes, and by the respect she naturally commands. *A woman like that would never be abused by anyone...*

"Are you coming, Rosa?" Francesca asks, when she notices I have stopped walking.

"Yes, sorry about that," I reply quickly. "I felt like I knew that lady, somehow."

"Maybe she reminds you of someone in your life," Francesca offers. "Maybe your mother? Or a teacher that was important to you?"

My mother…what does my mother look like?

I glance hurriedly at the lady in question, then catch up with the rest of our group. The entire walk back to the van is pleasantly peppered by Giulia's gushing about all we have seen today. Her innocence and enthusiasm are a breath of fresh air; I focus on her energy, to shut off the chatter in my brain. The drive back to the center is uneventful and peaceful. We are all physically exhausted from walking miles, still absorbing all we have seen.

I close my eyes and try to nap for a short while, but questions about my family echo through my brain, from my soul. What does my mother look like? Is she still alive? And most of all, is she looking for me?

CHAPTER SEVEN

Too many questions, not enough answers, and yet, the revelations of the last few days have left me drained. There are so many thoughts running through my mind — with blank spaces in between them — that I find it extremely hard to connect the dots. I thought getting away for a day with friends would help, but instead, I feel disoriented and alone. Seeing that woman in the gallery filled me with a strange anxiety, the depths of which I cannot comprehend. Knowing the love I carry in my heart for my son, I find myself craving the love of a mother. It's funny to think that a grown woman would miss her mother as much as I do right now, but deep down, I feel no differently than would a wounded child, needing someone to slay the dragons of confusion and restore the peace.

I don't know what to do. The shreds of information I have been able to retrieve so far are not enough to paint a picture, yet — much as I hate to admit it even to myself — I am terrified of what I will remember, once everything comes rushing back. There. I have said it. I suddenly remember a picture I have seen somewhere, depicting a man who must choose between killing his mother to avenge the death of his father, or letting his mother go free in honor of the fact that she gave birth to him, thus dishonoring the memory of his father. In the picture — a Greek myth, I believe, as I continue to examine the image playing through my mind — the man is frozen between the god Apollo, who holds him accountable to honor the patriarch, and the three Furies, who promise to haunt him for eternity if he commits matricide. Eight swords are laid out by his feet, but all the man can do is cover his ears to avoid hearing either of the conflicting voices, threatening to destroy his existence. I don't even know where I saw that picture, or how I remember it while everything else is shrouded in darkness, but I feel exactly like that desperate man. I need to remember, in order to go back and claim my son, and at the same time I am terrified of what my mind is so fiercely keeping under lock and key. I am standing at a crossroads, and I don't know which direction to go.

I should get up and get ready for group therapy, but I don't even know what I should share. My memories are so disjointed that they make absolutely no sense, even to me, but I feel that I must organize what I have recalled, so I can file the information away. Only then can I make room for more discoveries.

I get up slowly, my legs still aching from the miles we walked yesterday, and walk to the table, retrieving a notepad and pen before returning to bed. I cross my legs and adjust the pillows behind my back, to provide some support while I sit for some time. Maybe, instead of merely jotting down a "grocery list" of what I have remembered, I can write a letter to Iliana, and tell her that she is allowed to remember.

I like that idea: The thought of writing to my former self gives me the power to also comfort the woman I was, and let her know she is going to be okay.

Dear Iliana, I scribble, my hand shaking as soon as I start writing, *my name is Rosa, and I have some things I need to share with you. I hope that, as you get to know me, you will also feel comfortable in sharing personal details of your life with me. You see, I woke up in a shelter, a while back, confused and scared. I didn't know what had happened to me — I still don't know — and I am trying to remember as much as I can, though the doctor here, and some of the other residents, tell me I should be patient, and that my memory will come back when the time is right. I know they are trying to help me, but they don't understand how excruciating it is for me to sit here, day after day, knowing that I have a little*

94

boy out there who needs me; a little boy whose last name I don't even know, who probably cries himself to sleep at night, not knowing where his mother is. I am sure you understand how I feel, for I am sure you love your son Matteo more than your own life. In fact, I have no doubt that you would place your life on the line for him, especially if you had to protect him.

As I sit here on my bed, writing to you, my son absorbs most of my thoughts, and yet, I also think of you, and everything you have been through. I know some of the things Marco did to you: I know he controlled you, beat you, and made you feel like you weren't worth the dirt he walked on, but he was wrong. Now that my mind has been at rest for a while, I know how wrong he was: You aren't stupid, or incapable, or insensitive. You are a woman who tried her best...it's just that your best was not enough to slay the demons your husband carries within himself. You don't have to be ashamed anymore, and you don't have to believe the lies he told you. You are a beautiful human being who deserves to be loved and cherished, and if it's the last thing I do, I will find a way to remember and come back to you and Matteo...and, once I do, our lives will change.

For now, I need you to trust me, and I need your help to remember what happened. Think of me as your future self, stripped away of the pain you are carrying around like a cross.

Love always,

Rosa

I wipe away the tears that have been running copiously down my face and fold the letter, though I am unsure now what I should do with it. Maybe I should really mail it, just to create the visual image of sending a message. As crazy as that thought sounds, it makes sense to me, and I jump off the bed, still wearing pajama pants and without even washing my face, to go ask for an envelope and stamp from the front desk.

When I arrive downstairs, Pino — as always — is behind the desk, and I wonder if he ever leaves this place. He looks as impeccable as ever, in his blue suit and freshly-trimmed hair.

"Good morning, Rosa," he says cheerfully, then he takes a second look at my appearance. "Did you fall out of bed?"

"No, Pino, I didn't, but I need an envelope and a stamp, if you have one of each."

"Who are you writing to?" he inquires, a puzzled look on his face.

I want to tell him the truth, but I don't need the doorman to think I have gone completely insane, which would probably raise a red flag with the doctor. "I want to write to my mother."

Pino nods, but he keeps his eyes fixed on me as he opens a large drawer. "You remembered who your mother is?"

His question stops me in my tracks. Does the doctor share confidential information with the doorman? Aside from the question of it being unethical to do so, why would there be any reason for Pino to know personal things about the residents?

"Yes, I did. I just want to write to her, and let her know I am okay." I don't even know why I lied, but I am a little irked at having my dirty laundry out for everyone to see: Knowing that strangers know my secrets makes me feel vulnerable. What else does Pino know about me? Does he know that Marco beat me, or that he sexually assaulted me? I suddenly feel very self-conscious around this man I barely know; I take the envelope and stamp he has placed on the counter, and hurry back to the safety of my room.

I close the door and slip the neatly-folded paper inside the envelope. I just write, "To Iliana" on the front, where the address should be, and, "From Rosa" in the top left corner. I carefully affix the stamp to the top right corner, and leave the envelope on the table while I get dressed for the group meeting.

I still don't know what I will say when it is my turn to talk, but I will figure something out. There's no time for a shower before I have to go now, so I just pick out a pair of jeans and a sweater, brush my teeth and hair, and bolt out the door — hoping I have time to drop the letter into the mailbox at the front desk before going to the meeting.

Pino is still behind the desk when I arrive, organizing papers in a red binder, and he glances at me over his reading glasses when I approach the desk. "You are wearing real clothes now," he jokes.

Pino means no harm. If I have a dad, I hope he is as even-tempered and as sweet as Pino, and I smile, in spite of the embarrassment and anger I felt just 20 minutes earlier. "Yes…sorry about coming down like that, earlier. I don't know where the closest mailbox is, and I was wondering if we have a mail pickup."

"We sure do," Pino replies, automatically extending his hand across the counter, palm up, to accept the letter. He looks at the address and appears a bit disconcerted, but he doesn't say a word. I am sure that, if he has worked here for a while, he has seen his share of strange things.

I leave the letter with Pino and rush to the meeting room. I should have been there five minutes ago, and although we often make small talk for a short while, I hate to be the last person to walk into the room when everyone else is already sitting down.

"Good morning, Rosa!" Doctor Castelli exclaims as I timidly open the door and peer inside, "I'm glad you could join us."

"I am sorry I am late, doctor. I had something to take care of before I came." I am grateful he didn't ask me the nature of my engagement.

"No problem at all, dear, please have a seat."

I sit between Olivia and Romina, and make a mental roster of the other women in the room. Gina is not sitting in her usual spot, and I wonder if she is not feeling well, or if she is maybe sleeping in this morning.

"I am glad you all could make it," Doctor Castelli begins. "Who would like to start?"

Giulia raises her hand, and I am suddenly grateful. I hope we will run out of time before it is my turn to speak.

"Go ahead, Giulia," the doctor encourages her.

"I went to Florence with Olivia, Francesca, and Rosa, yesterday. We had a great time, and I would like to thank them for making me feel like we all belong to a family."

Doctor Castelli smiles. "That's great, Giulia. I am glad you and the other ladies enjoyed yourselves. Is there something you would like to share?"

"Yes," Giulia responds. "Spending quality time with my sisters made me think about the value of family. I know we all come from different backgrounds and different cultures, but the love we share for one another connects us beyond the divide of our individual experiences. Understanding such a profound concept made me think about my own family. I was so wrapped up in my own drama, when I was married, that I isolated myself from the very people who cared about me unconditionally. I wish now that I could have trusted them with what was weighing on my soul. If I had, maybe I would not be here."

"Maybe you could write them a letter and explain that to them." The words slip out of my mouth before I can stop them. "I did that this morning — wrote a letter to myself, I mean."

"That's wonderful, Rosa. Right now, you and your old self are barely acquaintances. Establishing a connection with the woman you used to be is a fantastic idea. She has to trust you before she decides it is safe to come out and tell you about herself."

I am glad the doctor feels this way. I thought he would consider it a crazy idea; instead, he seems to be enthusiastic about it. "That's why I was late coming to the meeting. I went to the front desk for an envelope and stamp to send it off."

"But how can you mail it when you don't have an address, or even a last name?" Romina asks.

"It doesn't matter," Doctor Castelli explains to her. "It makes little difference if it ever arrives at a physical address. What counts is that it was sent. You wrote your real name on the envelope, I am assuming, yes?"

I am ecstatic about the doctor taking the reins of the conversation and responding to Romina's question for me — aside from my not having to formulate a reply, his words convey that he understands exactly what I was hoping to accomplish.

"I love that idea!" Giulia squeals. "I think I am going to do that. I would like to write a letter to my husband's lover, and tell her that I forgive her for what she did. Ultimately, she had no obligations to me — he is the one who was obligated — and, although women should not intentionally hurt other women, I understand that, maybe, she was under Ettore's spell as much as I was, and she wasn't looking at the bigger picture. Her ego clouded her judgment, and she fell victim to his charm. I was very angry with her at first, and I blamed her for destroying my marriage and my life, but now I understand it wasn't her fault. He lured her into his trap, and it was he who had pledged loyalty to me. She had made no such pledge. I forgive her, and I plan to write her a letter to explain how I feel."

"This is wonderful!" Doctor Castelli says excitedly. "Thank you for the suggestion, Rosa. You have not only helped yourself by coming up with this great idea; you have also helped others identify a tool they can use in their own healing."

I lean back in the chair, satisfied with myself.

"I don't know that I can forgive my husband's mistress yet," Olivia offers timidly. "Maybe your husband's girlfriend was nothing to you, Giulia, but Dino's lover was supposed to be my friend. It was a double betrayal."

"It is okay for you to feel this way, Olivia," the doctor reassures her. "Losing a friend can hurt more than losing a husband. The bond in friendship sometimes runs deeper than the connection between two married people, especially if the marriage has been strained for a while. Discovering that your friend broke your trust is a hard pill to swallow. But, ultimately, by not forgiving her, you are not punishing her: You are punishing yourself. Forgiving someone does not mean that you condone what they have done; it means that you no longer allow what they did to affect you deeply."

I watch Olivia's face as she reflects on the wise words of the doctor. Theoretically, I understand what he is telling us, but putting that knowledge into practice is a different thing altogether. Could I forgive Anna for sleeping with Marco? A vision of the two of them, undressed, in the car flashes through my mind, and I feel anger. But then, I remember how she reacted when Marco became threatening to me, and I suddenly understand that she was not a monster; he was. Yes, I think I can forgive Anna. I don't know whether we can ever be friends again, but I can forgive her and evict her from my mind.

Rita and Arianna haven't said anything, but I notice now that they both nodded when the doctor explained the meaning of forgiveness. Have they forgiven their husbands for what they did? And what about Romina? Her husband was not cheating on her, but he couldn't let her out of his control. Could it be that something in his past made him feel that, if he lost control, he would be vulnerable? Could he have been a young boy feeling like a leaf in the wind, unable to harness the winds of life that tossed him around? Could it be that, at some point in his life, he was hurt because he had no control over the circumstances that affected his very existence?

"Would anyone else like to share anything today?" Doctor Castelli asks, as his eyes move from one woman to the next, making direct eye contact with each of us.

"I would like to share something, doctor," I say. "There are still a lot of holes in my memory, but I feel I am getting stronger each day, as I prepare to remember everything that happened in my past. The memories I have retrieved until now are painful, and there are moments when I question if I am pushing the envelope too fast, but I know I am safe here, and if I start spiraling down, you are all here to catch me."

Just as I hear myself speak those last words, an image of the two men carrying a furnace crosses my mind, but I quickly push it away. I *am* safe here.

"I am glad to hear you say that, Rosa. As you get stronger, it will become easier to process the information that rises to the surface," Doctor Castelli replies with a smile. He then pauses for a few seconds before dismissing the group. "Thank you all for coming today, and for sharing."

We stand and put away the chairs. Before we leave the room, I make it a point to ask about Gina. "Is Gina okay, doctor? When I first noticed she wasn't here today, I thought maybe she had just slept in, but it occurs to me now that I also didn't see her at dinner last night."

"As we discussed in my office, Rosa, you need to focus on healing yourself. Each of the residents here has a different journey, and sometimes, it is best for them to move to a different department, or to a different facility altogether."

I look at the doctor with surprise. "Do you mean that Gina left?"

"She did. She realized that she wasn't making any progress here, and she understood that there are other steps she must complete first. Again, please don't worry about Gina; she will be fine."

The dismissive tone in his voice curtails the brief conversation, and I go back to making sure the chairs are situated against the wall before I leave. Olivia is still in the hallway when I exit the room, and I quicken my pace to catch up with her.

"Did you know Gina left?" I ask.

Olivia nods. "Yes, the doctor told us she left, just before you arrived at the meeting."

"Do you know why she left?"

Olivia shrugs. "No, not really. I guess she wasn't getting what she needed."

"So, what happens in a case like that? Do the residents move to another shelter? Are there facilities that offer different resources?"

"I believe so. I think this is only a temporary place, Rosa. We come here for a while, but then we must leave and be ready to cross through the next doorway. Gina was not able to let go of some things, and she couldn't move forward."

"Is there a limit of time to live at this center?"

"Not necessarily. But if, after a long while, things don't improve, then your case is reevaluated—and you might be assigned to a new place."

I nod, feeling a touch of sadness at not being able to say goodbye to Gina. We hadn't bonded much in the time since I arrived here, but—like the rest of us—she, too, was struggling and needed our support. In the end, even if her circumstances were different, she was one of us.

"I understand. Well, I guess I am going back to my room for now. I feel tired again, and I think that maybe it is a good idea to rest a while," I say, as I stop by the elevator to go upstairs.

"Good idea. I am going to the recreation room for a bit, to check out the new fabrics that came in yesterday while we were gone."

Back on the second floor, I head straight for my room, happy to be alone with my thoughts again. My eyes are burning and my body aches, and I can't think of anything better, right now, than taking a nap. I welcome the feeling of being swallowed by the mattress as soon as I lie down, and in no time at all, I slip into deep slumber.

A man is standing near the front desk when I descend into the lobby; he is dressed in dark overalls, and I can't see his face while he is talking to Pino, but I am close enough to hear him speak.

"Can you tell me how to get to Iliana Landini's room?" he asks.

My heart stops…it's him! I silently gesture to Pino to be quiet as I back away, but before I can take a step, the man turns around, and I find myself face to face with a nightmare.

"Well, well…" he muses. "Look who's here." He grins first, then erupts into laughter.

I feel my heart implode. My breath catches in my throat and I think I am going to faint. What is he going to do to me now that he has found me? I take two more steps back and then run in the direction of the garden. I can feel him closing in, and I know he is right behind me. Jesus…why did you let him find me? Isn't this place supposed to be in a secret location?

I run to the building, but the door is locked! Marco is towering over me now, and he places a hand over my mouth. If this is an attempt to stop me from screaming, he is wasting his time. I am so frozen in fear right now, that I can't even move, much less scream!

"You thought you had gotten away from me, didn't you?"

I shake my head vigorously.

"No? Are you saying you weren't trying to get away from me?" he hisses. "Then you are not just stupid, you are a liar, too. And you should know what I do to liars."

He places his free hand around my throat and squeezes. "You should never have left me and our son. What kind of mother are you? I have told you time and again: You are lower than the dirt I step on every day."

I try as hard as I can to pry his hand away from my throat, but he is too strong for me to break free. I can feel the pressure of his fingers crushing against my trachea, and I can't breathe. I am going to lose consciousness and die. I will never be able to see my son again.

I jump up, and I am suddenly sitting on my bed, nearly hyperventilating and sweating profusely. Thankfully, it was a dream — but how do I know that he won't eventually find me here?

Once my breathing has returned to normal, I lay my head on the pillow and try to relax. Then, I drift off again, and Marco is no longer there. A woman is smiling at me, and she silently motions for me to follow her. She is an elderly woman with short silver hair, dressed in a powder blue suit. She looks almost like the woman I saw at the gallery, but her features are softer, and her build is a little thicker. She opens a door and, when Matteo comes running through, she scoops him up in her arms and plants a kiss on his cheek.

"See, Mommy?" Matteo says, his tiny arms wrapped around the woman's neck, "I am with grandma Angela now, but I miss you."

I watch them in awe as they begin to walk away, but then, the woman turns to look at me, and again, she invites me to follow. She opens one more door, and suddenly, Iliana walks through, her face bruised and her hair shaved to accommodate the bandages wrapped around her head. I hold my breath as Iliana walks over and takes my hand softly. She places something in my palm and gently closes my fingers into a fist. I try to open my hand to see what she gave me, but she shakes her head, so I close my fist again. There is so much I want to say to her, but the words are trapped in my throat and they won't come out. I reach out to touch her face, and she smiles back at me, before walking away through the door with Matteo and the elderly woman. I open my fist now, to reveal a folded piece of paper. I unfold it with shaky hands and I gasp, as the words *SAVE ME* scream inside my head.

CHAPTER EIGHT

My pillow is soaked with tears when I wake up, and my fist is clenched so tight, my knuckles are turning white. I open my hand and stare at my empty palm, my eyes still registering the piece of paper Iliana placed in it. *SAVE ME.*

I sit at the edge of the bed and I wipe my face with my hands. *How can I save you, Iliana? Please, help me help you.* And then, I suddenly remember...my last name! In the first dream, Marco mentioned my last name to Pino. *Landini,* he said. My full name is Iliana Landini, and my mother's name is Angela. I say a silent prayer of gratitude. It is not a lot, but it is something. I finally know my name, though I can't be sure if it is my married or maiden name. Iliana Landini...I like the sound of it.

I wonder what time it is. I keep forgetting to ask Doctor Castelli or Elena if I can have a clock in my room. Even if I was told there aren't many clocks in the facility, I don't see how having a wall clock could possibly hinder my progress. My stomach is growling, so I'm betting it is close to lunch time. I plan to go by the doctor's office anyway, to ask if I can be hypnotized again. I had planned to wait a while, but the sight of Iliana's bruises in the dream gave me a new sense of urgency. Maybe the dream is a premonition, and that's what will happen if Marco finds me.

I put shoes on and proceed to Doctor Castelli's office, hoping he will agree to hypnotize me again. Olivia and Rita are in the lobby when I step off the elevator downstairs.

"Hey Rosa, did you have a good nap?" Rita asks as I walk by.

"It was okay. I had more dreams..."

Olivia's attention is piqued. "Did anything important come through?"

I nod, and I am sure Olivia knows me well enough, by now, to see that I am shaken.

"What did you dream?" Olivia urges gently.

"I had two dreams. In the first one, my husband was here in this lobby," I respond, and point at the location by the front desk where Marco was standing. "He asked Pino where my room was. Then he saw me, and chased me into the garden, where he threatened to kill me. The only good part of that dream is that, when Marco asked about me, he mentioned my full name. I know my last name is Landini."

"Oh, my! That's a *huge* breakthrough!" Olivia exclaims excitedly.

"Yes, I think so, too. I don't know if Landini is my maiden name or my married name, but either way, I now have an identity."

"What happened in the second dream?" Rita asks.

My eyes fill with tears. "I saw my mom holding my son. And then, I saw Iliana."

"You saw yourself?"

"Yes. She — I mean, I — had a bandage wrapped around my head, and my face was bruised."

Both women are holding their breath, waiting for me to continue.

"She gave me a piece of paper, folded, and didn't let me see it until after she left. The paper had two words written on it in red ink: 'Save me.'"

Rita sighs and shakes her head.

"What, Rita?" I ask. "What do you think it means?"

"Iliana needs you to remember, so you both can live."

I agree with Rita completely. "I am on my way to see Doctor Castelli, to ask if I can be hypnotized again."

"Are you sure you can handle it?" A concerned frown darkens Olivia's face.

"I think so," I reply, trying my hardest to sound convincing.

"Don't overdo it, Rosa," Olivia warns.

"I won't. Well, what are you two doing down here, anyway"

"We are waiting for a new arrival — a girl named Paola. I guess Rita and I are the welcoming committee." Olivia replies for both, winking mischievously.

"Oh? Is she coming today?" I ask with curiosity.

"She should have been here already," Rita answers, her eyes fixed on the glass doors.

"Should I stay here with you? I mean…do you need an extra person on the welcoming committee?" I ask. Truth is, I want to see how the girl arrives here. I noticed, when we went to Florence, how secluded the center is, and I am still trying to figure out how I made it to this place.

"Suit yourself," Olivia shrugs. "The more the merrier, I think. She is going to be scared, and will feel out of place when she first gets here. Seeing friendly faces will help her feel more at ease."

"Do we know her story already?"

Rita nods. "It's not as bad as some others. Her father was abusive to her mother, and she grew up believing that it is normal for men to treat women that way. So, she put up with a man who put her at the bottom of his list of priorities, who waited until she had a baby and no job to party and run around on her. By then, she was stuck. With a young baby and no financial support, she had no choice but to stay. She was so emotionally distraught, one evening, that she ran her car into a wall. She is coming here from the hospital."

"That's terribly sad," I say, as Rita's words sink in. "What happened to her baby?"

"She is being taken care of by Paola's family."

"Poor Paola…" I say, a wave of sadness washing over me. "Her husband held her captive and stripped her of her dignity. There are still lots of things I don't remember clearly, but one fact I *do* remember is how I believed the lies Marco told, to manipulate me."

"We all did." Olivia whispers so softly I can barely hear her.

"Here she is!" Rita says pointing out the window, as an ambulance pulls up.

"Is she still injured?" I whisper into Rita's ear as we watch the doors of the ambulance open.

"No, I don't think so. It was probably the only transportation they could arrange for her," Olivia says, stretching her neck to catch a glimpse of Paola as she steps out of the vehicle.

Then we see her. A tall, nearly emaciated girl, with long, straight brown hair that tumbles limply over her shoulders like cooked spaghetti. She wears gray pants that look three sizes too big, and an oversize purple T-shirt, the collar of which is loose enough to expose her protruding collarbone. She stares at her shoes while scuffling along, and I notice she carries no belongings. She exudes such sadness, I feel my heart fill with empathy and my eyes with tears.

She reminds me of a lost little girl, as she walks through the large glass door, never once raising her eyes to look at us.

"Welcome to *Transitions*," Rita says gently, as she takes the lead in welcoming Paola.

Transitions? Somehow, this is the first time I remember hearing the name of this place.

Paola raises her gaze now, and her eyes register fear.

"Don't be afraid," I interject quickly. "I was scared too, when I first arrived, but you are among friends here."

Olivia nods, and she smiles in my direction. "Welcome, Paola. Rosa is right; you are safe now, and we will help you adjust. My name is Olivia, and that's Rita. And of course, this is Rosa."

"I am Paola. I don't know why I was sent here."

"This is a place of healing, Paola. Unlike a hospital, that only fixes your body, we can help you heal your soul. Our location is secret, so you have nothing to worry about." Rita explains gently.

I watch Paola as she absorbs our words, and I notice that, although she seems slightly more at ease, her body is still extremely tense and she stands with her arms wrapped around herself.

"We can show you your room when you are ready," Olivia offers with a timid smile.

Paola nods. "Yes, Madam."

I get the sense that Rita wants to point out there is no hierarchy at the center, and it is not necessary to address anyone as *Madam*, but thankfully, her thoughts don't materialize into words. This poor girl seems so fragile that I am half-afraid air itself could damage her.

I decide to postpone my visit to Doctor Castelli, and I accompany the rest of the group upstairs. Paola still looks at her shoes while she walks, her head pitifully bent and her hands clenched into tight fists at her sides. I know Doctor Castelli does not want us to use our energy by concerning ourselves with the healing of others, but the pain this girl radiates is so raw and powerful that I feel humanly obligated to do anything I can to help her feel better.

We stop in front of Room 108 — just two doors from my own — and Rita opens the door.

"Here we are," she says, before leading the way in.

Paola enters slowly, her eyes darting in all directions. We stand by the door, affording her some space to adjust to her surroundings.

"It is a nice room," she says timidly.

"I am glad you like it," Rita says. "We are all just down the hall from you, if you need anything.

"My room is just two doors down," I offer. "I am in Room 104."

"Olivia and I are just a little farther down, in 116 and 120."

I wonder if Paola even heard us. She is standing by the window, staring out with such longing that I want to run and hug her. I think about her story, shivering involuntarily. She grew up witnessing her father being abusive to her mother, just like Matteo. Is Matteo going to be as scarred as Paola is? Or, is she worse off, because her father's abusive behavior was continued by her husband, albeit in a different form? Both men abused her emotionally and robbed her of her innocence; most of all, they destroyed her self-worth. In that moment, I pray that, someday, my son will meet a wonderful woman who will love him and respect him, and will allow him to break the fatherly curse.

"There are some clothes in the cabinet in the bathroom, along with toiletries and shoes," Rita says, leading the way into the bathroom and opening the cabinet to show Paola where everything is. "Elena will probably check on you shortly, but if you need anything in the interim, don't hesitate to call on one of us."

Paola nods, and I can almost read her mind. She is feeling overwhelmed right now; she wants to be alone to gather her thoughts. I can feel her energy pushing herself back from us, but she is too submissive to voice her need.

"I think we should go and give Paola the chance to familiarize herself with the room," I suggest, making eye contact with Rita and Olivia in a silent plea for them to get my hint.

Paola looks at me and, for the first time, her lips curve into a tentative smile. "Thank you."

Olivia and Rita *did* get the hint, and they follow me outside without adding another word.

"She wanted us gone," I say as soon as we are a few steps away from Paola's room.

"How do you know?" Rita asks with a bewildered look on her face.

"I am not sure, really…I just *felt* what she wasn't saying," I reply, unsure myself at the bone-deep awareness I had while we were inside Paola's room. "Well," I add before they can ask me any further questions, "I'd better be going if I hope to catch Doctor Castelli before he leaves."

"Do you want to meet in the recreation room in about an hour?" Olivia calls out as I start walking away.

"Sure. I don't think the doctor will be willing to put me under hypnosis this afternoon, anyway."

I take the elevator down to the lobby, and then cross through the garden to get to the doctor's office. It is quite chilly today, and I wish I had thought to bring a sweater with me. I cross my arms in front of my chest, rubbing my arms vigorously to generate some warmth.

Doctor Castelli is in his office when I arrive. The door is ajar; I see him behind his desk, perusing a large stack of papers. I knock lightly to alert him of my presence, and wait until he raises his eyes to glance in my direction.

"Rosa. Please, come in."

I enter and stroll toward his desk, then sit on the chair across from him. "Good afternoon, doctor, I hope I am not interrupting something important," I state politely, inclining my head toward the large stack of papers in front of him.

"Not at all. How can I help you?"

"You told me that I could be hypnotized again when I am ready. I am ready, doctor."

Doctor Castelli seems disconcerted. "So soon? It's not safe, Rosa."

"I will take my chances. I had two dreams this afternoon. In the first dream, I remembered my last name. In the second one, I saw myself as Iliana, bruised and bandaged, and I was asking my Rosa-self to save me. I know it sounds crazy, but in the dream, Rosa and Iliana were two different people. At any rate, I believe mine was a premonitory dream, doctor. I strongly feel that if I don't remember and change the way events are unfolding, Marco is going to find me and, when he does, he will kill me."

114

Doctor Castelli weighs my words against the parameters of safety he feels compelled to enforce. "Your dream showed you your public persona and your higher self. Rosa — the personality who is functional right now — is your inner self; the one who, by some miracle, remained unscathed, despite the abuse. Iliana is the identity through whom people know you. You can liken Rosa with being the driver, and Iliana with being the car. Iliana cannot go anywhere without you, Rosa, and you are not ready to drive yet."

"I will be when I can remember!" I stand and slam my fist on the desk.

"I understand you are getting frustrated, Rosa, but I am talking to you not just as your doctor, but also as your friend. I know how the brain works, and there is only so much it can take." His voice is kind and steady despite my outburst.

"I met the new girl right before I came here. She is a ghost of the person she would have been if she hadn't been repeatedly exposed to the emotional strain of being treated like shit — excuse my language — by the men in her life. My son, doctor, is being exposed to the same, by his father. I have no doubt that Marco is probably already seeing someone else in my absence, and I can assure you that he wouldn't be sensible enough to keep his girlfriends away from our son. God forbid he starts abusing them, too, in front of Matteo. I don't want my son exposed to anything else. He deserves to grow up in peace."

Doctor Castelli reflects for what feels like a lifetime, and I hold my breath until he speaks again. "I understand, Rosa. So long as *you* understand the risks, I won't stop you. I am working tonight. Would you like to come later this evening? I must finish going through these admissions before I can do anything else. Let me know if you change your mind, but if you are still convinced in a couple of hours, come back and I will put you under."

"Thank you, doctor. I know I am a terrible patient, and I don't listen, but deep down, I know what is right for myself. Iliana asked me to save her, and I am determined to do just that."

I leave the doctor's office and head straight for the recreation room. Olivia said she would be there in an hour, and it has probably only been thirty minutes, but I can't really think of anything I want to do, and it is too cold to sit in the garden.

To my surprise, Olivia is already there, and Paola is with her. They are sitting at the quilting table, sorting through fabric.

"That was fast," Olivia says, as I pull up a chair.

"Yes. Doctor Castelli was busy sorting out admissions, he said, but he agreed that I can go back tonight."

"Are you absolutely sure you want to go through with this?" Olivia asks.

"Not a single doubt. I am scared — don't get me wrong — but I can't let fear take control."

Paola is just staring at me, two patches of material in her hands.

"I like those colors," I tell her. "They are happy colors." I smile and point at the pastel pink and purple hues she has chosen.

"I like pink," she replies, timidly. "My mom liked pink, too."

"Where is your mom now?" I ask, and immediately regret doing so, as the realization that she spoke of her mother in the past tense dawns on me.

"My mother is dead."

Jesus…

"She suffered a heart attack three years ago."

Probably from a broken heart.

"I like pink, too." My attempt to change the subject is pathetic, but thankfully, Olivia comes to my rescue.

"Let me show you how to sew the patches together, Paola," Olivia offers, and she quickly opens a small box containing quilting needles.

I sit back in my chair, watching quietly as Olivia introduces Paola to the magic of patchwork. I have no doubt that Olivia is a good mother — kind and attentive — and my heart swells as I watch her shower our new charge with such loving attention. Whoever her husband is, he doesn't deserve her.

"How old are you, Paola?" I ask, breaking the spell.

"Twenty-four," Paola replies, without looking up from her stitching.

"You are so young; do you have any children?"

Now Paola looks up. It's truly amazing, the effect children have on us. "I have a little girl, Amanda. She is my joy," she says, and her eyes sparkle for the first time since we met.

"I have a little boy. His name is Matteo and he is five. Or six. I don't know for sure."

Paola seems a bit puzzled by my answer, so I rush to explain. "I lost my memory. I didn't even know my name when I first arrived at *Transitions*, but I am slowly remembering…a little more each day."

Paola nods. "I wish I could forget everything. My life has been nothing but pain."

Olivia speaks. "I'm sure there were some good moments, Paola; when your little girl was born, for example. It is human nature to be swallowed by hardship and overlook the good days. Happy experiences don't have the same explosive impact that negative events have, so when we think of our lives in retrospect, the only memories that jump up are the ones that hurt us. Look at it this way: Did you ever do dictation at school? When I was a child, my teacher would read to the class, and we had to write down what she read to us, in our notebooks. At the end of the day, she would collect the notebooks and grade them. The next morning, she would give them back, so we could see the corrections—always in bright, red pen. Do you want to guess what it was that we saw first?"

"The corrections?" Paola asks tentatively.

"Exactly! The corrections. Our errors were highlighted in red, and thus they jumped at us quicker than the words we had written correctly. The correct words were what really counted toward our grade, but we hardly paid any attention to them."

I reflect on Olivia's words. She is absolutely right. And suddenly, without warning, I am watching myself sitting at a desk in a classroom. I appear to be around eight years old, and the boy behind me is poking me with his pencil. I tell him to stop several times, since the teacher, Mrs. Corradini, is explaining a lesson about the Etruscan influence on Tuscan artifacts. He ignores me, and continues to poke me, so I turn around and scribble on his history textbook. Mrs. Corradini notices the commotion, and when she comes closer to find out what is going on, he tells her that I wrote on his book. I plead with her, and tell her about the poking, but apparently scribbling on a textbook is a much more serious offense, and she takes my agenda to write a note to my parents. I start crying in front of everybody, and bury my head in my hands.

Mrs. Corradini. I remember her clearly now and, along with her, I remember my classmates — Federico, Roberto, Alessandra, Olivia, and many others.

"Your story led me to remember an episode from when I was a little girl, Olivia. I can see my teacher, and several friends from school, very clearly in my mind."

"That's great! You are remembering more and more each day," Olivia exults.

'You are really good at this," Paola compliments Olivia. "How long have you been interested in patchwork quilting?"

"Oh, it has been a couple of years, probably. I find it very relaxing. And the quilts are fun to keep around the house. I had to find something to keep myself occupied — something that was just mine, that didn't involve parenting — in order to keep afloat. I was like a single parent."

"Me, too!" exclaims Paola with conviction. "My husband ignored my very existence, and yet, I couldn't leave him; I had no family, no way to support myself and a baby. Even if I could have found a job, I wouldn't have been able to afford daycare and pay all the bills on my own."

"That's kind of like my story," Olivia replies. "My husband wasn't physically abusive, but he ignored the fact that I even existed. His attention was focused — as I would find out later — on his mistress. I was the maid, so to speak, and the babysitter. I think he stopped seeing me as a companion after the first few years of our marriage. By then, I had become nothing more than an impediment to his happiness, because while I was around, he couldn't be with his true love in the light of day."

"Would you have opposed a divorce?" I ask, intrigued.

"No, I wouldn't have, but he never agreed to it. It's all in the past, though. My goal is to learn how to let go of the way things worked out. I had no control over many of the events then, and I certainly have no control over them now. I had built this ideal in my mind, of how a good marriage should be, and I think — after considerable reflection — that what hurt me most was watching my dream of a perfect family shattered by the choices of others."

"I am starting to feel the same way. I think I could have found the courage to change my circumstances, if I had been able to see those circumstances with clarity. I allowed Marco to isolate me from anyone who might have alerted me to what was happening, and I let him chip away at my self-esteem. If I get out of here, once I remember, things are going to change."

"I am glad to hear you say that, Rosa," Olivia replies with a huge smile that makes her entire face radiate. "You still have time to change your future."

"I hope so, Olivia, I hope so."

CHAPTER NINE

"You are becoming a pro at this," Doctor Castelli says, jokingly. "Make sure you keep your eyes on the dot, and don't forget to breathe."

I stretch out my legs on the sofa and wrap myself into the throw blanket, while the doctor gets comfortable on the chair he has pulled up. He adjusts his glasses over the bridge of his nose, and looks at the script resting on his lap.

"I am ready when you are, doctor," I say with conviction. I take a slow breath and hold it in to the count of three, then exhale to the count of five. I do that over and over, until I feel my body relax and my extremities get heavy. I am gradually growing tired, and I struggle to keep my eyes open...

"I believe your entire duct system needs replacing, Mrs. Landini. You already knew that you need a new furnace, but I think that, unless we install new ducts, you won't get the result you desire. The new furnace will be ten times more powerful than the ancient one we are replacing, and the amount of air it will blow through will likely increase the pressure. Here, let me show you."

I lean in beside the technician to look at one of the tubular aluminum ducts hanging overhead. In the darkness of the crawlspace, the ducts look like giant black snakes, slithering through the separating walls, and I am grateful for the dim light provided by the man's flashlight, since we don't have a functioning light fixture down here. Marco is usually here when contractors come to the house, but this guy showed up an hour earlier than the scheduled appointment, and he asked me to show him to the crawlspace, to inspect the pipes.

I have never been particularly claustrophobic, but the crawlspace is so cramped, dark, and dusty, that it reminds me of a coffin, and I must keep my breath steady to avoid freaking out. I immediately feel compassion for this poor man, who spends most of his working hours tucked into small, dark spaces.

"See this duct?" The man directs his flashlight toward one of the snakes overhead. "The outer layer is worn through, and the insulating material is literally falling out." He extends his hand to touch the spot he wants me to see. "See? Feel this," he invites.

I reach out to touch the large tube, and as I do so, the sleeve of my shirt slides back to reveal two large bruises, side by side, on my forearm. The blue-brown marks stand out against my pale skin in the yellow glow of the flashlight. I yank my arm back quickly, and pull the sleeve back down. The technician redirects the flashlight and makes eye contact. "What happened to your arm?"

I am embarrassed, and I am grateful for the dim light shielding my face from additional scrutiny. My cheeks are burning, and I am sure my face is red. "I bruise easily, and I probably bumped my arm on something." My heart is drumming away in my chest, and my hands are shaking.

"As I said, the ducts need replacing. You saw for yourself how worn they are," the technician says, and I immediately notice his tone of voice has become softer, almost fatherly.

"You would need to speak to my husband, if you think we need such a complex job. He likes to oversee repairs, and I know very little about mechanical issues."

"Sure. What time do you expect him home?"

"He should be here shortly. We weren't expecting you until 10:00, and he had to stop by the office to take care of a few things."

"It's no problem, I will wait. Meanwhile, I can check the wiring, and make sure it is up to code."

"Iliana, where are you?" Marco's voice thunders from upstairs, and I involuntarily shiver.

"Down here!" I call up, my voice steady though my heart is flip-flopping in my chest, "I'm in the crawlspace."

I hear his footsteps in the kitchen, and I follow their echo to the front door. He goes outside, and comes around the house to the crawlspace.

"You were supposed to be here at 10:00. I thought I was pretty clear about the time when we made an appointment," he hisses at the technician. I am embarrassed for him, and for myself.

"I apologize," the man replies calmly, "I was done with my previous call and I figured you'd be happy to get this done. Most people complain about having to wait for service."

"I take care of home maintenance. My wife knows nothing about furnaces, she wouldn't be capable of making any decisions on my behalf." His eyes dart back and forth between me and the technician, daring me to defend myself.

"Just as I was telling you a while ago," I confirm. "My husband oversees all the maintenance of the house."

"No problem at all." The man replies gently, his eyes fixed on me as he addresses Marco. "I am sure your wife excels at other things."

For a moment, time stands still. Marco and this stranger — who is foolishly determined to defend my honor — stare at each other, and it reminds me of two cowboys in a low-budget western movie. Marco remains quiet, but, even in the dim light of the crawlspace, I can see his eyes firing up. I keep my own gaze low, to defuse any challenge he might be waiting for.

"Anyway, as I was explaining to your wife, the ducts are old, and they won't be able to accommodate the air pressure from the new unit. I strongly recommend you consider changing the ducts, before we install the new furnace."

Marco stirs the man's words in his mind. "It makes sense. This house belonged to my aunt, and it is over 80 years old. What am I looking at, financially?"

"Since your house is about 1,500 square feet, and we would need to replace the ductwork throughout, I estimate the total, including labor, would run around 1,500 to 2,000 Euros. You could save a little if we only replace the ducts that are visibly damaged, but I would advise against that. Even those that still seem to be in good working order are the same age as the ones in obvious need of repair. It is only a matter of time before they fail, and even before that happens, they will compromise the efficiency of the overall system, resulting in higher interim utility costs."

"What did you say the furnace will cost?"

"Depending on the model you choose, and its capacity, you are looking at a ballpark amount of around 3,000 Euros."

I hold my breath. Marco hates spending money, and I am sure he is not happy with this man to begin with, since he defiantly stood up for me. My mind runs in circles, trying to think of an errand I can come up with that will get me out of Marco's radar for a couple of hours, until he calms down. "I need to run to the grocery store, and I have a parent-teacher conference at Matteo's school. If you gentlemen can excuse me, I am going to go."

"Have a great day, Ma'am" the technician says with a soft smile.

Marco fixes his eyes onto mine, and in that moment, he reminds me of a snake ready to strike. "How come I am only hearing about this teacher conference now?"

I can feel heat rising to my neck and exploding into my cheeks, and once again, I am grateful for the dark surroundings. My hands shake a little, so I place them in my pockets. "I must have forgotten to mention it, Marco. I'm sorry."

"Is Matteo in any trouble at school?"

"No…I don't think so. It is just a routine conference."

"I'm going to stop by the school tomorrow, and ask her to notify me in advance, the next time she needs to see us, so I can take the day off work and be there."

"I don't think it is necessary for both parents to be there, Marco. I believe she only wants to discuss Matteo's progress."

Marco seems convinced, but I am holding my breath, all the while aware that this man — this stranger — is witnessing such an embarrassing discussion.

"Well, I am going to go, then. I will be back in time to prepare lunch."

I exit the crawlspace without looking back, leaving Marco and the technician to talk about details of the installation. I clamber into my car and speed away, not exhaling until I have driven around the curve. The prospect of Marco calling Matteo's teacher and finding out there was no conference scheduled is terrifying, and I am wondering if I should go by the school and make up an excuse about my husband's upcoming call. What the hell can I say to her? I don't think

I can explain that the only reason I lied was because I was scared and I needed to find a quick way out.

Despite the trouble it could cause, I feel strangely energized by the knightly attitude of the technician. Marco speaks to me in that tone all the time, and nobody before has ever stood up for me. I wonder what that man's name is…I wish I had thought to ask before Marco got home.

Breathe, Rosa, and go forward in time a little…do you see the technician again? Keep breathing…a few days have passed. Does he come back to your house?

Marco has taken the day off to be at home when the maintenance crew arrives, to complete the ductwork and install the new furnace. He goes outside to meet the men and closes the door behind him, which I take as a signal that I shouldn't venture out.

I can hear movement and muffled voices underneath the house, and I try to listen, to see if I can hear *his* voice. Marco would kill me if he could read my thoughts, and I feel an almost wicked satisfaction in knowing I am keeping something from him. He can own my body, and he can control every area of my life, but he can't stifle my mind entirely. I am still my own person, and one man believes I am worth fighting for — not physically, of course, but even challenging Marco, telling him that he is sure I can do many wonderful things, means a lot.

The curtains are drawn — Marco covered all his bases before going outside — and I can't see who came to do the work. I feel like a prisoner who has been hidden away, and I resent that, but, as outraged as I feel, I lack the courage to defy Marco's order to remain inside. I wish Marco could be like *him,* and I really want to know his name. The warmth of his smile has seared the image of his face in my heart, creating a safe place for me to go when I need to feel better about myself.

I hear footsteps approaching the front door, and I pick up the duster so it looks like I am staying busy. Marco comes in and slams the door, and my heart jumps in my chest.

"They are going to be here all day!" he thunders. "What have you been doing in here?"

"The usual chores. I am dusting the family room right now, then I need to go reorganize Matteo's closet."

He stamps his feet on the floor as he crosses the room toward me, and he gets so close I can feel the heat of his breath. "I don't want you anywhere near those men. I hope I am making myself clear." He whispers, sounding more like a hissing snake than a human being.

"I am not going anywhere. I have lots to do in here."

Apparently satisfied with himself, Marco retreats. He takes a step back, then turns on his heel and goes back outside.

Do you see the man again, Rosa? Continue breathing...does he come back?

I have just come in from sending Matteo off to school on the bus, when the doorbell rings. I almost don't answer the door, thinking it is a solicitor. Whoever is at the door seems determined to make their presence known, though, knocking several times.

"I am not interested! Go away!" I announce loudly through the closed door.

"I am not selling anything, Mrs. Landini. This is Stefano...I installed your furnace."

My heart stops. *Stefano?*

I open the door so fast that I must surely have startled him. "Hi...hi, Stefano, how can I help you?" I try to sound collected, but I wonder if he can see how flustered I feel.

"I was wondering if I can speak with you for a moment."

Can he hear the drumming of my heart in my chest?

"I...am not sure. My husband isn't here, and he...he..."

"Yes, I know, he oversees the house maintenance, but that's not why I am here."

"Oh? Why are you here, then?" I think I am going to pass out.

"Can I come in for a minute?" he asks gently.

"I...I don't think that it is a good idea..." I am about to burst into tears. I am not sure if it is embarrassment that's causing me to feel this way, or sheer terror that Marco will come home unexpectedly and find Stefano here.

"Would you prefer to talk here, on the doorstep?"

"Yes, maybe..."

"I just wanted to tell you that I have understood what is happening. I know you are afraid of your husband, and I wanted to give you my number. You can call on me anytime, if you need anything."

"I..." there is a lot I want to say, but I can't. Instantly, the fear and anxiety I have kept bottled up inside comes pouring out in liquid form.

Stefano touches my cheek and wipes the tears away with his fingers. "Hey, it's okay. I understand. I grew up with a mother who was abused. I know how hard it is. That's why, as soon as I noticed the signs, I wanted you to know I am here for you, no matter what you need."

To my own surprise, I want Stefano to hold me, and tell me everything is going to be okay, but I can't bring myself to make any type of physical contact. I lean my face into his lingering hand and I try to seal the warmth of his skin into my memory. I take the business card, on the back of which he has written his phone number, and I barely whisper when I thank him. He doesn't pressure me any further. Instead, he turns around and walks toward his van, then waves before he takes off. I look at the piece of paper in my hand, committing his number to memory. Just in case I should forget it, though, I go inside and frantically look for a hiding spot.

Did Marco ever go talk to the teacher? Go back to the day you left the house because you feared Marco, and you used going to Matteo's school as an excuse...

If Marco calls the teacher, she will be dumbfounded, and she will tell him there was no conference. Maybe he won't even call her, but I can't take any chances.

I decide to go to the school and talk to the teacher. I won't tell her everything, but I am going to find a way to explain why she should lie to my husband. I pull into a space in the school parking lot, and I go inside. I ask for Ms. Santorelli at the main office, and the secretary directs me to the classroom. I find it, and knock on the door before cracking it open a little to peer inside.

"Come in," a feminine voice calls out.

Matteo sees me at the door and jumps to stand. "Mommy!"

I place a finger in front of my nose to prompt him to be quiet and sit down, which he does with obvious reluctance.

"May I speak with you a minute in the hallway?" I ask the teacher, who is still sitting at her desk.

"Of course," Ms. Santorelli replies pleasantly. "Children, read over the paragraph again, and be prepared to answer questions when I come back." She walks across the room and joins me outside the door. "Good morning, Mrs. Landini. What can I do for you?"

What can I say?

"I have a situation that is a bit delicate, Ms. Santorelli, and I was wondering if you would be willing to help me."

The teacher's face grows serious. "Is everything okay?"

I force a smile. "Yes, of course. My husband's birthday is coming up, and I am throwing him a surprise party. He stayed home from work, yesterday, and I had to find a way to go out and order his cake without him knowing, so I told him I was going to a parent-teacher conference. He seemed a bit suspicious about it — he is like a big kid — and he might call you to confirm I was here. If he does, would you please tell him I came to talk to you? I would hate to spoil the surprise."

The young teacher smiles conspiratorially. "Your secret is safe with me, Mrs. Landini. I am sure your husband will be thrilled!"

"Yes, I think he will, too," I reply, smiling back at her. "I really appreciate your willingness to help."

I watch the young woman go back to her students in the classroom, and I secretly pat myself on the back for my Oscar-level performance. Now, even if Marco calls, he won't be able to catch me in any lies.

It is time for you to come back, Rosa...breathe, and listen to my voice as I count. Ten. Nine. Eight...continue to breathe. Seven. Six. You are beginning to wake up. Five. Four.

Continue to breathe evenly, and then you can open your eyes. Three. Two. One. Open your eyes slowly, Rosa.

I open my eyes, and it takes me a moment to adjust to the light in the room. I feel that I have no control over my body. My arms and legs feel heavy, and my chest feels compressed.

"You can continue lying down for as long as you need, Rosa. You were under for a little longer than normal, today, and it might take a few extra minutes for you to become fully conscious."

"I had a friend, Doctor Castelli. His name is Stefano. Like my Matteo, he grew up around abuse, and he wanted to help me."

"Do you remember if you called him after he gave you his phone number?"

I close my eyes, trying to remember, but I can't recall anything past the moment Stefano drove off. "I don't know if I ever did. But he did offer, and—unlike Marco—he saw me as a smart woman." Remembering just that one fact sets me at peace with the world.

"I like how you handled the teacher," the doctor says with a wink.

"Thank you, but it is sad in a way. When you get abused, you get really good at lying for your own survival."

"You are correct, unfortunately. Well, how do you feel right now?"

"Surprisingly well. I think knowing that at least one man thought I was okay restores my faith in the male species."

"Why do you think Marco was trying to keep you hidden away?"

"I think he sensed the connection between Stefano and me, and he couldn't handle it. He also felt challenged — I remember so clearly how they almost glared at each other — and his assertiveness was intended to make it obvious I am his property. It was nothing but territorial issue."

The doctor nods calmly. "I believe you are right, Rosa. Is there anything from today's session you would like to discuss?"

I think about all that I have remembered, and it all seems straightforward. "I don't believe so, doctor. I think I learned something important today, a huge piece of the puzzle: Even when I didn't ask for help, someone offered it because he wants me to be okay. My safety matters to him."

I sit on the sofa and get up slowly, surprised at how fluid my legs still feel.

"Take care, Rosa, and get some rest. You need to let some of this new information sink in."

"I don't feel tired, but my legs feel as though they are filled with Jell-O. I think I will just go to my room and relax."

I leave the doctor's office, and take my time getting back to my room. I could go through the connecting corridor to get to the residential building, but I opt to walk through the garden and get a breath of fresh air. It's already dark, and it feels cold, but it is so beautiful out tonight, that I sit on the bench and breathe in deeply. The air is so still and quiet that I wonder how long I have been under hypnosis. Has everyone already gone to bed?

As if answering my question, Paola slips out through the side entrance from the lobby and, when she notices me, she comes to sit beside me.

"I was getting restless, alone in my room," she says, timidly.

132

"I understand. I think loneliness is one of the ugliest monsters I have ever encountered, but I have made some friends since I have been here. You will, too."

"I have never had any friends, really. I was always socially awkward. I tried to belong, several times, but it never worked out. Either I couldn't connect with the people I met, or I tried too hard to be their friend, and ended up annoying them."

"I understand that, too. I am not a social butterfly, and I am painfully shy at first. I guess it is different here…we are all connected by the weight of our experiences, and we all understand each other. Our stories are not exactly alike, but they all share a common denominator: We were all stripped of our humanity by sub-humans who couldn't shake their own demons."

Paola stays quiet for a moment, then she smiles. "I like that. It's true. Neither my father nor my husband were happy men. Happy people don't enjoy hurting others. I think they were suffering in a different way, and they couldn't tolerate carrying the weight of their own lack of happiness alone."

I hug her, even though we are barely acquainted. "You are absolutely correct, Paola. And wise. I am just now learning how to forgive, but it seems to me that you are on the correct path."

"I hope so. I wish I could forgive myself as easily as I can forgive others."

"Is there anything in particular you need to forgive yourself for?"

She hesitates, so I change the subject and she appears relieved. "So, what did you do this afternoon?"

"I learned how to stitch patches of material, and I explored the art supplies. I would like to draw or paint, but I am not really good at it."

I can show you the basics, if you want. I am no Picasso myself, but I can hold my own…a little."

"Really?" Paola responds with enthusiasm. "I really would like that. I feel that if I can draw or paint, I can maybe unload some of the pent-up energy I keep locked inside myself."

"It is a little too late tonight, but I can show you tomorrow, if you want to meet me in the recreation room after group therapy."

"Yes, if you don't mind. I haven't been to one of the group therapy sessions yet. I am afraid I will feel intimidated."

"You will feel amazed how much you have in common with so many women out there! I felt apprehensive too, the first day. That was especially intense because I couldn't remember anything about my own life — including my name — but it did not take long for me to understand that we are all here to help each other heal."

"That makes me feel a bit better. Thank you, Rosa. I am always in a panic when I have to start something new."

"I am freezing out here," I say, rubbing my hands together. "I think I am going inside. Are you coming along?"

"In just a few minutes. I want to sit out here a little while longer. I will see you tomorrow."

I say goodnight to my new friend and enter through the nearest door, welcoming the warmth in the lobby. I don't meet anyone else on the way to my room, and I am silently grateful. I need to be alone for a while, to gather my thoughts. What I have learned today is not an earth-shattering discovery, but as I keep uncovering more and more pieces, I am getting closer to solving the puzzle. I lie on my bed after kicking off my sneakers, adjusting the pillows to get comfortable. I pick up my notebook and a pen from the side table, planning to jot down all I remember, using bullet points to organize names and situations…but all I write on the paper, over and over, is *Stefano*.

CHAPTER TEN

"The type of paint you choose depends on the effect you hope to achieve. Oil paint is more vibrant and dramatic; it offers a deeper contrast between light and dark shades. It is also permanent, and takes a long time to dry — as much as six months to a year, if the painting has several layers. Picasso's paintings are a good example of oil works. Watercolor lends itself to a softer look; it dries quickly, and a little paint goes a long way. The downfall of water-based paint, I would say, is that it is vulnerable to being ruined by a single drop of water. Acrylic paint is another popular paint, made of pigmented latex. Unlike oil paint which uses linseed oil as a binder, acrylic paint has water as the vehicle for a suspension of acrylic polymer, which serves as the binder. It dries within minutes, and can offer a unique look to your painting. If you paint over a canvas, though, you must prime the canvas with gesso and wait until it is dry before you paint. If you don't, the thinner paint will bleed through the weave of the canvas." I am glad our painting supplies include all three types.

"I am not sure which one I would like better…" Paola thinks out loud.

"Again, it depends on what you are trying to achieve, and how much time you have at your disposal for the painting to dry," I reply. "Maybe you should try all three, to see which feels most comfortable to you. I personally like oils the best, because I feel they help me bring my work to life. I went to Florence with Olivia and Giulia, the other day, and we saw many beautiful oils at the Uffizi Gallery."

"Do you paint a lot?" Paola asks, intrigued.

"Well…I am not sure. I painted here, the other day, and I am sure I have painted before, since I am familiar with techniques and the differences between types of paint, but I can't recall how long I dabbled with it."

"You really didn't remember anything when you arrived?"

"Not a single thing," I reply, matter-of-fact. For the first time since I have been here, I can accept the fact that my memory is gone without feeling particularly anxious, and I wonder what brought on this change in the way I feel.

"It must have been really scary," Paola ventures. "Is your memory coming back?"

"It was scary; still is," I admit. "But yes, my memory is coming back a little at a time. What did you think of the group therapy session this morning? I thought about going, but I felt so tired, and I preferred to remain 'unplugged' for a few hours."

Paola reflects for a moment. "It was okay. I met several women there, and they all talked about things that affect them. My situation was a little different — I think I mentioned this to you when we spoke before — my husband didn't beat me, he just treated me as though I wasn't even there. I think his unrelenting indifference eventually overwhelmed me; it made me feel worthless."

"Was your husband verbally abusive at all?" I ask, selfishly wondering why she is so sad if her husband only ignored her, and almost immediately I am ashamed of my own thoughts. All forms of abuse lead to sadness and a low sense of self; not one is better than the others.

"Oh yes, he was that! But I didn't care; my father used to call me names, too, and I was used to it."

Paola's face darkens with sudden sadness, and I scramble to find a way to change the subject and shift back to a happy mood. "So, which paint would you like to try first?"

Paola seems lost in thought for a moment, then a smile blossoms on her delicate face. "I would like to try oil paint first, if that's okay. I long for something vibrant and passionate in my life."

Stefano...why am I thinking about *him* right now? I feel myself blush, and hope that Paola won't notice.

"Hello, ladies! Can I join you?" Francesca cheerfully calls from the doorway, and we both turn to look at her.

"Hi, Francesca! This is Paola, a new resident. Paola, meet Francesca. She lived at *Transitions* for a while, a few years ago."

"Yes, I know about Paola." Francesca approaches us with a huge, warm smile. "I stopped by to pick up some paperwork from Doctor Castelli, and he told me about Paola joining the group. It is great to meet you, Paola! I hope you will make the most of your time here."

"I will try," Paola replies quietly. "I don't even know for sure what I am supposed to learn."

"You are still a little confused, sweetie; it's quite normal," Francesca says, nodding her head slowly to emphasize her words.

"I guess," Paola thinks out loud. "Rosa is showing me how to paint. Olivia taught me how to sew patchwork sections together."

"You know," Francesca replies, gazing gently at Paola, "my story was similar to yours. My fiancé was verbally abusive, and he ignored me after the honeymoon stage of our relationship, but he never hurt me physically."

Hearing Francesca talk about her fiancé piques my interest, since I don't know much of what happened to her. I pull up a chair and sit quietly, while she chats with Paola.

138

"He was quite charming, Marco was," she begins. Hearing that name makes my teeth grind.

"I met him through work, and was struck immediately by his looks and his confidence. I came to understand, later, that he was not confident — merely arrogant — but I guess that, at the time, I couldn't distinguish between the two. He invited me to lunch one day, and we went to a small café near our office. He was one of the salesmen and I was an accountant for the firm, so we weren't at the office together often, since he traveled extensively."

My heart stops at Francesca's words. *A salesman? Her Marco is a salesman?* I shift uncomfortably in my seat, pretending to be busy sorting paint colors.

"Anyway, he invited me to lunch, and I had the time of my life. We ate and talked, and we laughed a lot. I had just ended a toxic relationship, and it felt good to have fun with a man again. I felt comfortable with Marco right away, and by the time we got back to the office, we had already decided on the next date. We went out for a while, and then moved in together; that, unfortunately was the biggest mistake. It was like someone had cast a curse on us, changing Marco from a prince into a toad. He was snappy and controlling, and then he started not coming home until very late at night. I knew he was seeing someone else, I could feel it, but when I confronted him about it, he told me that I was crazy and I was making things up in my head." Francesca pauses.

This guy doesn't sound like my Marco, but deep down I am still freaking out, and I can't get my heart to stop pounding. I turn to look at Paola, and I see that tears are flowing down her face. She is so quiet that I hadn't even realized she was crying.

"So, Marco and I didn't talk for a few days, but then, of course, we made up. He convinced me that he never had anyone else, and, in fact, he pledged to be with me the rest of his life. To prove to me how much he cared, he asked me to leave my job and only worry about our home. I thought it was very romantic, and I envisioned having a little family with him, being a happy homemaker. It wasn't long before my dreams of having a family suddenly seemed quite real: One morning, I took a pregnancy test. I sat on the bathtub while I waited for the result, and thumbed through a magazine to stay busy, but I couldn't take my eyes off the wand. It turned in less than a minute, and I just stared at it in disbelief. I was pregnant!"

I gasp. *Francesca has a baby? I thought she said she didn't have any children...*

"I spent the afternoon fantasizing about the baby I was carrying, and I made a special dinner to break the news to Marco that night. I was excited beyond belief, almost literally coming loose at the seams, thinking about the family we were starting. I saw myself baking cakes, kissing our child off to school, and welcoming my husband home with a kiss at night. Well, he wasn't my husband yet, but I was positive he would propose now. He wouldn't want the mother of his child to live in dishonor, would he? It took all the control I could muster to not leap into his arms when he walked through the door. Instead, I walked slowly to him, wearing my prettiest dress, and I led him to a beautifully prepared table, where two candles were already softly glowing. Marco was puzzled, though I could read in his face that he was enjoying the surprise. I served the dinner I had spent the entire afternoon preparing, and I sat at the table across from him." Francesca pauses briefly, and swallows hard. "He asked me the reason for such a sumptuous dinner, and that's when I told him I was pregnant. Marco was speechless. He stared at me for what felt like an hour, his hand still clutching a chicken leg. 'What did you say?' he asked. I smiled and got up quickly to go hug him. 'I am pregnant, Marco, we are having a baby!' I said again, placing my hand on his shoulder."

"What did Marco do?" Paola asks, entirely absorbed in the story.

"He pushed my hand off his shoulder and threw back his chair. 'What the hell are you talking about?' he hissed through his teeth. His outburst caught me by surprise; for a moment, I thought he was just playing around, but after one more look at his face — twisted in anger — the truth washed over me like a gelid downpour. I began to cry, collapsing on the chair closest to him. My legs were trembling, and I shook my head back and forth. 'What are you saying, Marco? Are you not happy?' I pleaded with him. He looked at me with disgust, and then he left the room."

"Did you have the baby?" I inquire.

"No" Francesca replied. "The baby was never born. After that night, Marco barely came home. Here I was — emotional, hormonal, heartbroken — and I no longer had even a job to distract me."

"Did you lose the baby?" Paola asks, and I am grateful she is doing her part to clear the questions we both have.

Francesca pauses a moment to think. "Yes, I lost the baby, unfortunately."

"Did you go back to work?" I venture.

"No...I wish I had. I brought it up one night, and Marco became very agitated. He told me I was ungrateful, and I didn't appreciate all he did for me. I didn't have the strength to fight that battle."

"Wow..." Paola shakes her head. I can't say anything — anger is strangling my words before they can rise to my lips.

"After that fateful night, I fell into a deep depression. Marco barely acknowledged me as a human being, and was determined to destroy me at every turn. He belittled me in front of the few friends I had left, making them so uncomfortable that they soon stopped coming around. One girl, Amanda, warned me that I should leave — even offered to let me stay with her for a while, until I got on my feet — but I was so confused that I couldn't even take her suggestion seriously."

"How did you finally leave?" I ask, now as riveted by Francesca's story as Paola.

"The hard way. I tried to kill myself."

Silence settles over us like a prickly wool blanket, and I am too stunned to utter a single word.

"I wasn't successful. I took a bunch of pills, but the same friend who had offered me a place to stay found me. She had come over one morning to check on me, and I didn't respond when she knocked on the door, but she saw my car parked in front of the apartment building. I had given her a key to water the plants if we were ever going to be out of town, so she let herself in and found me unconscious; she called the emergency number and I was transported to the hospital. I was sent here right after."

"My story is extremely similar to yours," Paola offers. "My husband Giuliano was verbally abusive, but he never crossed the line to physical violence. I grew up with domestic abuse; I was used to hearing the insults, and the verbal beatings, so I lived through it by making my daughter my reason to live. She was beautiful and smart, and she never failed to make me smile. I had no family other than my husband and daughter, and I never saw walking away as an option. I also became depressed, but I did my best to hide it. I held my breath if my daughter was loud when my husband was asleep, because I was worried he would yell at her, and I lived for the hours he was gone to work. Those hours were peaceful; my daughter and I would spend time cutting out figurines from magazines, and filling coloring books with pretty colors. Then, I don't know what happened to me. My mood became sullen, and my outlook on the future turned darker each passing day. I didn't even think of going to see a doctor. Instead, I started sleeping a lot when my daughter was busy watching children's programs. One day, I went to the grocery store after Giuliano got home. I told him I had forgotten one of the ingredients I needed to make dinner, and he didn't even bother to look away from the TV. I kissed my daughter, and I drove away. I took the ramp for the highway and pushed my foot down on the accelerator until it reached the floor. The car began to shake from the high speed, but I was almost in a daze. I don't know exactly what happened next, but — like you, Francesca — I was taken to a nearby hospital, and was sent here after I was discharged."

I am crying openly now. Both these women had experienced such overwhelming anguish that they had tried to take their own lives. Even in my darkest days with Marco, I don't think I ever wished to die. My heart breaks for them, and I stand instinctively to hug them both.

"I have made peace with my past," Francesca tells me calmly. "You don't have to worry about me."

"I am trying to get where you are," Paola interjects. "There are still moments when I am confused, and I don't know how to cope with the feelings of anger. You know, I would walk down the street and see happy couples cooing at each other, and I was jealous of them. I didn't understand why they had love, while I didn't — not as a child, and not as an adult. I can't compare my life to those of others, since I don't know what is happening behind the closed doors of their homes, but bitterness was a large part of my existence. I felt like that

143

as a child, too, when I saw my mother constantly being treated like garbage by my father — and I had no control over those circumstances. As an adult, I probably could have changed the way my life unfolded, but I became so numb to it that I didn't realize how much it affected me, until it was too late. I lost all objectivity and clarity."

"I share many of those feelings," I admit. "I, too, looked at other women with envy. I didn't understand why they deserved to be loved and I didn't."

"I believe that we all felt that way. It is the first chip off the block of self-worth. Just like children who are adopted into a loving family, but who will forever wonder why their birth mother gave them away, we also fed our own feelings of inferiority when we compared ourselves to women who seemed to have it all," Francesca says calmly. After what she has been through, I am in awe of her inner strength.

"Well," Francesca says, rising from the chair she had pulled up, "I only stopped by to say hi, since I had been told of your arrival, Paola. The doctor and the front desk staff — and pretty much every other person in here — can get hold of me, if you need anything. I like to help as I can. Rosa, do you think we could talk privately, in a little while? I am headed to the kitchen to see if they need help with anything, if you want to meet me there."

I am a bit surprised by her request, but I am determined to go with the flow. "Sure," I reply with a shrug. "Give me a few minutes to show Paola where everything is, and I will be there."

My eyes follow Francesca until she walks through the door and disappears down the hallway. Then I turn my attention back to Paola, and focus on helping her choose some colors she can use for her first painting.

"As I was saying before Francesca stopped by," I say, "these are primary colors." I point at the handful of tubes I had separated from the others while Francesca was talking. "You can mix these colors to obtain any color you wish, and to help you figure out which colors combine to create others, you can use this color wheel." I pick up a small paper color wheel and show it to her. "See? If you mix blue and yellow, for example, you get green. Depending on how much of each color you use, the resulting mix will look different. The brushes are here, next to the canister of turpentine. You need turpentine to clean the brushes after you use them, because oil color does not wash off with water. If I were you, I would first take a piece of paper and practice strokes with all the different brushes, just to have an idea of what each brush can do. Once you feel comfortable with the brushes, think of something you would like to paint. You can start with something small, like a piece of fruit. Trace the shape, and then fill in the details. All that matters is that you have fun with it. Let your imagination guide you, and don't worry if you make a mistake — or a lot of them! It is very common, especially when you are just beginning."

"Rosa," Paola whispers. "What will happen when we leave here?"

I know Paola did not consciously intend to upset me, but for some reason her question fills me with anxiety, and I struggle to keep my voice steady. "I am not sure, Paola. We can probably go back home. I can't wait to see my son."

"I would like to see my daughter, too."

I smile at her. Her innocence and her raw approach are simultaneously disarming and heartwarming. "I am sure you will, as soon as you are able to take care of her again. Well, I'd better go to see what Francesca wants to discuss. You go ahead and start painting. I am sure you will do a great job."

I get up to leave and, just as I glance over my shoulder on my way out, I notice Paola is weeping softly. She did say she was severely depressed, and I am not surprised that she is feeling overwhelmed. I don't want to put any pressure on her, though, so I continue out of the recreation room without further questions.

Francesca is in the kitchen, helping the cook, Mrs. Bonaviti, prepare lunch. Mrs. Bonaviti reminds me of a cartoon grandmother. She is around sixty years of age, with a plump, round figure, brown hair that is graying at the roots and is always tucked inside a hair net, and she wears little round glasses that are held in place by her rounded nose. She is also a heavenly cook. If I could personify Mrs. Santa Claus, Mrs. Bonaviti would be a good fit.

"Hi, Francesca. Did you want to see me?"

Francesca lifts her head from the muffin pan she is carefully coating with butter, and meets my eyes. "Hi, Rosa. Yes, I will be done in a second."

The aromas of baked meatloaf and roast potatoes permeate the air, and even though I ate breakfast only a couple of hours ago, my mouth is watering. I lean against one of the stainless-steel counters watching Mrs. Bonaviti, as she vigorously whisks egg whites in a large steel bowl, and I wonder if she is preparing Tiramisu for dessert. Francesca sets the muffin pan on the counter, wiping her hands clean with a white bar towel.

"Thank you for meeting me, Rosa."

"Not a problem. What can I do for you?"

"Olivia tells me you are remembering a lot more each day."

"I wouldn't say it is a lot, but I am happy with the progress."

"What do you plan to do when you remember everything?"

"Hopefully, if everything goes as planned, I am going home to my son."

Francesca sighs, but says nothing further.

"I am sure you didn't ask me to meet you here, only to ask about my post-release plans. What did you want to talk about?"

"I want to talk about you, Rosa."

I am honestly puzzled by her answer. "About me? What do we need to discuss?"

"Your plan to go home."

"Look, Francesca," I say gently. "I really like you, and I am open to talking about anything with you, but I am having a hard time understanding what you are driving at. I have a child out there, and he needs me. I am going back to take care of him, as soon as I know why I came here to begin with. If you know anything about me that I should know, perhaps you could share it."

"I don't know anything about you, Rosa. I never met you until the day we went to Florence, and I would never have heard your name if Doctor Castelli hadn't called me, to let me know you were here."

"Why would Doctor Castelli call you? What is it that he thinks you can do to help me?"

"As I have told you, I was a resident at *Transitions* a few years ago. I still come by to help."

"I got that much, but why would he call you about me? Is there something you can tell me, or show me, that will help me remember the memories that are still obscured?"

Francesca shakes her head and smiles gently. "No, I can't do that, and even if I could, it would be unwise of me to tell you anything that could put you at risk."

"So, what is the purpose of this private meeting?"

"Let's go sit somewhere, Rosa. Can I get you a cup of coffee?"

"No, thank you."

"Very well, let's go then."

I follow Francesca out of the kitchen and into a small office.

"Whose office is this?" I ask with curiosity.

"Nobody's, to my knowledge. It is just a place where we can talk in peace, without fear of being interrupted."

"I am all ears," I say, plopping onto a yellow sofa.

"I knew your husband."

I suck in my breath sharply. *This is just surreal. Am I dreaming again?*

"I wish I didn't, Rosa, believe me. Knowing Marco has ruined my life, and I need to make sure he is not going to ruin yours."

"Is this a joke?" I say with a grin, silently praying that, at any moment, Francesca is going to start laughing and tell me I am being pranked.

Her solemn face quickly kills that thought, and I can feel my mind crumble.

"You really knew Marco?"

She nods, then sighs. "As much as I hate it, yes, I did."

"But, how?"

"You heard me tell my story to Paola. Marco and I met through work, several years back. I lost the baby after I downed all those pills, and believe it or not, he never felt a twinge of remorse. I honestly believe that man is incapable of love, or any other higher emotion. He is just very angry. I have been able to forgive him over time, but I know he never owned any responsibility for what happened."

I must ask. "Had you already left him, when I married him?"

Francesca smiles. "Absolutely. However, I believe that he met you right after we split up. How long did you two date?"

"Not for long at all. He proposed almost immediately, and Matteo was born shortly after that," I say, surprised that I suddenly remember that detail. As soon as I say those words, I regret doing so, remembering what Francesca shared in the recreation room. She wanted to marry Marco, and he never proposed to her. I am confused by my feelings. Here is a woman who lived with my husband, a woman I should despise — just based on her relationship with him — and instead, I care about her! And I wish neither of us had ever met Marco. She seems completely unaffected by my disclosure.

"Just as I thought," she responds, serenely.

"This is absolutely bizarre, you must admit," I offer, as her words filter through my brain. Somehow, no matter how crazy it sounds, and how surprising this revelation has been, I feel as though, deep down, I have known it since I first heard Francesca speak my husband's name.

"Bizarre, yes, but there aren't many places like *Transitions,* and it is not so strange that we both ended up here, given that we lived with a man like him. When did Marco become physically abusive to you?"

"I couldn't say for sure — I don't remember, exactly. I *do* recall one early episode, when he got upset because I asked him about coming home late."

Francesca listens attentively. "Hmm…he wasn't like that before. When he got upset, he would just leave."

"Francesca…"

"Yes?"

"I don't know how to ask you this, because it is kind of private. I mean, *really* private."

"Ask away. Nothing Marco does affects me anymore."

"Was he ever…did he ever force you to have sex? And by sex, I don't mean regular sex. Did he ever ask you to do things you were uncomfortable with?"

Francesca laughs. "Are you asking me if he was ever kinky?"

I blush profusely. "Yes — was he?"

Francesca sat back on the sofa. "I guess he was. Nothing crazy, but I think that sometimes he had trouble…"

Francesca's words hit me at the core. *Could it be it? Maybe he was angry during sex because his male pride was compromised! That might explain the violence.*

"Bottom line, Rosa, you can't go back to him. As you can see when you compare our stories, his violent tendencies escalated from one relationship to the next, and that's the cycle abusers follow. If you go back, he will kill you. Not right away, maybe, but he will."

Francesca's words chill my spine, and I sit with my back straight. "So, what can I do? I can't forget I have a son out there. I miss him."

"You need to go home and claim your son, Rosa, but then, you need to walk away before it is too late."

"I fully intend to do just that, Francesca. After the horrible things I have remembered, I don't think I can go back to sharing a life with him. We might share a child — and, because of Matteo, I will never fully regret meeting Marco — but we are no longer in love. We haven't been in a long time — and I knew that — but I couldn't see clearly. My judgment was blinded by his lies."

"I am glad you feel that way, Rosa. Please know that I am here if you need me. You will be able to go back soon, if you so choose, and I needed to make sure you understand how important it is for you to fight for yourself…and for your son."

I hug her before standing up to leave. "Thank you, Francesca. Among all the strange occurrences since I have been here, this one probably takes the cake, but I am grateful I had a chance to know you."

"Same here, Rosa. Just remember: You must choose to live."

CHAPTER ELEVEN

"I can't tell you how surreal it felt to hear the stories Francesca shared, Olivia — first with Paola, and then with me alone." Olivia and I are sitting side by side at the breakfast table, across from Romina and Rita.

"I can imagine…" Olivia says, after swallowing the last bite of a croissant. "It's not every day when you meet someone who used to date your own husband, let alone someone who lived with the man."

"How did it make you feel?" Rita inquires cautiously. "I mean, did you feel jealous at all?"

I need a minute to think about Rita's question. Was I jealous in any way? I feel like I should have been, but I wasn't. Marco and I share a son, and that part will never change, but I feel certain there is no love left between us. God is my witness that I did love that man, when we were first married, but all the years of control, abuse, and fear have taken a toll — not just on my self-esteem, but also on the core of our marriage. The only thing I felt, when Francesca talked about the relationship she had with Marco, was compassion. I felt heartbroken for the woman who tried to make a home for him; who was happy to give him a child; who, in the end, allowed him to crush her, so that she no longer valued her own life. Francesca was Marco's victim, just as I was, and I am glad she had the courage to walk away. I am also grateful that she had the guts to warn me. I had already decided to leave Marco, once I go back home. Knowing that this woman — who was a stranger only a few days ago — cares enough to urge me to leave, though, brings my friendship with her to a whole new level. It also strengthens my resolve to turn my own life in a different direction.

"No, I wasn't jealous, Rita. If anything, I felt sorry for her. She loved him, and he turned on her. She even lost the baby she was carrying. Marco deserves to burn in hell, as far as I am concerned."

"So," Olivia asks while she gathers her dish and mine to take them to the counter, "I really should be going. I promised Paola to teach her a little more about patchwork quilting."

"Olivia," I say quietly, "Did you know that Francesca's fiancé and my husband are the same man?"

Olivia sighs, then she sits back down. "I did. When you shared his name, and you told me what type of work he does, I connected the dots, and I asked Doctor Castelli to call Francesca."

"Is that why she went to Florence with us?"

"It was her idea, but I hoped she could give you some suggestions that would help you remember, since she was indirectly connected to you. I am sorry if it upset you; I didn't mean to stick my nose into something that wasn't my business."

"Oh no, I am not upset at all! I just thought it was strange that I would meet my husband's ex by chance, in a shelter for abused women. I am glad I got to know Francesca."

Relief floods Olivia's face, relaxing the lines of stress I had not even noticed there at first.

"That's good. We are all here to help one another, Rosa. Each woman needs the strength of all women." She walks over to the counter, and deposits our dishes in the tub there.

"What are you going to do today, Rosa? Are you coming to the meeting?" Rita inquires.

"Not today, Rita. There is something else I must do. Francesca's words have made me feel more empowered, and I am ready to go home. If I can convince the doctor to let me go under one more time, I know I am ready to bring down the wall."

Rita stands and comes around the table to hug me. "Be careful, Rosa. I am cheering for you, if you think you are ready. Just don't make the same mistakes we made, and you will be all right."

Rita's words are puzzling, but I don't have time to explore their meaning further, if I want to catch Doctor Castelli before the group session. "I won't, Rita. I promise." I hug her back and I am on my way.

Doctor Castelli is sitting at his desk when I knock on the door to his office.

"Come in, Rosa. I have been expecting you."

"You were? Why?" I raise my brows.

"You are ready to go back, I know, and you are only a veil away from remembering the event that compromised your memory. I knew you would come to see me soon."

I blush. If I hadn't thought before that Doctor Castelli could read me, now I know otherwise.

"I am ready, doctor. I have enjoyed my time at *Transitions,* and I've made friends here, but this is not where I belong. I need to get back to my son."

"What about your husband, Rosa?"

"I will file for divorce as soon as I get back. Once I had a chance to step back, to distance myself from the madness, I understood that nobody should be feeling the way I did. I will also file for full custody of my son, and I am confident that I will win."

Doctor Castelli nods, his hands joined beneath his chin as if in prayer, and a huge smile erupts on his kind, fatherly face. "That's what I was hoping you would say, Rosa."

"You didn't warn me about remembering too much, this time, doctor."

"I don't need to. Not this time. Well, are you ready?"

I am a bit confused. "Ready for what?"

"I thought you wanted to have another go at hypnosis…"

"Oh, I do, if you think it is okay!"

"You know the steps, Rosa." The doctor comes around the desk and carries the extra chair over to the sofa, setting it down nearby.

"We are doing this right now?" I ask, incredulous.

"Yes, unless you object."

"No, of course not! I just thought you would have to lead the group session first."

"Rita can lead it for me. She has been here long enough that she knows how to keep the place running."

"It sounds great to me!" I exclaim excitedly.

"What is holding you, then? You know what to do."

I almost run to the sofa. I lie down and relax my arms over my abdomen, waiting for Doctor Castelli to bring the throw blanket. I scan the white wall to detect the small black dot that, in the time I have been here, has become my ally. "I just need the blanket, and then I am ready for take-off, Captain," I say, following my words with a few deep breaths, to stifle the excitement pulsing through me. I am vibrating so much right now, I wonder if I can calm myself enough to be hypnotized.

Doctor Castelli comes back with the blanket, and hands it over to me. Wrapping myself into it, I focus on the dot, breathing deeply, in and out. The doctor begins to read his script, and after a few minutes, his voice starts to draw progressively farther away...my focus on the dot fades...

Continue to relax, Rosa, and breathe fully...you are going deeper today, back to the time after you met Stefano. What happened after that?

Marco waits for me to come back from the store. I see him pacing in the kitchen, back and forth, while I carry the grocery bags inside, and I immediately detect his mood. I can smell his anger, if that's possible; I feel a knot developing, growing like a cancer in the pit of my stomach. He doesn't say anything to me right away, and waits for me to put the food away, but I continue watching him with the corner of my eye, careful not to be caught staring. And then, as I put the last purchase in the refrigerator, he is ready to attack.

"Say, Iliana," he says in a mocking voice, "did the furnace stop working after it was installed?"

"No, of course it didn't, why would you ask?" I answer, hoping to sound nonchalant. I feel myself blush, and even if Marco believed my words — which I managed to deliver in a half-steady voice — the flushing on my face and neck is sure to give me away.

"He left his business card here, along with his cell phone number written on the back. Stefano — a *charming* name — I guess he is a real *conscientious* worker, focused on making sure his customers are *satisfied*." Sneeringly, he flashes the business card in my face, and I can hardly breathe. How did

156

he find it? I thought I had hidden it well, inside the bathroom cabinet that contains my feminine supplies. Why would Marco look in there?

"So…when did he come back, Iliana?" His voice has lost its disdainful quality. Instead, each syllable rolls off his tongue like a threatening clap of thunder.

"He…he left it in the mailbox. For you, probably." I try to control my voice, but the words come out shaking like leaves.

Marco takes one step back and glowers at me. I know that, at any moment, he will pounce. "Oh, he did, did he? Why did you put it in with your tampons, then?"

"I…I am not sure. Maybe I had it in my hand when I went to put a new box of tampons in the cabinet, and I left it in there by mistake. Then I forgot."

"You are a fucking liar, Iliana! A liar and a cheat!"

He raises his arm so quickly, and I have no time to duck. His hand slams against the side of my face with such force that I lose my balance, falling against the stove.

"I didn't do anything, Marco, I swear!" I cry out, lifting my arm to shield my face and head.

Marco stands there, towering over me, and he kicks me in the side. I feel a sharp pain, and I am sure he cracked my rib cage. He kicks me over and over, the point of his leather shoes hammering repeatedly against my already sore body.

"Tell your boyfriend he'd better stay away from you, and away from this house! In fact, I will tell him myself! And I will tell that sorry son of a bitch to send someone to take back the furnace. I want nothing of his in my house!"

When he leaves, I remain crumpled on the floor, like a discarded doll that has been chewed and shredded by a dog. I don't know how long I lay there crying — frightened that, if I move, I will discover I can't get up because he has broken my bones — but the entire time, I worried about Stefano. I don't want Marco to surprise him, because — even though Stefano is not a small man and he would be able to defend himself — it would be unfair to him, to be caught unprepared when confronted by a madman. I am glad I had already committed his phone number to memory, because Marco took the business card. I drag myself across the floor, until I can find something to use as leverage in order to stand up. I grab the leg of the chair and take a deep breath as pain surges through my entire body. I am finally able to stand, so long as I can lean on something. I steady my back against the wall and rest there for a moment, hoping my legs will stop shaking. I inch toward the counter, where I left my purse and my phone, but then I decide against it. Marco could surely check the call log on my phone and see Stefano's number; it is safer to use the house phone. Thankfully the phone is in its cradle on the wall, only a couple of steps away.

"Hello, this is Stefano, how can I help you?" My heart skips a beat when I hear his voice.

"Stefano, this is Iliana Landini. You installed a furnace at my house the other day." I whisper as quietly as I can. Although I heard Marco's car drive away, one can never be too sure.

"Of course, Mrs. Landini. How are you?"

"Not good, Stefano." Quickly, I add, "My husband found the business card you gave me, and he is really upset. He said he is going to look for you, to tell you to stay away from me." I can't stop the tears. Hearing Marco's volatile threats crystallize in my own voice, they seem that much more real to me, and I am terrified.

"Are you okay, Iliana? Has he hurt you?" All I hear in Stefano's voice is concern for me.

"I will be fine, Stefano, don't worry about me. Look out for yourself."

"Where are you right now, Iliana? Are you at home?" I can hear his voice shaking with anger, but I know it is not directed toward me, and his anger does not scare me.

"I am at home, but don't come. He will kill you if he finds you here," I plead through tears.

"The hell I won't! I will be there in less than five minutes. Lock the door until I get there." And with those last words, he hangs up the phone.

What happened next, Rosa? Did Stefano come over?

I haven't often called the emergency team myself, but I remember somebody calling 118 once, when an elderly customer collapsed while shopping. I was astounded by the speed of the first responders. Stefano got to my house just as quickly. I have barely made it to the bathroom to wash my face, when I hear someone pound on the door.

"Iliana, are you in there?" I can hear the fear in his voice.

"I am here, Stefano!" I call out. "Go away!"

"Not a damn chance! Let me in!" He sounds desperate, and my heart constricts.

"Wait, then. I'm coming..." The pain in my side is making me feel dizzy, and I am afraid I will pass out before I can make it to the door.

My legs buckle about two feet away, but I gather all the strength left in my body to crawl and turn the lock, then I collapse on my back, exhausted. Stefano opens the door, nearly tripping over me.

"Jesus Christ! What did he do to you?" He is on his knees, carefully threading an arm under my head.

"He is going to kill you, Stefano…please leave before he comes back." My voice cracks, and I plead with him, but he won't budge. He lifts me into his arms, and he kicks the door wide open with his foot to get clearance.

"You are going with me. He could have killed you, Iliana." His voice is filled with emotion, and he bends his head to caress my forehead with an innocent kiss. I raise my face and return his kiss, barely grazing the side of his mouth.

"Well, well…what a beautiful family picture we have here!" Marco's voice slices the air like a knife. I turn my head to look, and Marco is blocking the gate. "Where are you heading, lovebirds?" His voice slurs…he has been drinking!

"Get out of the way, Mr. Landini!" Stefano roars. "Iliana is going with me."

"Iliana?" Marco says derisively. "Oh, we are down to first names now, are we?"

"I have already asked you once, sir: Get out of the way," Stefano says, with a steady voice. He either has nerves of steel, or he is one hell of an actor.

"Please, Marco, leave us alone!" I cry out.

"Shut up! Shut up, you stupid whore!"

He charges forward and, as his body slams into us, Stefano falls to his knees, dropping me to the ground. Marco reaches into his pocket, pulls out a gun and, in that moment, I go blind with rage. All the pain, the fear, the anxiety I been bottling up for years, rushes up from the depths of my soul, and I leap toward Marco, to deflect the shot aimed directly at Stefano. In the instant before I make skin contact with him, Marco's eyes lock with mine, and in them I see all the hatred he bears me, and the anger that turns him into a monster. In those eyes, I see madness. And then, a gunshot explodes in my ears, and everything goes dark.

It's okay, Rosa, you're safe. Breathe…it's okay to come back…come back, Rosa, right now! Three…breathe…two…one…Rosa, wake up! You're safe here, wake up!

I can hear Doctor Castelli's voice from a distance, but he is too far away for me to reach. I want to talk to him, but my body is not responding. My lips feel cold and inanimate, and my words are frozen somewhere inside me. I hear the doctor run, and then the sound of a door opening.

Please, come help me, she is not coming back!

I want to tell him I am okay. The panic in his voice breaks my heart. This kind man has tried to help me, just like Stefano, but he couldn't, until I was ready to help myself. I hear a lot of noise in the room, and several people talking at once. Wait…I think I hear Rita's voice. Yes, it's her, I am sure. And Olivia! Why is everyone here?

Rosa, it's Olivia, I can feel Olivia's energy hovering over me, but like the doctor's voice, her essence feels as if it is moving farther away. *You rest now, my friend,* I can hear her whisper, *we all worried this would happen, but we couldn't stop you. You will be okay…it is different for you than it was for us. You reacted, and chose love over fear. It took you a while to remember, but now you are ready to go. Goodbye, my little painter, and be happy. We will always watch over you, I and the others, and sometimes you might catch a glimpse of us, dancing in the light of the moon…*

CHAPTER TWELVE

"She is waking up! She is coming back! Nurse! Nurse!" My mother's voice filters through layers of consciousness, but although I try to open my eyes, they feel glued together.

I hear footsteps rushing toward me, then I feel cold hands touching my face, and someone raises one of my eyelids, flashing a bright light into my eye, and releasing my eyelid again. I don't understand the commotion, and I am too tired to think. My mouth is dry, and I can't formulate any words.

"Her eyelids fluttered, doctor, and her eyes opened for a few seconds!" My mom's voice is overcome with emotion.

"Are you sure, Angela?" My father's voice filters through, also, and I can feel his concern.

"Yes, yes! I am positive."

"Would you mind stepping aside for a moment, while I check the patient?" A man's voice interrupts gently.

I feel cold metal on my chest, and I think it is a stethoscope, maybe. Did I pass out at the shelter? I remember being in Doctor Castelli's office, but I am a bit confused as to what happened after that. And why are my parents here? Did Doctor Castelli call them, too?

"She is definitely back," the man's voice declares. "Give her a few minutes, then we will take her for a scan to check her brain waves. Her heart is strong, and her breathing is regular. Nurse, leave the oxygen hooked up for now, but if she continues to breathe on her own, we can probably remove it today."

I hear someone weeping softly, and I think it is my mother.

"Mom..." my voice sounds scratchy and foreign, even to myself.

"Iliana!" I can feel her warm hand now, touching my face, caressing me gently like she did when I was a little girl and I feared storms.

I open my eyes slowly, just for a few seconds at first, and then I close them back because the light in the room is overwhelmingly bright.

"I think the light is bothering her, nurse. Can we dim it a little?"

"Sure," the nurse replies. "The doctor turned it on when he came in."

I hear steps, and then the muffled click of a switch. I open my eyes again, and this time I feel more comfortable looking around. My mother and father are hovering beside my bed, my father standing by my mom with a protective hand over her shoulder. He looks older, his face an intricate pattern of lines etched by worry, and his tired appearance makes me want to cry. He is a ghost of the man he was. I remember my father as a tall, imposing figure, with dark hair and eyes that were always aflame with a deep passion for life, but now he looks like time has shrunk him, and the luster in his eyes is gone.

"Dad..." I whisper, and I make an effort to extend my hand and touch him.

And then my father cries. He cries like I have never seen him cry before, his body shaken by powerful sobs. "Iliana, I am sorry I wasn't there to protect you, princess."

Everything comes back, and I see my life flitting through my mind, like slides in an old film projector. I see snippets of my childhood, of going to school, of my first Communion.

And I see Marco, his handsome face, and then the way he turned on me. I see my wedding, and the dreams I had of a fairy-tale life with a husband and a cute little house…and then I see Matteo being born, and I can smell that baby-scent emanating from him, and I feel intoxicated.

"Matteo," I say with a raspy voice. "Where is he?"

"He is at school, Iliana. I will go pick him up shortly and we will come right back here. He is going to be very happy to see you."

"Where is everybody else?"

My parents look at each other, a little confused. "Everybody else, who?"

"Olivia, and Doctor Castelli. Francesca, and Rita, and Paola. Paola is new, but we have become friends really fast."

"Iliana, I don't think I know those people. Who are they?"

"Didn't one of them bring me to the hospital from the shelter? I remember being in Doctor Castelli's office, but I can't remember anything after that."

"Nurse," I hear my father ask. "Is there a doctor named Castelli at this hospital?"

I turn to look at the nurse shaking her head. "I don't think so," she says.

"Doctor Castelli isn't a hospital doctor, Dad. He was a doctor at the shelter I was living in. I guess he was the director of *Transitions*; he was the person who oversaw everything at the center."

"Honey," my mom says gently, as she picks up my hand and holds it in her own. "You were never in a shelter. You were brought here, barely alive, after a bullet from Marco's gun nearly killed you. The bullet pierced your skull, and we can

164

thank the good Lord that it only grazed your brain. It was removed surgically, and you've been in a coma for nearly two weeks."

The memories come through as a torrent, flooding my mind. I see Stefano carrying me outside to the safety of his van, and I see Marco, standing by the gate and threatening us. I remember seeing the gun, and I jumped on Marco because Stefano had fallen to the ground and he didn't see Marco aiming at him. I couldn't let Marco kill him, not after Stefano had risked his life to come save my own. I remember the gun going off, but I can't remember anything after that.

"Jesus…he shot me…"

"We all thought we were going to lose you, Iliana," my father says. The deep sobbing has subsided, but his voice is still filled with emotion. "I don't know what we would have done, how we could have coped if you hadn't made it."

"Where is Marco now?" I ask, anxiety rippling through my insides.

"Awaiting trial. He was arrested when he attacked you, and a trial date was set, but his father posted bail, so he is free for now." My father responds with a disgusted look on his face.

"He is free? After he tried to kill me?" I can't believe what I am hearing.

"Yes, unfortunately. Money can move mountains. He is not allowed to come near you or Matteo, and that nice man who was with you the day you were shot has been camping outside of your room, at night, to make sure Marco won't surprise you. I have explained to him that Marco is not stupid enough to come to a place full of cameras while he is awaiting trial, but Stefano won't take no for an answer." My father adds.

"Stefano has come to see me while I was in the hospital?" I ask, incredulous.

"Every day. He even calls Mom to check on you when he is at work." I can see a twinkle of excitement in my father's eyes. "He really is a nice man."

Stefano's face suddenly fills my mind, and I feel my heart swell. Marco had come back with a gun that day, and if it wasn't for Stefano, I would be dead right now. "I need to call him. To thank him, at least."

"He will be here shortly, I am sure. He is like clockwork, that one. He comes every day on his lunch break," my mother says, with a conspiratorial smile.

"Mom…you said I never lived in a shelter, but I am sure I did. I met some friends there, and I would like to let them know I am okay. I think I passed out in Doctor Castelli's office, and they are all probably worried about me."

"Iliana, I can assure you that you were never in a shelter. You came directly to this hospital after you were injured, and you have been in a coma since." My mother's eyes are shadowed with concern.

"But it's not possible…I met those women! They were all victims of domestic abuse, and we were in a shelter to learn how to get on our feet again. They told me their stories, and they helped me regain my memory which, I gather now, was blocked by my refusal to accept the fact that I had been shot. I can see their faces clearly in my mind and, if I close my eyes, I can hear their voices. We even went on a couple of day trips, in San Gabriele and Florence. We went to the Boboli Gardens, and to the Uffizi gallery. Olivia enjoys patchwork quilting, and Giulia is a chatterbox. Oh, and Francesca! I almost forgot about her…she used to be engaged to Marco before I met him. She was so overwhelmed with his behavior, especially when she told

166

him that she was pregnant and he told her he didn't want the baby, that she tried to kill herself. And there was Romina…her husband was controlling her so much that she wasn't even able to buy her own groceries without his permission. Can you believe that?!"

I catch my breath and I see sadness in both my parents' eyes.

"You never met those women, Iliana. They were only characters in your dreams while you were in a coma." My father breaks the news to me as gently as he can.

He is lying…he has to be lying. I *know* I didn't dream those people.

"I am tired," I say, suddenly. "I would like to rest for a little while," I whisper, then turn on my side facing away from my parents, the needle in my hand digging into my flesh as I move.

"Rest as long as you need, sweetheart," my father says. "We will be in the waiting room."

I hear them leaving and closing the door, just as my tears overflow, spilling down my face. Is my father right? Was this all a dream? Did my mind make up the wonderful, sad women I met on my journey? I close my eyes, and see Olivia's beautiful face, her piercing blue eyes suffused with wisdom. I see Rita's impish grin, and her motherly attitude toward the rest of us. And Paola, the scared baby bird who found her way to us, even with a broken wing. How can they not be real?

I cry. How long, I cannot tell, but at some point, the nurse comes into the room and asks if I need to remove the breathing tube. I nod my consent, since I am congested and would like to blow my nose. I am so mentally depleted, I don't even react when the nurse warns me *it will hurt a little.* It hurt a lot, but I don't even care. I feel like I am losing my mind all over again. When I arrived at *Transitions*, I had lost my memory; now, I have lost all my friends.

I hear a soft knock on the door, but don't even respond to that. Then the door opens slightly, and my heart skips a beat when I see Stefano peering inside. "May I come in?" he asks.

"Of course…" my lips curve into a timid smile.

My eyes follow him, as he pulls up a chair and sits down. He is even more handsome than I remember, with short, dark hair and deep brown eyes. His temples have a touch of silver, and he looks like he has been out in the sun. His eyes meet mine, and he smiles.

"See what happens when you try to be a knight in shining armor?" I joke to lighten the atmosphere, then my face turns serious. "You could have been shot, Stefano."

"Let's not talk about sad stuff, Iliana. Today is a happy day. I have been praying for this moment since that horrible afternoon, and I have to tell you…I have feared, a few times, that you wouldn't wake up."

"Marco is crazy," I state. "I can't believe he is out!"

"Not for long, hopefully. With my testimony — and the accounts of the neighbors who heard the commotion and witnessed everything — he should be put away for quite a while. We just have to make sure he stays away. until we get to that point."

"Stefano…have you ever heard of a shelter for victims of domestic abuse called *Transitions*?"

Stefano thinks for a moment, then he shakes his head. "I don't think so. Where is it?"

"I think it is somewhere near San Gabriele, because I know that when Olivia and I went to town, we didn't drive far. I still remember the roads we took. Could you take me there, when I leave the hospital?"

"Sure, if you know how to get there. When did you visit last?"

I don't even know what to say, and I try to formulate something in my head that is not going to sound completely crazy.

"My mother says that I have never been there, Stefano, but I know I have. I made some friends who helped me cope with the abuse I suffered. My parents think I dreamt the entire thing, that I never met the women I am so sure I know."

"It's not that hard, these days, to find out if something — or someone, for that matter — exists. I can bring you a laptop, if you want. They might not allow it in ICU, but I am pretty sure that, since you are alive and kicking right now, and breathing on your own, you will be moved to a regular room soon."

"Would you do that?" I exclaim excitedly. Then I think of a small detail, and my sudden joy fizzles out. "I don't know their last names, or maybe even their real first names: Everyone at the shelter picks a new name, so they can more easily dissociate from their painful past, and heal."

"It makes sense," Stefano says. "Do you know anything about them that could help you identify them?"

I am grateful that he, at least, is taking me seriously, and not immediately thinking I have lost my mind.

"Well...Olivia is a beautiful woman, tall, with deep blue eyes and long, dark hair. She has two children — an older girl and a little boy. Her husband didn't abuse her physically, but made her feel unwanted and unloved. She felt trapped in a gilded cage she could not break free from. Her words to me were that the same owner who fed her every day also clipped her wings, so she couldn't fly. He had a long-lasting relationship with a friend of hers, which he had no intention of breaking."

"That's odd...her story is extremely similar to a case that took place in San Gabriele, but the variable is that the woman in San Gabriele is probably dead. She disappeared from her home a few years ago, and her body was never found. Everyone thinks her husband murdered her, but so far there hasn't been any solid evidence to prove whether he did or didn't. Her name is Milena Mariani. It shouldn't be hard to find some pictures of her, since it is a local case." Stefano says calmly. I scan his face to see if he is just being condescending, but I see no trace of lies.

"Can you please bring the laptop later?" As soon as the words leave my mouth, I wish I could take them back. "I am sorry...I didn't mean to be so forward...or demanding. Would you please bring a laptop the next time you have time to come by?"

Stefano grins. "I will be back this evening, Iliana. I've been here every night."

"So my father says," I reply, "and I think he is very grateful to you for it. So am I."

"I wouldn't have it any other way. If Marco ever shows his face around here, we won't have to worry about him going to trial." He says, a shadow darkening his face.

"There was another woman there, who has short, blond hair and an impish glint in her eyes. Her name was Rita while she was at the center. And then there was Romina. She and I became good friends. She has medium-length brown hair, and glasses, and her husband was so controlling he wouldn't let her even buy groceries. She met some friends online, including a man, who became her special friend..."

"And her husband killed her, because he couldn't cope with her being unfaithful. Her children's testimony is, ultimately, what put her husband in jail, when they testified about their father asking them to lie. All four of the children had similar stories. Her body was found in a creek a few months later."

My eyes fill with tears. "What did you say?" I can barely hear my own voice.

"It is the story of another woman who was killed by her husband, somewhere up north."

I burst into tears. Stefano touches my hand and lifts my chin gently. "You just woke up, Iliana, and there is still a lot of confusion in your mind. What you lived through just two weeks ago is a hard pill to swallow, and it is not uncommon, after such a trauma, to experience strange things."

"But Stefano, that woman, the one you said died because of the friends she made online, I have met her. Her name at the center was Romina, and she was quite alive."

"Don't think about this for right now, Iliana. I will bring a laptop tonight, and we will look together. Do you think it is possible that maybe you've heard of those cases before, and your mind threaded their stories into the fabric of your dreams? Or maybe your mom was watching a TV show about those cases while she was here in your room, and the words filtered through?"

I think about what Stefano is saying. I never watch TV, so I am sure I didn't know about those cases, but could it be that I heard about the women's stories while I was asleep? That's certainly plausible. "I don't know, Stefano...they seemed so real, and the doctor...he was very helpful."

"I am sure he was, but now, let's get you to rest, a little. I am going to go see if your parents need anything in the waiting room."

"That's fine. Thank you for everything, Stefano."

Stefano stands to leave, and in that moment the door opens.

"Mommy! Grandpa told me you were awake!" Matteo comes flying toward me.

"Easy, easy, Matteo," my father says. "Mommy is still hooked up to a lot of machinery."

"Oh, Mommy!" he says, as he buries his little face into my neck. "You finally heard me. I asked you to wake up so many times, but you never did."

I suddenly remember the voice of the little boy I heard in the recreation room when I fainted. Was it Matteo's voice filtering through? An unbelievable sense of sadness washes over me. Maybe my father is right, and *Transitions* doesn't exist. Maybe it was all concocted by my mind, as I fought to stay alive in the aftermath of Marco's attack. And maybe Stefano nailed it, too, when he said that my mother could have been watching a TV show featuring cases of women who had died due to domestic violence. After all that happened, it is very possible my mother would have been interested in a program like that.

My mind is reeling. Dead or alive, real or not, those women were my friends, and their stories helped me make up my mind. I look at my sweet son, his little head cradled on my chest, and I inhale deeply when I kiss his hair. Those poor other women never made it back to their children, and I feel exceedingly grateful.

It is so strange how destiny works, sometimes; how it puts us in touch with ourselves and with those whose paths we cross, who will help us find our way. I read a book once, about contracts we write with other souls before we come to Earth, to support each other on the journey. Did I have a contract with Giulia, and Olivia? Did Francesca and I sit at

172

a café in Heaven, before we were born, and discuss a contract about sharing the same monster? And what about sweet Paola? Did she sign a contract with her abusive father, or with her husband who pushed her to attempt suicide? Who are the abusers? Are they demons who haunt our souls, are they angels in disguise who take us to the brink of madness to kill our egos? And if all that's true, why would we agree to undergo a life of such turmoil when we could have signed a different contract with fewer struggles and more perks?

My head hurts. I close my eyes, savoring the time with my son. I don't feel like talking to anyone right now, at least for a little while.

Tomorrow is a new day, and I will live again. For right now, I need to sleep, and maybe see my friends one last time.

CHAPTER THIRTEEN

I had no dreams — none I can recall, at least. I remember closing my eyes while Matteo snuggled against my chest, and slipping into a pocket of darkness, but none of the friendly faces I grew to love came to visit. I feel as though my life at the shelter was suspended, with the door left open; I had no sense of closure. I could not, now, thank Giulia and Romina for the bond we shared, nor was I able to hug Paola and Francesca one last time. All those women, and their stories, helped me glue together the pieces of myself that were shattered and scattered, and I will forever be grateful to them. It was Rita who had patiently explained how important it was for Rosa to listen to what Iliana was trying to say, and it was the kind-hearted doctor, whose eyes always searched the depths of my soul for clues to help, who ultimately showed me the door to return. Those people, who meant so much to me, are all gone, and I can find no way back to them, to say goodbye. I would have given anything, when I was at the shelter, to come back into this reality and see my loved ones. Now, I would give everything I have ever owned for the chance to go back there one last time, and tell everyone how much I love and appreciate them. No matter what anyone says — and no matter how irrational it might sound — I know *Transitions* exists. There is no doubt in my mind that, although I can't explain it rationally, my soul — my Rosa persona — was there.

"Did you have a good nap?" Stefano's voice jolts me away from my thoughts.

I turn toward the door, smiling. "I did. I slept like the dead."

"Thankfully," he says with a grin that illuminates his entire face, "you slept like the living. I still can't believe you are awake, and as strong as you are. The doctor told your parents that, if everything continues to look up, you will be out of the hospital in a matter of days."

My eyes hone in on the black leather bag he carries on his shoulder. "Is that a laptop?" I ask, hopeful.

"Yes, I told you I would bring it tonight," he replies, as he perches at the edge of my bed. "How are you feeling?"

"I am not too sure. 'Confused' probably sums it up." I can't bring myself to explain how sad I feel for the women I left behind.

"Well, it is to be expected, Iliana. In two weeks, you have gone through more than most people ever will in their entire lifetimes. I don't know a whole lot about the type of toll a coma takes on one's body, but I imagine it is huge."

"I gather," I reply, still unsure how I should feel.

"Well," Stefano says calmly, "should we research the case of Milena Mariani?"

The name sounds foreign to me, not evoking much of an emotional response. "Sure."

Stefano opens the laptop, and types something in the search field. "Here she is!" he exclaims excitedly. He turns the laptop for me to see, and my breath gets trapped in my throat, as a photo of Olivia — a bit younger and thinner than I remember her — smiles at me from the screen. My eyes immediately fill with tears, and my mind screams silently, as my entire body begins to shake, uncontrollably. I can't take my eyes off the screen, even to escape the overwhelming reality that Olivia is dead. A guttural sound breaks free from the denial I have clung to until now — screaming through my parted lips with the desperation of a wounded animal blinded by pain — before becoming choked by sobs.

Stefano waits without saying a word, until I can weep no more. He makes no attempt to remove the laptop, knowing that, however painful, this moment is crucial in my path to healing.

"It's her…it's Olivia," I manage to whisper. "It's not possible, Stefano. How can it be?"

"I don't have an answer for that question, Iliana. Nobody really understands the human mind completely, and surely no one knows where one goes during a coma. I have read of cases in which people came back knowing things they didn't know before; I've heard of people near death, watching their own body as medics have frantically tried to save them. Nobody — regardless of smart, or how well-educated on the subject they are — really knows where our minds travel."

"What does the article say?" I ask with a shaky voice. Do I want to know what happened to Olivia? A part of me wants to remember her as vibrant, and as alive as she was when I met her; the other part of me wants to know her story…all the way to the end.

Stefano scrolls down to scan the article. "It talks about her disappearance, and how everyone thought she left willingly at first. It goes on to relate how, over time, it was discovered that her husband had been having an affair, and how troubled their marriage was."

"What was her husband's name?" I ask, fervently hoping that Stefano will speak a name different from that which Olivia related in our conversations.

"Dino Orlandi."

"Dino never had time for art, and he thinks art is a waste of time. If it doesn't make him money, it has no value."
My heart breaks, as my last shred of hope is ripped away by the memory of Olivia, talking of her husband's lack of

artistic interest. I sigh, drawing a deep breath to steady my voice. "He didn't love her, Stefano. He kept her on a shelf, like any of his other possessions. Does the article say anything else about her?"

"Not this one, particularly, but there is an extensive collection of articles, ranging from the time she disappeared until recently. There is a lot of circumstantial evidence that links Dino Orlandi to her possible murder, but since her body was never found, there is nothing solid that can be pinned on him. Meanwhile, he has moved on and lives with his mistress, still sticking to his story of innocence."

"Can I see, please?"

Stefano lays the laptop on the bed while he adjusts the pillows behind my back, then he picks it up again and lays it gently on my lap. I scroll down the list of articles, and I notice a headline that stops me in my tracks. "Sisters in Tragedy," it is titled. In the teaser, I see names that don't ring any bells, but I click on the article anyway, because, at *Transitions*, we were all sisters.

My heart pounds as I wait for the article to load, and I swallow several times. Finally, here they are: Picture after picture, story after story, the women whose lives have become strangely entwined with my own are all there, their sad smiles a brave front, masking the truth.

"Oh, my God..." Again, I can't stop the tears from coming, pouring straight from my heart, it seems. I point at the first picture with a shaky finger. "This is Giulia," I explain. "She was married to a man who, like Olivia's husband, had an extramarital affair."

"I remember that case," Stefano nods, when he sees the woman I am pointing at. "That's Marilena LoBianco. It was concluded that her husband killed her after she refused to have sex with him."

"She mentioned that," I interrupt, "but her husband had a relationship with another woman, and Giulia knew it."

I close my eyes, thinking of Giulia and her bubbly personality, and I swallow hard to keep from crying again. "She is beautiful, Stefano, and she loves so many things! I remember the day we went to Florence, and how interested she was in the history of everything we saw. She walked around with a travel guide, reading to us from it, and excited to learn new things. She wanted to go visit a leather factory, and we never went. Now, we won't have a second chance to go." I glance at Giulia's picture again, tracing my finger over her long dark hair, and the smile that, in times of despair, warmed my heart and gave me the strength to fight for my own life.

I scroll down to the next picture, and see Rita. According to the information in the article, her name was Elisa Campo. Elisa was separated from her husband, and the separation was not amicable. She met him the night before she disappeared, when she visited his home to drop off their daughter, and he was the last known person to see her alive. The next day, she was supposed to pick up her daughter from school, but she never showed up. One of her close friends revealed that Rita feared her husband, but the stories neighbors told, about strange cars parked in front of her house the night before, supported her husband's claim that she met other people that night. There were even reports that her disappearance could have been the result of an association between Elisa and the Freemasons, but no evidence was ever found to confirm such an association. One detail in the article catches my eye: Elisa Campo disappeared in 2008, nearly ten years ago! I allow my mind to travel back to the day I heard her introduction during the group therapy session: *I have forgiven and, like Gina, I am here mostly to offer support.* Rita was at peace…she had forgiven the person — or people — who murdered her, but she chose to stay and help those of us who needed a steady guide, in order to find our way out of the swamp.

"I loved Rita." A mix of emotions trails from my voice, like moss from an ancient cypress. "She was like a mother to us all. She was a bit older than the rest — she and Gina both were, but Gina left, and I didn't have a chance to ask where she was going next — and she looked out for us. I remember Doctor Castelli telling me that Rita could even lead the group discussions. He respected her, too."

"Are you sure you want to do this, Iliana?" Stefano ventures. "You've been through a roller-coaster ride of emotions already, and you need to focus on healing."

I grin. "You sound like Doctor Castelli. He always not to concern myself too much with the events that affected others, because my focus had to remain fixed on my own healing."

"I didn't meet this doctor, but I agree. It is good to be compassionate, but you must be aware of your own limits. If what happens around you becomes too much, and you don't remain centered, your external world will come to own you."

"You ignored your own safety to ensure mine," I remind Stefano, smiling.

"Yes, but it was an emergency situation. With all the respect due to those women, Iliana, you have plenty of time to find out more about their stories. I am sure they would want you to put your own health first. They are gone, but you are still here, and it is imperative that you become strong enough to resume your life."

I think about Stefano's words, and I am sure he is right. I scroll quickly to the end of the article and, as I do so, I see Romina's picture, but — instead of clicking on it to read the story — I close the laptop and hand it back to Stefano.

"Thank you for bringing this. It hurts to discover that what I thought was real is instead something my mind concocted, but if I hope to heal fully, I must be strong enough to accept facts for what they are."

179

A quick knock on the door interrupts the conversation, and Stefano stands up to put the laptop back in its case.

"Please come in," I call out, as the door opens and a young nurse walks in. She has short platinum hair, tucked behind her ears. Her skin is very pale, and she wears a bright red lipstick that makes her thin lips stand out like colored pencils. When she gets closer, I notice her eyes are crystal blue.

"Hi, my name is Adriana. The morning doctor left orders for you to be moved to a regular room if everything continued to improve through the day, and the doctor who came by earlier while you were asleep didn't even bother waking you up, since the numbers he read on the monitors were good, but he confirmed that you can be moved. I was waiting for you to awaken from your nap before I came in. I will leave soon for shift change, so if you are ready to go, I can start the process. We have to get you unhooked from the monitors, and then you will be ready to go."

"I would like that. Thank you, Adriana," I reply with a smile.

"Would you step outside for a moment, sir?"

"He can stay…" I offer.

The nurse shrugs. "If you are comfortable with it, I have no problem with him staying, as long as he stays out of the way."

"I am going to stand in the corner," Stefano assures the nurse, winking at me as he does so.

She caps the IV line and carefully removes the needle from my hand, then she removes the tubes connecting me to the monitors and looks at me. "I can leave the catheter in, if you want, unless you want to try getting up and walking to the bathroom on your own."

"I'm going to step outside," Stefano volunteers, before I have a chance to reply. The sensitivity this man shows, over and over, is something I am not used to.

"I would like to try walking to the bathroom on my own," I state, as soon as Stefano closes the door quietly behind himself.

"Very well," Adriana responds. She removes the catheter, ordering me to sit on the bed for a moment, before attempting to stand up. "You might feel dizzy the moment your feet touch the ground."

I do as I am told and — as I had been warned it might — my head spins the moment I stand, so I sit back down and place my hands on the bed to steady myself.

"I can call one of my colleagues to help, if you think you need additional support."

I shake my head. "No, I'm okay, I just got up too fast."

I take a deep breath and try again. This time, holding on to the nurse's arm for support, I can stand on my own. I take a small step, and then another one. I let her help me to the bathroom and back, and by the time I lie back down, I feel exhausted.

"Don't feel discouraged," she says, noticing the look of disappointment on my face. "It takes a lot of strength to do what you just did. In no time at all, you will be running."

I appreciate her words of encouragement more than she can imagine. In this reality or any other, we are all sisters, and we support each other on different levels.

"I am going to get the wheelchair," Adriana says with a smile. She opens the door, and as she walks out, Stefano comes back in with my mother.

"Hello, Iliana. How are you feeling, sweetheart?" My mom asks as she quickly comes to stamp a kiss on my forehead.

"I'm good, just a little tired."

"I see all the tubing is gone; it must be a good sign." She sounds very excited.

"Yes," I confirm. "I am being moved to a regular room. The nurse just went to fetch a wheelchair."

"That's wonderful news, darling. Dad should be here momentarily. We couldn't find a parking spot nearby, so he dropped me off and went driving around to look. Hopefully, he found something not too far. Did the doctor come by?"

"I haven't seen him this afternoon, but the nurse said he came by while I was sleeping, and he only checked the monitors. He left orders to move me out of ICU as soon as I woke up."

"So," my mom inquires, "what have you done since you woke up?"

"I woke up only a short while ago, and then Stefano came in and we checked a few things online."

"Oh? What sorts of things?" my mother asks.

"We were looking up articles about women whose lives were cut short. By the way, Angela," Stefano asks, "do you remember watching a show about domestic abuse cases while you were in this room? About Milena Mariani, maybe, or Marilena LoBianco?"

A puzzled look descends over her face. "I can't remember, why?"

"We all know Iliana has been in this hospital since she was shot, and she never physically went to a shelter, but is sure she met women whose stories are exactly like those of Milena Mariani, Marilena LoBianco, and a few others. Not being someone who watches TV, nor someone who keeps up with crime-related news, she would not know the details of those stories, unless someone told her about them. We both wonder if, maybe, she heard of those cases while she was in a coma, and somehow, the names and events traveled through layers of consciousness and were worked into her dreams."

"It's possible," Mom agrees, "but I really can't remember. The Mariani case has been back in the news lately, and often, many of those cases are grouped together."

"Do you think it makes sense, Angela?" Stefano inquires. I am sure asking my mother her opinion just earned him several points.

"It does...it really does. When my alarm rings in the morning, or if someone knocks on the door while I am sleeping, those sounds usually become part of my dreams. It is possible that Iliana heard someone on TV talking about those cases, and she dreamt about meeting those women," she allows.

I listen to Stefano and my mother discussing this issue as if I am not even in the room, and I feel annoyed. Of course, what they are saying makes absolute sense, rationally, and it would explain why I met women who were dead before I was even shot. One thing, though, that neither of them is thinking of: If I heard about those cases while I was asleep, I can see how I would know what happened to them. But how — since my eyes were supposedly closed this entire time — how did I know what they look like? How could my mind have made that up out of whole cloth?

I don't feel like arguing with either of them, so I keep my thoughts to myself.

"What do you think, Iliana? Could it be possible?" My mother tries to involve me into the conversation.

"It could be, I suppose," I reply, nonchalantly.

I am glad when Adriana opens the door and comes in, pushing a wheelchair.

"Oh, you have company," she says. "I hate to bother you."

"No bother at all!" I chime in. "I am ready to move to a normal room. ICU rooms are a bit gloomy." I am also happy and grateful that the nurse's arrival interrupted a conversation I want no part of.

"Do you need me to help?" Stefano offers.

I glance at my mother, and I see appreciation glowing in her eyes. She likes Stefano, not only because he saved my life, but also because he is attentive and thoughtful. What a relief it must be for a parent to know someone else also loves their child as much as they do. I wonder if Stefano cares about me, beyond the level of friendship. He helped me, and continues to do so, but it is possible that he became involved in my situation because — after witnessing the abuse inflicted on his mother — he feels he should react, now that he can. Children can only watch helplessly, but a grown man can change the course of things, and I feel almost sure that a sense of duty is the biggest reason why Stefano is here.

"Sure!" the nurse replies appreciatively. "If you don't mind supporting her, I will adjust her gown beneath her as she sits."

We leave the intensive care unit and take the elevator up to the third floor. The nurse pushes my wheelchair, and Stefano follows behind with my few belongings, while my mom waits in the old room for my father.

The new room looks much cheerier, and although I am ready to go home, I think I will like it better than being in ICU. It has a lot more space, and it resembles a hotel room.

"Fancy!" Stefano exclaims. "It looks like a room at the Hilton." I love his sense of humor, and I am grateful he is around to lighten things up.

Adriana helps me to my bed and, once again, I feel tired. My father must have been right around the corner when we left the intensive care unit, because just as the nurse is finished, he and mom walk in.

"Good evening, sweetheart!" He says, and he blows a kiss.

"Hey dad, did you have a nice afternoon?"

"I did. I went to the hardware store with my favorite shopping partner."

"Yeah?" I ask. "Who is that?"

"The one and only: Matteo. He is my favorite shopping partner because he never lets me spend too much money. I am so busy keeping after him that I don't have time to browse for anything else I might need or want. That kid is great if you are trying to save money."

Stefano laughs at my father's affectionate joke. "I need to borrow him, then. I always spend too much money at the hardware store."

184

Good job, Stefano…if you were looking for a way to win my dad over, you just hit the bull's eye.

"Where is Matteo, anyway?" I ask

"He is with Aunt Veronica. She was going to feed him dinner while we are here, and then get him to bed. His class is going on a field trip to the zoo tomorrow."

I smile. Aunt Veronica is a peculiar old lady, but her heart is as big as the universe. She is eccentric and funny, with blue hair. At the young age of 82, she is always wearing bright pink accessories — and Matteo loves her dearly — but we could never visit her when I was married to Marco, because he wouldn't have his son around that "crazy old bat," as he called her.

"I'm sure he is having the time of his life," I say, with a big grin on my face. Stefano has never met Aunt Veronica — so he is clueless — but he will meet her soon enough, I hope. Once I get out of the hospital, I intend to make regular visits to Aunt Veronica part of our weekly routine.

"Oh, yes, I almost forgot…" my mother says. "I spoke with the prosecutor who's handling your case, this afternoon. I updated him on your condition, and he asked if you would be willing to talk to him tomorrow, or the next day."

"Of course," I reply. "Is he coming here?"

"I'm not sure yet. I told him I would call him back after talking to you," my mother says, shifting her gaze from me to Stefano. "Maybe you should be here, too, Stefano. You already told him your side of the story, but in case Iliana forgets any details, it might be helpful for you to be around."

"Sure, Angela. Just keep me posted about the time he is coming, and I will make sure to be here," Stefano confirms to my mother. Knowing my parents, I am sure they are totally sold on his charm by now, and I can't blame them.

"You really should go home, Stefano," my father says. "Spending every night here is probably exhausting, and it is not necessary. The room is right beside the nurses' desk, and I really doubt Marco would be that stupid. He is angry, and surely twisted, but he is not completely obtuse. If anything, he is too smart for his own good…unfortunately. He fooled everybody."

"I don't know…I just don't feel comfortable leaving Iliana here alone, no matter how nearby the hospital staff is," Stefano replies.

I look at him, and my heart swells. And then I realize what my father is seeing in Stefano's face. He looks exhausted — spending the night in a chair for two weeks, only going home long enough to take a shower before heading off to work, has taken a physical toll on him. His forehead is etched with lines, and he looks like he needs a vacation day. "Dad is right, Stefano. I will be fine. I can call for help if anything happens, and I agree: Marco is evil but he is no fool. He knows he is already in trouble with the law, and he is not going to do anything that will get him into deeper waters."

Stefano reflects for a moment. I can read in his face the desire to sleep in his own bed, but he feels conflicted. "I don't know, Iliana…"

"I agree with Iliana," Mom joins in. "You need a little time for yourself, Stefano. Iliana will be home in just a day or two, and she will need all of us even more at that point. She is safe here. I will make sure to let the nurse on duty know they need to be extra vigilant."

"Are you sure, Iliana? I don't feel good about this. I really don't."

"I am positive. Go home and get some rest. Mom has a good point: If I am ever going to need a security guard, it will be when I am home. There are people walking in front of the room at all times of the day and night. Nobody would be foolish enough to do anything stupid," I say with conviction.

"Okay, you talked me into it — all of you. But, I am going to sleep with my phone on the pillow. If you need anything at all, call immediately. I only live ten minutes from the hospital."

"I promise," I say with a smile.

Stefano walks to the bed and kisses me gently on the forehead. "I will call you in the morning, then, and I will stop by at lunch time. Rest well."

"You, too. And don't worry…everything is going to be okay," I say, secretly excited that he cares this much.

"Well, goodnight, then. Angela and Giacomo, call me if you need anything."

"Goodnight, Stefano," my parents reply, both smiling at him with appreciation.

"I am glad this issue came up, Iliana," my father starts as soon as the door closes. "We need to think of a security plan to implement, once you leave the hospital. We don't know how long Marco is going to remain free and, as long as he is able to walk the streets, he is a potential danger. I know there is a restraining order against him, but honestly, I don't think a piece of paper is much of a defense against a maniac, if he has it in his mind to do violence. He knew what he was risking when he came back with a gun, too, but he did it anyway. I just wish you hadn't kept us in the dark, Iliana. We could have helped…"

"Don't go there, Dad. If I could go back, I would, but I wasn't thinking straight at the time, and I can't change the past. And of course, I agree with you. A piece of paper is not going to stop Marco."

"I have already removed your personal belongings from that house, but I will need you to look through the things I picked up to see if I forgot anything," he says.

"I don't care if you did, Dad. I don't ever want to set foot in that place again."

"Fair enough. Let's talk this over with Stefano tomorrow, and see what he suggests, too," my mother joins in.

"You guys have gotten really close with Stefano the last two weeks, I see. You know, I barely knew him the day of the accident."

"Yes," my dad nods. "He told us what happened, and how you two met. I am glad he came over, Iliana. I owe him a lot, and he has truly been a rock for us."

"I am so grateful to him," I think out loud. "I am happy he didn't listen to me that day, when I told him to stay away. Well…you guys probably need to get some rest, also. Why don't you go home?"

My father glances at his watch. "We should listen, Angela. The last two days have been intense, especially for you. We need to be ready and strong, when Iliana comes home."

My mother is a bit reluctant, but she doesn't argue. She stands and stretches, then grabs her purse from the side table and loops it over her shoulder.

"Goodnight, honey. Sleep well, and call us if you need anything at all," she says, as my father wraps his arm around her shoulder, ready to go.

They close the door on their way out, leaving me alone with my thoughts. So much has happened that my head is still spinning. I have lost dear friends, and found my old life; I have lost Rosa so that Iliana could awaken. I am back with my son, and excited to see if there is a future in the cards for me and Stefano…and I am worried about Marco, and what will happen if he finds me. What if he *is* that crazy? What if he feels like he has nothing to lose? What if his anger is massive enough to cloud his judgement? I try, as hard as I can, to be strong for my parents, pulling out every ounce of courage I could find to reassure Stefano, so he could get some rest. Truth be told, I am scared. I am terrified Marco will find me and, if he does, will finish what he started. I can sense his anger, even from a distance…and I know I am not just imagining things.

The phone on the nightstand rings shrilly, nearly making me jump out of my skin. I glance at the clock on the wall

— nine o'clock. It's probably Stefano, or Mom, calling to say goodnight.

"Hello," I say into the receiver, but silence is all I can hear on the other end of the line. "Hello! Stefano, is that you? We must have a bad connection…"

I hear smashing glass. The line goes dead.

CHAPTER FOURTEEN

"Are you ready to remove the bandage, Iliana?" the doctor asks, as he picks up the shears from the tray. "There is still a bit of swelling, but the wound looked good yesterday. You're healing fast."

"I couldn't be any readier, doctor," I reply, as he unravels the gauze. I can feel cool air reaching my scalp with every layer he peels off. Once the entire bandage is removed, he inspects the wound. "Looking good. Once more of your hair grows back, you won't know there was ever a scar there."

It hadn't occurred to me that my head had been shaved — but, of course, it would have to have been! — and I immediately feel self-conscious, glancing at Stefano standing in the corner. I wonder if he can read my mind, because as soon as I raise a hand to touch my head, he smiles and tells me I am beautiful.

"Can I have a mirror?" I ask the doctor.

"Sure. The nurse can bring you a mirror, or, if you would like to get up and go look in the bathroom, I will wait here. I also want to run a few neurological tests, and it would be helpful if I can observe how you walk."

"Yes, I would rather get up and go see for myself," I reply, sitting for a moment at the edge of the bed.

"Do you need help, Iliana?" Stefano inquires when he notices it takes me a while to get up.

"No, I can manage, thank you." I smile gratefully, and stand on my feet.

The doctor's gaze follows me until I enter the bathroom and close the door, and I hear from his comments to Stefano that he is satisfied with my progress. I am alone in the bathroom, ready to face my reflected image — but I am honestly shocked at what I see when I look up. A large patch of my hair is gone; in the center of the bald area is a scabbed, red scar. I seem to have lost weight, and my cheeks are sunken in, causing my eyes to look bigger than I remember them appearing the last time I looked in a mirror. My skin looks dry, my lips are rough and chapped, and there is a scar on my upper lip. I barely recognize myself in the woman who stares back at me, and I remember the dream I had, as Rosa, seeing a bruised and bandaged Iliana walk through the door...

"You are a survivor, Iliana," I whisper to myself. "Be proud of your scars." And as those words escape my lips, I think back about the phone call last night. The operator was not able to provide any information about the number that called, and I tried hard not to panic. I thought of calling my parents, or Stefano, but then abandoned the idea. It was only a phone call, likely from someone with a twisted sense of humor. Perhaps someone who had dialed a wrong number...or, it could have been just kids, goofing around and pranking a random number. I tried not to think about it too much at the time — otherwise, I wouldn't have been able to fall asleep. Instead, I slept like a stone all night, and woke up this morning ready to leave this joint.

Stefano and the doctor watch me walk back to the bed, and the doctor asks me how I feel. The truth is that just taking a few steps is exhausting, but I keep those thoughts to myself in fear he will give orders for me to stay longer. I want to go home and be with my son, although that issue requires extra thinking, as I no longer have a home to call my own. The house I lived in belongs to Marco; we no longer share it and, even if Matteo and I are welcome to live with my parents as long as we need, I make a mental note to look at listings as soon as I am out of here. I need my own place, and I need to find a job to support myself.

"Well," the doctor begins, when I am again comfortably in bed, "what do you think?"

"I look like I have been through a meat grinder," I joke.

"You have. You had three broken ribs — which have healed nicely, thankfully — and a deep laceration right below your nose. You look a lot better today than you did when you first arrived," the doctor informs me.

"Still beautiful," Stefano says again, and I am intrigued by the light dancing in his eyes.

"When will I be able to leave, doctor?"

"There is nothing physical holding you back, Iliana. It will take a while to heal completely, but you are okay to go home if you wish. Your vitals are good, and the scans show that the swelling on the brain is continuing to recede."

"Really?" I am suddenly excited. "I need to talk to my parents, and work out the logistics."

"They will be happy to have you home," Stefano says with a soft smile.

"I said you are okay *physically*, Iliana," the doctor continues. "The question is: Are you okay *mentally*?"

"I think so…I am still a bit shaken, but, as you said, it will take a while to heal."

The doctor nods. "Yes, that's certain. What concerns me is the fact that your assailant is still free, and that thought alone might cause you stress that could hinder your progress."

"Well, there is nothing I can do about that, doctor. I can't hide in a hospital the rest of my life. At some point, I must face Marco," I reply firmly.

"We will face him together," Stefano says, calmly, but I can detect a spike of anger in his voice. His eyes are no longer dancing.

"I will leave you to discuss this. A social worker will see you before you leave, to inform you of all the resources the community offers, in case you need additional support. I will sign off on you going home, if you are ready, but please talk about it with your family before you decide. I would not mind keeping you under observation for another day or two." the doctor concludes, before leaving the room.

"I don't mean to sound too forward, Iliana, but I live alone — and you are welcome to stay at my house," Stefano offers haltingly.

I think about it for a few seconds, then shake my head. "I really appreciate it, Stefano, but I don't want to impose, and it would feel like we are moving too fast. I will not hide the fact that I am attracted to you, and God knows how grateful I am, but I am just beginning a new chapter of my life, and I need some time alone to do that." While the last thing I want to do is sound unappreciative, I have a bone-deep conviction that what I need most is to be certain I can be a whole person, without needing someone else to validate me. I have never taken my own stand; instead, I went from being Daddy's little girl to being Marco's wife. I have never been Iliana. It is time I give her a chance.

A light tapping alerts us that someone else is at the door. Stefano goes to open it, and he welcomes the visitor, whom I do not recognize.

"Good morning, Mrs. Landini. My name is Alessandro Toglietti, and I am the assistant prosecutor in the case against your husband. I spoke with your mother this morning, and she said it would be okay for me to stop by."

"Oh, yes," I reply. "Please come in."

"How are you feeling, Ma'am?"

"I am alive," I reply with a smile. "To my husband's disappointment, I am sure."

"What do you remember of the day you were injured?"

I take a deep breath. "Before we start, sir, I need to give you a little background information that you probably haven't heard before, since my parents weren't really aware of what was going on in my marriage..."

"Go ahead, Ma'am. Is it okay if I record the conversation?"

I nod. "My husband, Marco, was abusive to me — physically and emotionally. I lived in a state of constant fear, never knowing what would set him off. Over the years, I learned not to push certain buttons, but he would snap over the smallest things. That's how Mr. Puccini and I met," I say, glancing at Stefano. "He installed a furnace at my house, and Marco became preoccupied about my relationship with Mr. Puccini, although we had just met — and only for professional reasons."

"Was your husband customarily jealous of other men?"

"Marco was jealous of anyone or anything he thought could undermine his authority. I believe he is a very insecure man, who uses arrogance as a shield."

"I see. What angered him the day of the incident?"

As I was saying," I continue, "Mr. Puccini came over to install a furnace, and he noticed some bruises on my arm. Marco came home shortly after that, so we couldn't talk at all. Stefano — Mr. Puccini — came back the next day, while

Marco was at work, and he gave me a business card with his cell phone number written on the back. He explained that he had seen his mother being abused while he was growing up, and he couldn't bring himself to just stand by and do nothing."

I pause for a moment, and the prosecutor waits patiently, trying not to pressure me.

"A few days later," I pick up my narrative, "I got home from the grocery store to find Marco at home. It was an unusual time for him to be home, but since he worked as a salesman and he traveled a lot, I didn't think anything of it when I pulled up and saw his car. I brought my purchases inside, and found him pacing in the kitchen. He didn't say anything. He just watched me as I put the food away, taking a deep breath from time to time — he reminded me of a tea kettle getting ready to boil. My senses were on high alert: I knew he was upset about something, and it was only a matter of time before he would explode. As soon as I finished putting everything away, he started in. He flashed Mr. Puccini's business card in my face and asked if I'd had trouble with the new furnace. He immediately called me a liar, and he accused me of having an inappropriate relationship with Mr. Puccini."

The prosecutor raises his eyes and looks at both of us. "But you didn't…"

I blush. "No, we didn't. We barely knew each other, and only spoke for five minutes the day he came by to deliver his business card."

"Did he attack you right after this?" The prosecutor asks.

"Yes. He slapped me and made me lose my balance, and I fell against the stove. He then kicked me several times and said he was going to find Mr. Puccini, to tell him he wanted the furnace removed from the house. I didn't want Mr.

Puccini to be caught up in a confrontation he didn't expect, so as soon as Marco left, I called him to warn him."

"How long did it take Mr. Puccini to get to your house?" He asks.

"I'm not sure. Ten, fifteen minutes, maybe."

"How long had your husband gone, by the time you got to the phone to call Mr. Puccini?"

"I am not sure. I remember lying on the floor for a while before I could manage to drag myself across the room and pick up the phone."

"How much time, would you say? A rough estimate."

"I probably lay there about ten minutes; and then, it took me several minutes more to get across the room."

The prosecutor nods. "What did you tell Mr. Puccini when you called?"

"The truth. I told him Marco was looking for him."

"What did Mr. Puccini say?"

"He asked me if I was okay, and he told me he was going to come over. I tried to discourage him, but he didn't listen."

"What happened after that?"

"I dragged myself to the door, so I could unlock it. I felt very weak, and I didn't know whether I was going to make it, or faint. When Mr. Puccini arrived, he found me collapsed on the floor. He picked me up, said I wasn't safe there, and that he was going to take me with him. He had just carried me out the door when we heard Marco's voice. He was standing by the gate, and Mr. Puccini told him to move. He refused, and charged toward us, instead. When he body-slammed us, Mr. Puccini lost his balance and we both fell. I saw Marco pull out a gun from his pocket and aim it toward Mr. Puccini, and I don't know what came over me. It was as if the courage I had lacked throughout the years burst through me all at once, and I literally jumped on Marco."

The prosecutor smiles. "You had broken ribs, and you still managed to jump."

"I felt no pain in that moment. Adrenaline was rushing through me so furiously that I could have been running with broken legs. I remember hearing a gunshot, but I have no recollection of what happened next."

"Mr. Puccini?" The prosecutor asks.

"I was trying to get up, when I heard the gun go off. I jumped up and saw Iliana fall down."

"What did Mr. Landini do?"

He seemed stunned, and just stood with the gun in his hand for a second or two — just long enough for me to react, and jump on top of him. The police arrived within seconds. I think a neighbor called when she heard the commotion outside."

"Would you say that Mr. Landini was intoxicated when he arrived?"

"Yes," I reply. "He slurred his words. I thought it was odd because he was only gone for about thirty minutes, but there was something different about him."

"We found half a bottle of Bourbon in his car," the prosecutor confirms, "along with a small bag of cocaine."

I am honestly surprised. "Marco was doing drugs?"

"Apparently. There was cocaine in his system, and his blood alcohol level was above the legal limit. You've never noticed changes in his behavior?"

I realize now that I was married to a stranger. "No, sir. I guess I hadn't."

"Mr. Landini is out on bond. You are aware of that, correct?"

I sigh. "Unfortunately, yes."

"Is there anything else you would like to share, Mrs. Landini?"

The thought of telling the prosecutor about the strange phone call last night crosses my mind, but I decide against it. I don't want Stefano to start camping outside my room again. "No, sir. Nothing I can think of."

"I guess that's it, then. Here's my business card," the prosecutor says. "Please call me if you remember anything else."

"I will."

Stefano walks the prosecutor to the door, then returns to sit on the bed. "I won't sleep until I know that man is behind bars," he says.

"Me neither. I can't wait for the trial, and unfortunately, it won't be for another two months."

"Are you going to file for divorce?" Stefano asks.

"Absolutely. My father has been asking around to find the best divorce attorney in town."

I see relief on Stefano's face. "Hopefully, this nightmare will be behind us soon."

The phone rings, and Stefano lifts the receiver. "Hello," he says.

His face darkens immediately. "Hello," he repeats, more forcefully this time. "Who the hell is this? It's not funny!"

"Stefano, just hang up." My heart is racing in my chest. It can't be a coincidence that someone called the wrong number twice within the last twelve hours. "It happened last night, too."

Stefano looks at me, surprised. "Why didn't you say anything to the prosecutor about it?"

"I thought that maybe someone just had the wrong number, and I didn't want to jump to conclusions…but it is strange that someone got the wrong number two days in a row."

Stefano dials zero to call the hospital operator. "Operator," he says when a woman picks up, "can you please tell me what number just called this room?"

He waits on the line, and we make eye contact. I have no doubt his nerves are on edge, too. When the operator comes back, she informs him that the calling number has been withheld, and she is not able to provide any additional information. He places the receiver back on its cradle and takes a deep breath. "Do you think it was Marco?" he asks, as he sits at the edge of my bed again, running a hand through his hair. "Hospitals have a policy of masking the identity of abuse victims for safety. Did your parents not request that?"

"They probably didn't think about it…I hope it wasn't him. I wondered about that last night, when I received the first phone call, but I tried to calm myself down and rationalized that someone probably had the wrong number."

"That settles it," Stefano says. He stands again and walks in nervous circles around the room. "You are coming to my house when you leave here, and I will take a leave of absence from work, until things calm down. I am not leaving you alone. Did you hear anything in the background last night?"

"I heard something…it sounded like smashing glass, but I couldn't tell for sure. Maybe the person that was calling dropped a glass."

"Or maybe he threw a bottle into the wall…" Stefano replies. "We need to call the prosecutor and tell him about the calls."

"But we don't know for sure it is Marco who's calling," I protest.

"We don't know for sure it is *not* Marco, either, and that's enough doubt to make it scary," Stefano states gently. "We need to tell the prosecutor, Iliana. Marco was forbidden, by court order, to contact you in any way."

Stefano is right. I was trying to convince myself that it wasn't Marco last night, but who else could it be? If someone had called the wrong number, they would have apologized — or hung up right away — but the caller remained on the line in complete silence.

"I think he is only trying to scare me, Stefano. Fear is the tactic that has always worked for him, and he is probably desperate to regain control right now…but you're right: It is best to report these two incidents."

"Do you want me to call, or would you prefer to do it?" Stefano asks.

"I will." I glance at the business card to get the number, and punch it into the phone. Assistant Prosecutor Toglietti answers at the third ring. "Hello, this is Iliana Landini. It didn't occur to me, while you were here, to mention something that might be important. I received a phone call last night, after my family left, but when I answered, nobody spoke. All I heard was glass shattering. I first assumed that it was a wrong number, but then the same thing happened just a short while ago, right after you left, and I don't even know if the two calls are related, but I figured I should call

200

and let you know. We tried to see if we could trace the caller, but the operator stated that the call came from a private number, and she could not retrieve any information."

The assistant prosecutor's voice remains steady, and I hear him shuffling paper, so I think he is writing something down. "I am still in the building, Mrs. Landini. I will do my best to find out who called. Meanwhile, until I can assess what is going on, make sure someone is with you at all times."

CHAPTER FIFTEEN

After much reflection — and in the face of the loving pressure from my parents and Stefano — I have decided to postpone my quest for independence until Marco is safely locked away, and I have temporarily moved both myself and Matteo into Stefano's apartment. It felt a bit awkward at first to accept this arrangement, but Mom, Dad, and Stefano all felt so strongly about this, that I finally gave in. I have fought this battle alone for long enough; I have given myself permission to accept help.

Stefano's apartment is a small, two-bedroom place, with a quaint kitchenette and combined dining and family room. It only has one bathroom, but I am sure we can manage. The furniture is sparse — as one would expect to find in a bachelor pad — and it lacks a feminine touch, but it is clean and comfortable, and I am grateful we are here.

My mother and Stefano have been a constant presence. As he promised, Stefano took a leave of absence from his job, and he sleeps with one eye open. That's what he tells me, at least; he has been sleeping on the couch, to leave the two bedrooms for Matteo and me. I protested immediately, telling him that Matteo and I could share a room, but he said that I need my space, and Matteo needs his. My parents think Stefano is the human equivalent of sunshine, and they coo every time his name is mentioned in conversation.

Marco hasn't tried to contact me again — if it was he who called those two times — and my anxiety is beginning to wane. Assistant Prosecutor Toglietti keeps me updated daily, and I feel like I can finally catch a breath. The police were unable to trace the calls made to the hospital, and there was not much they could do without solid evidence that Marco tried to contact me, but I try to keep myself busy and not obsess on those two isolated incidents.

"Iliana," Mom says, as she helps me fold a sheet, "I spoke with Luciana, yesterday. She feels terrible about what happened, and she says she would love to come and see you, if you are comfortable with the idea. She is worried about you."

I raise an eyebrow and stop folding. "Luciana? I don't think that it is a good idea for Marco's mother to see where I live, Mom."

"I don't think she would tell him, honey. She sounds heartbroken about the whole thing. You can't blame her for what her son did."

My mother's words anger me. "I am not blaming her for anything, Mom, but I don't know if it is safe for her to come here."

"I think it would be fine, Iliana," my mother responds defensively. "Luciana is a victim of her son's actions, not a supporter. She told me she hasn't even talked to him since the incident."

"Really? And do you talk to her often?"

"No, just occasionally. She has called me a few times to see how you were."

Stefano walks into the family room from the kitchen, and overhears the conversation. "Do you know for sure she is not talking to her son?"

My mom reflects for a moment. "Well, I can't be completely sure, but that's what she told me. And besides, Stefano is here with you, and if she comes over today, I am here, too."

"Today?" I ask, a little irritated that my own mother doesn't feel she needs to give me time to think things over.

"She has a dentist appointment near here, and I told her I would call her cell phone and let her know if you agree."

I feel cornered. "I guess that's fine. I just hope she is not going to tell Marco where I am."

"I am sure she won't, sweetheart. Here, let me call her before she goes into her appointment." She drops her side of the sheet and scurries to the kitchen to retrieve her phone, returning just a moment later. "Her appointment was delayed — an emergency patient walked in — so she will actually be here in just a little while."

I don't even know what to say…am I ready to face Marco's mother? What if she asks me details of her son's behavior while she is here? What can I — or should I — say to her? I just nod to my mother, and I finish folding the sheets and pillow cases myself.

Stefano prepares a simple lunch for us, setting a sandwich aside for Matteo. My father is going to pick him up shortly from school, and then they will be over. It sounds like it is going to be a full house, and I am sure to feel entirely uncomfortable, talking with her about my situation in front of everyone.

"I think I would feel more comfortable if she and I meet at the café around the corner," I say, hoping my mother will understand. Before I can formulate any other words, though, the doorbell rings.

"Is her dentist in the same building as this apartment?" I joke, sarcastically. "It couldn't have been more than thirty minutes since you called her."

My mother shrugs and goes to open the door. Luciana walks inside, and looks around before focusing on me.

"Iliana..." she says, tears immediately filling her eyes. "I don't even know what to say."

I stand to hug her. "Hello, Luciana. Thank you for coming by." She appears sincere, and I feel more at ease.

"Why didn't you ever tell me what was happening, Iliana?" she asks, tears still streaming down her face.

"I don't know, Luciana. I guess I was scared, and probably embarrassed."

"But you knew I would have done something to stop it, right? You knew that much, I hope."

"I was blinded, Luciana. The abuse went on for so long, that I lost touch with my own judgement, I believe. I lived in a state of constant fear."

"You aren't the one who should have been embarrassed, Iliana. I am embarrassed that my son would do something so horrible."

"It is not your fault, Luciana. Marco is a grown man, and he makes his own decisions."

Luciana sighs, then smiles through her tears. "Thank you, Iliana. I know you will never be able to forgive him, but I hope you can forgive me, someday, for not being more vigilant."

"I have nothing to forgive you for. I need justice to be done, Luciana, and I am sorry to say this to you about your son, but I won't rest at ease until I know Marco is behind bars."

Luciana nods, then her gaze falls. "He wasn't always like this, Iliana. I don't know what happened to change him."

"Drugs probably didn't help. Neither did alcohol," I say. I am sorry to twist the knife in the wound, but she needs to know who her son really is.

"The police said they found cocaine in his car," she admits. "I still can't believe it. He was always so confident…"

"Cocaine will do that, Ma'am. It boosts confidence," Stefano offers. Luciana raises her eyes to look at him, but she doesn't respond.

"Luciana…there is something I need to ask, since you are here," I say gently.

"Sure, Iliana, anything."

"Did Marco have another serious relationship before he met me?"

Luciana shifts uncomfortably. "Why would you ask me that?"

"Please, Luciana, I need to know."

Luciana draws a deep breath, then she slouches against the back of the couch. "He lived with a woman for a while. She was a nice girl, and she really seemed to care about him. He was always a bit restless, so I was happy when he settled with her. He seemed happy, too, at first — but gradually, he grew restless again, and sometimes he reminded me of a caged animal at the zoo. Marco had a wild streak in him that nobody could tame — I recognized that from the time he was a boy and he became defiant toward any form of authority."

"Did they break up?" I ask, and I hold my breath while I wait for Luciana to respond.

"No…she became depressed, and she committed suicide. She was home alone, one morning, when Marco was out of town on a business trip…and she ingested a bottle of sleeping pills. The saddest part — something we didn't discover until an autopsy was performed on her — was that she was pregnant at the time of her death."

I feel dizzy. Everything Francesca told me in my dream really happened. I might have heard about the names and stories of the other women from a TV show my mother watched while I was comatose, but what about Francesca? How would I have known about her if we hadn't met?

"Was she dead when they found her?" I ask.

"No, she was still alive. One of her friends stopped by to check on her, the friend reported, and she found her unconscious. They took her to the hospital immediately, but they couldn't save her. The baby died shortly after."

"Do you know if Marco was abusive to her as well?" I inquire.

Luciana shakes her head. "I don't think so…she never gave any signs that anything was wrong."

It figures. Victims rarely expose their abusers. They keep the dirt carefully swept under the rug, to avoid creating waves and angering the abusers more, and — even when they are questioned — they lie, to cover up what is happening to them. In my case, it wasn't only my safety I worried about: My larger concern was Matteo, and what would happen to him if I left. Marco's family has the financial ability to hire good lawyers, and he made it clear, many times, that I wouldn't be able to take Matteo with me if I left. Not that I ever threatened to leave, but I think Marco knew I was feeling overwhelmed by our reality, and he felt obligated to remind me on multiple occasions.

"Is she buried somewhere around here?" I ask. I glance quickly at Stefano, curious about his reaction to this revelation. He hadn't voiced disbelief of my story, but I could tell he was trying to find a rational explanation for all that happened to me, for the things I knew.

Luciana nods, weeping softly. "Yes, she is buried in the cemetery right outside San Gabriele."

"I would like to go visit her grave, sometime." I say more to myself than to Luciana.

"I understand," Luciana says. "I have been there, myself. She had no family, and I have gone by to bring her flowers from time to time. Well, I should be going, Iliana. I really appreciate you being gracious enough to see me."

"No problem. Again, it is not your fault," I reply. I stand when she does, so I can walk her to the door.

"Take care, Iliana, and let me know if you need anything."

I smile. "I will. Thank you for understanding."

I close the door after she leaves, and turn the lock, then I return to the family room where my mother and Stefano are busy exchanging opinions.

"So, what impression did you have?" Stefano asks. "Do you think she will tell her son she came to visit you?"

"I am not sure…she seemed genuinely sorry about what happened," I respond.

"I am sure she is, Iliana. I know I would be, in her place. As a mother, you feel like you own your kids' mistakes."

"That's true," I agree with Mom's remark. "Let's hope she at least keeps the location of the meeting a secret. I don't even care if she tells him she spoke with me." I run a hand through my hair and feel the large square bandage over my wound. "Ugh…I also need to schedule a haircut. The shaved patch is so large that the hair in that spot is not going to be able to catch up with the rest. Maybe I just need a shorter hairstyle — at least, for the time being."

"You will look beautiful either way," Stefano says immediately, smiling at me. I return his smile warmly.

The doorbell rings again.

"It must be Dad and Matteo," my mother estimates after she glances at her watch. "They were going to stop by the bakery to buy some fresh bread on the way here, but I called Dad and told him we already ate lunch." She gets up and goes to open the door.

"Mommy, Mommy!" Matteo squeals, as he runs through the door. That boy doesn't know the meaning of "walk." He drops his backpack in the corner and hugs my waist.

"How was school, sweetheart?" I ask.

"It was great! Did you know that there was a man who discovered America? His name was Christopher Columbus. People before him believed the earth was flat. People were stupid."

"It's not nice to say the word 'stupid,' Matteo. It is not a kind word," I remind him gently. "Yes," I add, "I know about Christopher Columbus. He made a great discovery."

"Grandpa said he is taking me fishing today. At the river!" Matteo exclaims excitedly. "I am going to catch a big fish, Mommy."

I ruffle his hair. "The biggest."

"I am hungry, Mommy."

"I bet. Stefano made you a sandwich; it's in the refrigerator."

Feeling suddenly guilty, I turn to my father. "Would you like a sandwich, Dad? It'll only take a minute…"

"No, I am good, honey. Let Matteo eat his, and then we will be on our way."

They leave within half an hour, leaving Mom, Stefano, and me alone again.

"You heard Luciana confirm Francesca's story earlier," I remark to Stefano, eager to know what he thinks. It can't be mere coincidence that I dreamt of a woman telling me her story, then find out she really existed, and that her story is the same as the one I heard *from her*.

"It was surreal…" Stefano admits. "I honestly don't know what to make of it."

"What are you two talking about?" Mom inquires, unaware. I have told her about the other women at the shelter, but I don't remember mentioning Francesca.

"The pregnant woman Luciana was telling us about, Mom. I met her."

My mom is confused. "You met her? But Luciana said that poor girl died before you and Marco even met."

I breathe evenly before I reply. "I met her at the shelter, Mom. She is one of the women I talked about."

"Iliana, we have discussed this already…"

"I know, Mom. We have — but I couldn't have heard about Francesca from a TV show. She wasn't murdered, her death was self-inflicted because she was depressed, and somehow, I knew her story. How would you explain that?" I look directly into my mother's eyes. I don't mean to be defiant, exactly, but I need to get across to her that I am not crazy, either.

My mom reflects for a few moments before saying anything. "I don't know, Iliana. I get what you're saying, but you must admit, it is quite strange. I *know* you were asleep in that hospital bed, sweetheart, and you never went to a shelter."

"Her body never went to *Transitions*, Angela," Stefano interrupts. "Her mind might have traveled there."

I want to hug him. Not only has he said something that could seem feasible — even to my mother — but he also called the shelter by its name, unintentionally confirming to me that he believes my story.

My mom's attention is piqued, and Stefano takes the chance to make his case. "Nobody knows where a patient's mind travels while in a coma. There are a lot of things science still can't explain, Angela."

"It's pure sci-fi, Stefano," my mother protests. "But, you are right: No one really knows."

I stare at Stefano in awe, and I wonder if the man should run for politics. His serene magnetism and rational certainty are overwhelming, and could easily sway the masses.

My mother glances at me. "So, the story this Francesca told you is similar to the one Luciana shared with us?" I can see she is still a bit skeptical.

"It is exactly the same story," I confirm. "I met Francesca when I went to Florence with Olivia and Giulia. Francesca drove us there. That day, she shared with all of us that her fiancé's name was Marco, but it wasn't until a few days later that she confided to me that she knew *my* Marco, and that they had a relationship. I voiced to her how odd it seemed to me, that she and I could have been connected to the same man and end up in the same shelter — and she explained that she had been called in to help me make an important decision, specifically because of her intimate connection with the man who had abused me."

"Who called her?" My mother asks.

"Olivia suggested it to Doctor Castelli. My memory was completely wiped out when I first arrived at *Transitions*."

"You both realize that this entire concept sounds crazy, right?" my mother blurts out, still unsure of what she can accept.

"Crazy, but not impossible," Stefano counters.

My mother nods, but doesn't say anything. I simply smile at him, for having my back.

Stefano rises from the sofa. "I am going to take a shower, while you two ladies relax and chat."

He leaves the room, and I stand to stretch my legs. I walk to the window to look outside, while my mother gathers the sheets and such that we folded earlier, carrying them to the linen closet. It is beautiful day, and I step out on the balcony to soak in the sunshine. The weather has surely taken a turn for the better; although it is only mid-March, the temperature is quite pleasant, and it draws people out of their homes. I sit on one of the two metal chairs, watching passers-by go into and out of the small shops nearby, and I inhale deeply. I love the fragrance carried by the breeze, bursting with the sweet smell of budding flowers and the sultry aroma of coffee from the café around the corner. For the first time in many years, I am at peace. And then I see it: Marco's black SUV, parked across the street. My heart seizes in my chest, and I try to formulate the words to alert my mother and Stefano, but the words die before I can open my mouth. Apprehensively, I look at the driver's window, hoping I am wrong, but Marco's face glowers back at me, aware now that I have seen him. Even at a distance, I can see the threat in his eyes, and I continue to watch in a daze. Marco's eyes are fixed on me, challenging and dangerous. He knows I am scared, and he is trying to break me down. He watches me for a moment longer, then he drives off, and I am sure I see scorn and rage etched on his face, before he disappears around the corner.

CHAPTER SIXTEEN

"What, Mommy?" Matteo asks, innocence shining from his beautiful eyes. In his six years of life, Matteo has seen more violence, sensed more tension, than any child his age should have. Thankfully, he has managed to survive through it, and to hold onto the magic of being six years old.

"I want to know how you feel, Matteo. I know you probably feel confused from all that's happening."

I watch him think, and I wonder what is going through his mind. Is he upset? Is he relieved to have me home? Does he miss having his father in his life?

"I'm all normal…" he shrugs, his words lingering in the air.

"What do you mean by that, Matteo? What is 'normal'?"

Matteo shakes his head slowly, but I can't read his body language. "I don't know. I am okay."

"Do you have any questions?" I ask gently. "Is there anything you are curious about?"

"Where is Daddy?"

"Daddy is at his house. It used to be our home, too, but we are no longer going to live there."

"Is Daddy going to jail, Mommy?"

Matteo's question makes me want to cry. I want Marco in jail, I want justice to be done, yet I must also try to see things from Matteo's perspective: Marco is his father, and no matter what he did to me — to us — Matteo will always have a bond with him. I am sure he feels conflicted right now, and I hate Marco even more for forcing his son into a corner, making him feel he must decide which parent he loves more, to whom he should be loyal.

"I don't know, Matteo. Daddy made some bad choices, but he didn't mean to," I lie. "He needs help to see that what he is doing is wrong. He is sick, you know?"

Matteo looks at me with such concern in his eyes that I feel disarmed. "Is he sick like I was mommy? When I had the flu?"

"Yes, sweetheart, but instead of having a fever and a stuffy nose, his brain is sick. He has a hard time seeing things the way we do."

"Is Daddy crazy? I know somebody crazy — Gianluca, at school. He gets mad when the teacher yells at him…when he doesn't do his homework."

I smile. Even if he is looking at the situation from the perspective of a child, Matteo just hit the nail on the head. I don't know the little boy he is talking about, but the comparison sounds appropriate. Marco is angry, just like the boy Matteo knows, but instead of simply stomping his feet, Marco lashes out, and hurts others. I wonder for a moment if we should raise a flag of concern with the school — as well as with this boy's parents — and maybe prevent the making of a new Marco. Could Marco's parents have rerouted his inner anger and channeled his aggression toward something positive, if they had been honest with themselves and recognized their prized son had a problem?

215

"I don't think Daddy is crazy, Matteo — just as I don't think your friend at school is. I think they are both sick, and they need help."

"Oh no, Mommy…Gianluca is not my friend. He's a bully! I'm scared of him."

I raise my eyebrow. "Oh? Why have you not told me this before? Have you shared your feelings with your teacher?"

Matteo looks down, blushing extravagantly. "No. He would beat me up if I told on him."

Hearing this is heart-wrenching, and that reaction is intensified by knowing that my son felt uncomfortable coming to me, to tell me about being bullied at school. What can I say to him? I set the example, by allowing his father to bully me around. Matteo responded to the violence he encountered in the same way he had seen me respond to it; he swept his feelings under a rug and pretended everything was okay.

"We need to tell your teacher, Matteo."

"Don't want to!" Matteo explodes, and it shocks me to see just how scared he is of this kid. Anger surges up from the pit of my stomach, threatening to erupt with force, but I swallow hard and breathe purposefully, to control my own emotions.

"Would you at least be willing to talk to a doctor, Matteo? Someone who will listen and help you understand?"

Matteo is sitting on the couch, stiff-backed with his knees drawn up, his arms wrapped around himself in self-protection. "No!"

I don't pressure him, as I understand first-hand how he feels. "We don't have to talk about this right now, Matteo. I know it is hard. There are a lot of emotions attached to being exposed to violence, even if the violence hasn't physically happened yet. Feeling threatened is just as devastating."

Matteo looks directly into my eyes. "Like when Daddy was being mean to you, Mommy? Were you scared, too?"

I swallow the knot in my throat. "Yes, Matteo, I am sure we felt the same way."

"I wanted to tell Grandma…what Daddy was doing. But I was too scared."

My hands are shaking, and I clamp them together to remain in control. "Is there any specific moment you would like to talk about? A moment when Daddy and I were fighting that you might have witnessed?"

Matteo lowers his head, and I just want to hold him in my arms and wipe away all the bad memories. A tear runs down his face, followed by others that he angrily wipes away in an attempt to appear strong.

"One night I got up to look for you. I heard Daddy's voice. He was mad. He was pushing you. I screamed at you to make him stop."

Make him stop, mommy! Make him stop!

I shake the memory of the words I heard after the first group meeting at *Transitions*, and I let Matteo continue his story.

"Daddy looked at me. And he yelled at me. Said I should go back to my room. I was scared! I thought he was going to kill you, Mommy! I hid in the hall."

The image I painted in the recreation room…a little boy watching from a distance. I had seen Matteo that night, hiding, and watching Marco's violent outburst. I can't control the tears, and I instinctively pull my son into my arms. "I am so sorry, Matteo! Nobody should ever have to see their Daddy acting like that."

Matteo nods and continues his story. "I was scared to go to school the next day. Daddy was at work. But I was scared he would come back. I wanted to say I was sick, so I could stay home. I wanted to stay with you. Wanted to make you happy…and I made you a card. I really thought you would like it. You cried when I gave you it. I didn't want you to be sad, Mommy."

"You didn't make me sad, Matteo — Daddy did. You were a victim, just as much as I was."

Matteo comes to sit in my lap, resting his head against my chest. "I love you, Mommy. I was scared."

"I was, too. But it is over now, son. We don't have to be scared anymore."

I wish I could believe the words of assurance I am giving Matteo. Images of Marco looking at me from his car two days ago still haunt me, and I am terrified he will be back. Stefano has not left the apartment at all. We notified the prosecutor about Marco's actions, but nobody else was with me when I saw him and, by the time Stefano and my mother joined me on the balcony, he was already gone. Once again, Marco had an opportunity to hurt me — though not physically this time — and he got away with it. History repeats itself.

"Are you going to marry Stefano, Mommy?"

I hadn't seen this question coming, and I blush profusely. "Stefano and I are friends, Matteo. He is looking after us to make sure we are safe."

I scan my son's face to see if he believes my words, fully aware of the warmth spreading into my cheeks. Matteo seems more serene, now, and I am amazed at his resilience. I remember someone telling me how animals that are typically preyed upon hide their symptoms when they are sick, to mask their vulnerability from potential predators. Is that what my son has learned to do? Is his sudden shift of mood a survival mechanism to hide his true feelings? Matteo is going to need therapy to overcome what he has observed over the years, and so will I. No matter how much stronger I feel right now, there are moments in which I still feel anger burning through me, and I am now keenly aware of how dangerous it is, allowing anger to fester under the surface. I will heal completely, and so will Matteo; we just need time, and the support of those we love, to get to the finish line.

"I like Stefano," Matteo continues. "He is nice. And he lets me win when we play 'Scopa.' He thinks I don't know he lets me win…but he really does, Mommy." Matteo laughs, and the burbling trill that escapes his lips warms my heart. Stefano has been amazing to me, and to my parents, but knowing that he has brightened my son's life, even if only by playing a game of cards with him to distract him, touches my heart in such a way that I want to run to the kitchen and give him an enormous hug. He has kept himself distanced from my conversation with Matteo, but I am sure he has heard every word, and I am just as sure he is happy that Matteo likes him.

Of course, Stefano enters the room at just the right moment, carrying a tray of butter sandwiches filled with all sorts of goodies. "I think I heard myself being summoned," he says with a grin. "Anybody want a sandwich?"

Sitting on the couch so that he and I are surrounding Matteo, he places the tray on Matteo's lap. "You are king of this house, little man, so you get to choose first."

Matteo's eyes sparkle, and the two share a conspiratorial look that melts my heart. It is no longer Mommy and Matteo against the wrath of Daddy; it is Mommy, Matteo, and Stefano, all connected by a bond of kindness and respect. Matteo selects a tiny bun stuffed with prosciutto, and chomps into it gleefully.

"The queen is next," Stefano says, nudging the tray in my direction.

I am not hungry, but I grab one of the sandwiches, anyway.

"Finish your snack and then go get ready, champ" Stefano says. "Grandpa will pick you up shortly, to take you to the park."

I look at Stefano in awe. I am grateful for all he is doing for me, and I am amazed at the way he plans things ahead to help me out. He has a way of arranging things without controlling them, in direct contrast to Marco's approach, and I revel in the way he outrageously pampers me. "I didn't know my parents were taking Matteo to the park."

"Oh, yes…I am sorry. Your dad called a short while ago, while you were talking to Matteo. It's a beautiful day, and they are going to come over in a little while," Stefano replies, as he picks up the tray and carries it back to the kitchen.

Matteo gets up, then stops, turning toward me with his small face serious and focused. "Now that Daddy is not living with us anymore, can I have a puppy?"

"Umm...not right away, Matteo, but we will talk about it once we have our own place."

Satisfied with my answer, Matteo runs to his bedroom to get ready, and I stretch out on the sofa. Stefano comes back and drapes a small throw blanket over my legs. "Why don't you rest for a little while?" he asks.

It sounds good to me. I don't know whether it is due to the receding, but still present distension of my brain, or because I am stressed by the thought of Marco still free and lurking about, but I am tired.

"Just for a few moments," I say, allowing my eyes to close.

I am sitting in the group therapy room; Olivia, Romina, and Giulia are already there. Francesca walks in just before we start, arm-in-arm with Doctor Castelli.

"Thank you for coming one last time, Rosa. We have so much enjoyed having you with us, but even though we hate to see you go, we are happy you are going back. You can change things, Rosa; now that you have chosen to fight back, a wonderful life awaits you." Doctor Castelli says with a soft smile.

"I don't want to leave you behind," I say through tears.

"You can't change what happened to us, Rosa, but you have awakened in time to change your own life. Live for all of us, and be happy. Your joy will be our joy." Francesca whispers, her kind face serene.

I am crying openly, and Francesca rises from her chair come give me a hug. "It will all work out, Rosa, just don't be afraid. I have a favor to ask of you…"

"Anything…" I reply, and I mean it.

"Bring my baby a flower, to represent the life that would have blossomed, if it had realized the chance to be born."

"I will, Francesca. I am so sorry…"

"No time to be sad, Rosa. Today is a happy day."

Are you okay, Iliana? Stefano's voice filters through my dream and I wake up.

"I am sorry…I must have dozed off," I say, apologetically. I am immediately aware that I have been crying. I sit up on the sofa, and wipe my face with my sleeve. "They came back to see me one last time, Stefano. They are still around me."

Stefano runs a hand through my hair, and he touches my cheek. "Let's dry those tears before Matteo comes back," he says with a smile. I want to drown in his gentle eyes.

My parents arrive, and Matteo opens the door. "Grandpa! I want to go on the swing with you! I am going to go faster than you!"

"We'll see," my dad says with a huge grin. "I think *I* am going to be faster—my legs are longer!"

Matteo ignores the challenge. He grabs my father by the hand and the two of them run out the door, but I notice my mother lingering behind.

"I thought you were going with them, Mom," I say.

"I thought of it, but there is something I need to share…"

"What is it?" Stefano inquires, immediately taking my hand in his.

"I talked to the assistant prosecutor before we came over. He didn't go into many details, but essentially, he said they have evidence that Marco was in this neighborhood the other day. He made the mistake of carrying his cell phone with him, and his phone connected with a nearby tower, just a block away from here. They issued a warrant for his arrest, for violating the restraining order."

"Are you serious, Mom?" I literally jump onto my feet, my hands holding my head. "This is amazing! Is he already in jail?"

"I think they are picking him up today," she replies, relief flooding her face. "He will be held until the trial."

Stefano hugs me, and I start crying. All the fears, all the anxiety, instantly melt away like snow in midday sun, only to surface again like a punch in the gut. I feel safer knowing he is behind bars, and at the same time I know it will only be a matter of time before he's out on the streets again, hunting me down. I can't forget the look in his eyes when he last looked at me from his car — the hatred burning in those eyes will haunt me for years to come. Will he come after me even more aggressively, more violently, once he is released? I don't want Mom and Stefano to see the fear that still grips my soul; I want them to believe everything will be okay moving forward. I swallow hard, forcing myself to smile, steadying my voice with effort. "That's wonderful news, Mom! I can definitely breathe easier now."

"We should go out and celebrate!" Stefano says. "I think dinner is in order!"

"We can watch Matteo, if the two of you want to go out," my mother suggests. I feel increasingly sure that she is trying to set Stefano and me up romantically.

"We can…or, we can stay home and all have dinner together," I reply. "This is a victory for all of us, and we should be together."

The word *home* triggers a thought: "Mom, will you help me find a place for myself and Matteo?"

I notice a slight tinge of disappointment in Stefano's eyes when I utter those words, but he doesn't say anything to oppose my wish.

"Already?" my mom asks. "Why don't you stay here for a little longer? Until you are healed, at least. I am sure Stefano does not mind," she coos, and I laugh, wondering if she is even aware of how transparent her intentions are.

"Yes," I reply calmly. "I hope there is a future for Stefano and me, but I need to get on my feet, first. I don't want to approach a new relationship as half a person. Stefano deserves a whole woman by his side, and I still have work to do on myself."

I see appreciation in Stefano's eyes, and I know that no matter how long it takes, I will heal, and the two of us will be together. Someday, when Rosa and Iliana are one again.

CHAPTER SEVENTEEN

"Follow this road until the end, and take a left at the yellow, two-story house. Then we need to go for another half a mile, and there should be two dirt roads to the right. *Transitions* is about a mile up, on the second dirt road." I can see the directions clearly in my head, from the day Olivia and I visited San Gabriele. If I close my eyes, I can see the two of us, Olivia and me, riding back to the shelter in a blue compact car. I wonder why it never occurred to me to ask who the car belonged to, at the time.

"Are you sure this is the right road?" Stefano asks. "It looks abandoned...I don't think there is going to be a yellow house at the end of it, unless it is a haunted one."

I look at him from the side, amused. "Are you getting scared?"

"Who? Me? Never," he replies, and a grin flashes onto his face.

To Stefano's apparent surprise, the yellow house is there, and it appears to be inhabited by the living. A swing-set in the yard looks new, and toys are scattered everywhere, seeded around a hammock that is suspended between a large oak and a smaller tree.

"See? I told you there was a yellow house at the end of the road..."

"You got me," Stefano replies, still incredulous. "Did you say I should take a left here?"

"Yes, and then we need to drive another half-mile."

Fields sprawl on both sides of us, with no other sign of civilization beyond the fact that the road is paved.

"It is beautiful. I rarely venture out into the deeper pockets of our countryside," Stefano says, his eyes darting across the fields. I wonder what they grow around here."

"They grow corn in that field," I say, point to the left. "I am not sure about the other ones."

"Here's the first dirt road. How far is it from the second one?" he asks.

"Just a quarter of a mile, or so," I reply. I can feel a ripple of anxiety in my stomach…my rational self knows that *Transitions* is probably not going to be there, and yet, I am still clinging to hope. We turn at the second dirt road to the right, but before we can go further, Stefano slows the car in the middle of the road until we almost stop.

"Are you sure you want to continue, Iliana?" He asks gently.

"I am. I know there is only one chance in a million that the center will be there. I am prepared for that, if that's the case, but I have to know the truth — all of it."

Stefano resumes a normal speed. "How much longer did you say we have to go?"

"About a mile," I reply without hesitation.

We drive in silence, but after a mile, all we see is more fields. We go a bit further, the road comes to a dead end after another quarter of a mile. "This is it," Stefano says. I can tell he is disappointed for me, although he shouldn't be. "Would you like to get out of the car and walk around?" he asks.

"Yes, if you don't mind," I reply. He pulls over so I can get out of the car. He gets out, too, and comes to sit with me on the grass.

"Are you okay?" he inquires, still clearly concerned about me.

"Yes. Deep down I already knew I was not going to find the building I remember living in, but I needed to come, to get closure. I hated it, and loved it there, at the same time. Not remembering anything drove me insane, but I loved the people I met…if that makes sense," I say calmly.

Stefano nods. "It makes a lot of sense. I remember going to a camp as a kid. My dad wanted to send me, and I didn't want to go — in part, probably because I was worried about my mom being home alone — but I made so many friends that week, and I so enjoyed the different activities, that I was sad when it ended. I hated to come and I hated to go. Of course, I wouldn't give my father the satisfaction of knowing how much fun I had, but I secretly enjoyed every moment."

"That's a great comparison, Stefano!" I smile, grateful for his understanding.

We walk across the empty field, and I notice a mimosa tree on the side of the path. My heart leaps into my throat — we had a mimosa tree in the garden at *Transitions*! Is this the same tree I remember? "That tree…" I whisper.

"What tree?" Stefano asks.

"The mimosa tree, over there." I point at it.

"What about it?"

"That tree — at least, I *think* it was that tree — was in the center of the shelter's garden."

Stefano looks surprised. "Are you sure?"

"No…it looks the same, but I can't be certain it is the same tree."

"Can I help you folks with anything?" A throaty voice calls from behind us. We turn to look at an old man, about 70, maybe, wearing jeans and a casual, button-down shirt. He has a toothpick in his mouth, his hair is snow white, and he appears to be in excellent shape for his age.

"My friend thought there was an old hospital here once. We came by to see for ourselves whether it is here or not." Stefano replies.

"There was no hospital here," the man replies. "It's just an empty field."

"This field doesn't get cultivated like the other ones? Does it belong to anyone?" I ask.

"No, ma'am. Nothing grows here. The land belongs to me, and it belonged to my daddy before me, but none of us have ever been able to use this field for anything. The people who live nearby have come up with a whole lot of theories, but none of them are true…ghosts live here, they say."

"Do you believe them?" I ask.

"Nah…there is no such thing as ghosts. When the good Lord calls us home, we just go up, we don't stay here on this messy planet," the old man says with conviction.

"What if we have something unresolved when we die?" I venture.

"Then I guess we go to purgatory until we figure it out." The old man says.

Purgatory…

"Well, I need to get back, but you kids be careful. There are a few artesian wells in the fields, and if you don't know where they are, you might trip over them and fall. I will never forget the story of a little boy, nearly forty years ago, who fell into an artesian well, and he couldn't get back up. The rescuers tried to save him for an entire night, sending food and water down to him with buckets hanging from a rope, and trying to chip the rock to open a passage large enough for one of the men to go down and fetch the boy, but nobody could get to him. One rescuer almost made it, but the little boy slipped off and fell even deeper. It was a sad night. It took ten days to pull his body from that well. It didn't happen here, but I just want to make sure you pay attention."

"Thank you, sir," Stefano says. "We are getting ready to leave, anyway."

The old man waves goodbye, then he disappears down the dirt road at a trot.

"Are you ready to go?" Stefano asks. I nod, and we crawl back into the car. Neither of us speaks, until we nearly reach the township of San Gabriele.

"Do you think we could go visit Francesca's grave?" I ask. "The cemetery cannot be too far.

"Sure," Stefano replies. "See if you can pull up the directions on my phone."

We arrive at the cemetery in less than ten minutes. It is surrounded by a six-foot wall, tall enough so that one can barely see even the tips of the tallest monuments. We park the car and approach a black, cast-iron gate. Before we go in, we stop by a truck, parked adjacent to the entrance, its apparent owner selling flowers and candles. I buy a bouquet of flowers and two candles — one for Francesca and one for her baby. The moment we pass beyond the gate, I feel overwhelmed by a sense of solemnity, and I cross myself out of respect for the souls resting in this place. There are oven-vaults on both sides, some featuring beautiful artwork. We pass two mausoleums, and we peek at the graves ensconced there. They look particularly expensive, with stunning statues, and fresh flowers carefully arranged inside marble-based vases.

"I wonder where Francesca's grave is," I muse.

"Didn't Marco's mother say Francesca had no living family?"

"Yes...so I doubt she is buried anywhere that is well-maintained, if the burial was financed by the town."

"Maybe she had distant family — cousins, or maybe an aunt or uncle," Stefano suggests.

"Maybe. Sadly, we will likely never know."

We follow the gravel path to an overgrown lawn, where below-ground graves are separated by rusty chains and an assortment of weeds. Some of the headstones are chipped and dirty, littered with exhausted seven-day candles that finished burning long ago. A few of the graves have flowers, but most don't, and many of the names and dates have even been partially erased by the elements. I glance at some of the pictures—beautiful young women and valiant men smile charmingly, making me wonder about their lives, and their individual stories.

"Iliana, come here! Is this your Francesca?" Stefano calls out.

My heart skips, but I don't want to get overly excited before I can confirm that the grave Stefano has just stumbled upon is, indeed, Francesca's. The inscription is of poor quality, and her picture is from many years before, when she was barely out of her teens, but it is undeniably the Francesca I know. *Francesca Pellegrini, born in Florence on 09/09/1980, died in San Gabriele on 02/05/2008.*

"She was so young when she died," Stefano says, sadness clouding his eyes.

"Yes," I reply, "only 28." I wish her picture could look more like the real Francesca, instead of a high-school girl, but this is probably the only photo of her that a distant relative could manage to find.

"Stefano," I ask timidly, "do you think I could be alone for just a moment?"

"Of course," he replies. "I will be over by the vaults, when you are ready."

I wait until Stefano is out of earshot, then I kneel, to wipe Francesca's gravestone with the sleeve of my jacket, and her photograph with a corner of my shirt. I put fresh water in the empty plastic vase, and arrange the flowers in an appealing way. I light both candles, placing them side by side on the stone.

"I brought some flowers for your baby, Francesca, and some for you, too. I wasn't sure what flowers are your favorites, but you seem to be the type of girl who would like daisies, so I bought a bouquet of assorted daisies. I hope your baby likes them, too. I wish I knew his or her name! So much has happened since I spoke with you last, Francesca. Do you remember the last session of hypnosis I had with Doctor Castelli? Well...you all warned me about it, but I went through with it anyway, and I was catapulted back into my own reality. Lots has changed. The most important thing is that Marco is in jail, and he can no longer hurt anyone. Charges were pressed against him even before I woke up, and there was a restraining order in place against him. He tried to harass me anyway; he parked across the street from the place where I am living now, and was arrested for violating a court order. Hopefully, he will be behind bars until the trial, and after that, I am hoping he will be convicted. He shot me, Francesca...he almost killed me. That's why I lost my memory. My son almost lost his mother, thanks to him, but I have met a wonderful man now, and I am working hard to heal. I guess I just wanted to tell you how much I appreciate you. I wish things had worked out differently for you, that you could have taken a different turn than the one you chose. I know you mentioned you had no family, but you have me now, and I will come by regularly to see you and care for your grave. Thank you again, Francesca, and rest in peace." I cross myself before standing, then I lean to kiss the picture, and I make a mental note to find a better picture of her.

I find Stefano reading birth and death dates on the oven vaults, and he wraps his arm gently around my shoulders to lead me back toward the car.

We must have been inside the cemetery longer than I thought, because, by the time we drive back, the sun is already setting.

"I would like to care for Francesca's grave regularly," I say.

"That's a sweet thought," Stefano replies. "I wonder if she has anyone at all who is still living."

"I am determined to find out. I have her birth date, and the place where she was born. I will start with that information and work my way up to somebody in her family, even if it is a distant cousin or uncle." I am on a mission to find someone, or something, from Francesca's past.

"Your father called a few minutes ago," Stefano says. "They are on the way to my place from the park, with Matteo, and your dad would like to take me out bowling. I am not even good at bowling, but I didn't have the heart to say no. Do you want to go?" he asks.

"I think I am going to pass, Stefano. I am tired, and I think you and Dad need some 'father-son' time. You are the boy he always wanted." I grin, and his answering grin warms me.

When we arrive at the apartment building, we see my parents' car, so we park and go upstairs.

"About time you two got back," my mom says. "We picked up pizza on the way here, to speed up dinner a little. Did Stefano tell you that Dad is taking him out bowling?"

"Yes, Stefano is excited about going," I reply, winking at Stefano.

We eat pizza amidst a flurry of conversation. We tell my parents about the visit to Francesca's grave, omitting the details of our conversation with the man at the field. My mother is already skeptical about the entire story, and volunteering the information that there is no building is like confirming that she is right.

Dad and Stefano leave right after we finish eating, while mom stays behind to help me with the dinner dishes. She tucks Matteo into bed and reads him a story, then she joins me in the family room.

"A lot has happened, Iliana," she says gently, sitting on the sofa beside me. "How are you feeling?"

"Safe, for the first time in a long while." I am not exaggerating. Knowing that Marco is behind bars has closed the door between my world and anxiety.

"Hopefully, he will remain locked up for a long time," my mother continues, adding, "if his father stays out of it. It is time for that man to grow up and take responsibility for his own actions."

"I can only hope. Meanwhile, I need to focus on reinventing my own life. Next week I will start applying for jobs, but I need to put together a résumé first."

"There is no rush, Iliana; Dad and I can help."

"I know you can, Mom, but that is hardly the point. I am a grown woman, with a child of my own. It is also time for *me* to grow up, and prove — to myself — that I can take care of myself and my son. I allowed Marco to chip away at my self-esteem, and make me believe I have no skills, but it is not true: I am a smart, capable woman, and I will make it out there."

"What about Stefano?"

"Stefano is my friend for now. Someday, maybe, we will be more, but neither of us is in a rush to jump into a relationship."

My mom doesn't say anything, but she nods to acknowledge my words.

"I understand, Iliana. You know I am here for you, no matter what you need."

"I know, Mom. I love you."

"Well, before we get all sentimental, I'd better head out and get home. I have to be up early tomorrow morning, for a hair appointment."

I stand to say goodbye, and walk my mother to the door. "Goodnight, Mom; drive carefully." I kiss her lightly on the cheek.

I lock the door of the apartment and, for the first time since waking up in the hospital, I am alone. It is a beautiful evening, so I wrap a scarf around my shoulders and go outside to sit on the balcony. The moon is almost full, and it casts a mystical glow on the darkened roads a floor below. Although there are still a few cars around, and I hear voices from the café around the corner, everything else is calm. Someone who has never been afraid cannot fully comprehend how — over time — fear and anxiety become your constant companions, and you become oblivious to their presence. Now that Marco is gone, I feel like the weight of the world has been lifted from my shoulders, and I am convinced that feeling safe is the fundamental building block of self-evolution.

It is peaceful out here; I feel as though I can be one with this moment. There may be more storms ahead, more heartache to be revisited, but in this moment — in in this one beautiful moment — I am whole. It took a village to get me to this point and, although we inhabit different realities, I can still feel the energy of the women I met at *Transitions*.

"Where are you, Olivia, Romina, Rita, and Giulia?" I say out loud, hoping that the night breeze will carry my message on, to the heavens. "The four of you were my closest friends, and it is thanks to you and Francesca that I have been given a second chance. When I met you, Iliana was dying, and that's why Rosa emerged. If it hadn't been for you, and the things you helped me reflect on, I might not have made it back to Iliana in time. The man I met today in the field said that the dead who are still dealing with unresolved issues go to a purgatory. Is that what *Transitions* is? Is it a holding limbo for souls who need to work out earthly issues before moving on? The fact that we met in this place between worlds makes me think that I, too, would have died, if things had gone differently. My mind refused to accept that the man I married, the father of my child, tried to kill me, and Iliana couldn't wake up until Rosa — my inner persona — accepted what happened, and made a different choice for Iliana and Matteo. I don't know why you were there, but maybe your final mission was to help me find my way in this world. Do you remember the movie that relates how an angel's quest to get his wings required him to help a desperate man? I wonder if you were angels, too. It was too late for you in this world, but there was still time for me to change my life, and you knew it. I pledge to you that the help you gave me will be paid forward. I don't know what I am going to do yet, but I promise that I will do *something*. Please, bring my love to Doctor Castelli, and to Elena, and to Mrs. Bonaviti, who made the best Tiramisu I have ever eaten! I will miss all of you, but my life is here, now. Someday, when my time on this earth is over, I will see you again, and maybe we will visit Florence together one more time. We will go visit that leather factory, Giulia, I promise! Rest in peace, my friends…my sisters…and, if you can, continue to watch over us. Goodbye for now." I blow a kiss to the sky, and close my eyes, as a single tear trickles down my face. I feel an overwhelming sense of peace…but I no longer feel their energies around me. In this beautiful night, under a gorgeous Tuscan moon, my sisters have gone home.

CHAPTER EIGHTEEN

Often, when I was married to Marco, I would lie awake in bed at night, praying and trying my best to stifle the bitterness I felt. Growing up, my religious faith taught that God never puts a cross on our shoulder heavier than we can carry, and yet — many times — I wondered why, if our father in Heaven is real, I had been punished with Marco.

I once saw a film in which God is so disappointed with the way humans carry themselves, that he sends his angels to destroy humanity. The angels in the film were depicted as demons, and, after watching the movie, I thought of how difficult it is for our limited minds to see the big picture. Was Marco an angel in disguise? Did God send him into my life to destroy me, because I had done something wrong, or maybe to simply push me to the edge so that I could learn how to take a stand?

I realize now that I had always been passive. My parents took care of me while I grew up, and my mom worried about everything. With her in my corner, I never had to worry about anything on my own; she always took the lead. Then I met Marco, and he made it clear from the beginning that he was going to be in charge. I was okay with that—with him calling all the shots, I never had to make difficult decisions...or *any* decisions, for that matter. I traded in my parents for a man whose power crushed my soul.

Now my life has changed. I am at a crossroads, and I must learn how to be my own person. I appreciate my parents, and Stefano, but the time has come for me to step out in front of the curtain and claim my place on the stage. Rosa took a stand, against the advice of all who tried to keep her safe. She knew what needed to be done, and she was ready to face the risks. Rosa made it possible for Iliana to come back, and

I won't let her down. As tempting as it is to let Stefano take charge of my life, I know in my heart that I must not travel that road. I have been given a second chance, and I cannot — *will* not — allow myself to fall back into the complacency of being sheltered. One thing I have learned is the responsibility we each have for ourselves, to identify the patterns of our lives, to see what needs to change. Coupled with this is the importance of making the effort to shift the energy in response to a situation that demands change. If we fail ourselves in this, history will repeat itself. One can bring a dog to the dog park once, and if that dog is being attacked by more than one other dog, it could mean that the dogs are vicious. If that same dog is attacked during future visits, by different dogs, it may indicate that the dog being attacked is submissive. Alpha dogs and other animal predators can smell weakness — maybe human predators can, too. Marco preyed on Francesca first, and then on me, and I have no doubt that, if given the chance, he would go after a new victim next. Francesca and I were both weak and, ultimately, we paid the price for our weakness, but Iliana is no longer going to be passive. I owe it to Rosa to change myself, not just my circumstances.

The *old* Iliana wishes she could be cocooned in Stefano's kindness, and allow him to pamper her like a princess, but I can't allow myself to be that woman anymore. I care about him — maybe someday I will be ready for a new relationship — but, for the time being, I need to be my own mate.

Stefano and I are sitting outside a café, sipping cappuccinos, and I couldn't feel more relaxed. Mom and Dad have taken Matteo to the park again, and Stefano and I went to see two apartments I found listed online. I am excited about starting my own life, and I am happy he is here to support me without stifling my need to feel independent.

"So, did you like either one of those places?" Stefano asks.

"I liked the first one. The second apartment looked a bit cramped, though the lower rent makes it attractive. Which one did you like?"

"Hmm…I like small places, so I thought the second one was more appealing. Very quaint," he replies.

"I would like to see a few more before I make a final decision. My parents are going with me to the bank to co-sign a small loan, but it is imperative I find a job as soon as possible."

"What are your skills?" Stefano inquires.

"I am good with art, and I can be very organized. I have a degree in business administration, but I have never done anything with it. I guess I could do anything to start—a secretarial job, maybe, or a position running a small business. I need to see what is available on the market, and then I will make a decision."

"I will ask around, too. I know a lot of people, thanks to my job. Maybe I will hear of an open position."

"I am not going to worry about it. I have worried about a multitude of things for the greater part of the last eight years, and I have learned that worrying doesn't help prevent or overcome problems. If anything, it clouds one's ability to see opportunities," I say, calmly.

"I am really proud of you," Stefano says, "and, although I wish we could be more than just friends, I understand."

"I also need to speak to a lawyer. I need to file for a divorce, and take back my own name. You know, women in Italy usually keep their maiden names, but I allowed Marco to talk me into using my married name on all official papers."

"It was a way for him to state his ownership of you," Stefano says. "I am glad you are changing your name back."

"Iliana Giannelli…I can't even remember the last time I used my maiden name, but I like the sound of it. Marco said that, if we were a family, we all needed to have the same last name. It didn't seem a battle worth fighting, so I went along with his wishes."

"I wish my mother could have had the same resolve. My father was horrible to her, and she did nothing about it. She never worked a day outside of the house, and my father treated her like a maid. He was a terrible alcoholic, and he was so incredibly abusive in the way he spoke to her, that my brothers and I grew to believe that it is normal to speak to someone like that. It wasn't until we were older, and went to our friends' houses, that we realized how differently their parents interacted with each other. I remember being in my friend's kitchen, one day, and his mother accidentally ruined dinner. His father came into the room when he heard her complaining, and he told her that it wasn't a big deal, and they could go out to dinner instead. I was flabbergasted by the father's reaction. My father would have surely been furious, and aside from verbally assaulting my mom, he would have probably smacked her around to 'teach her better.'"

"I can totally identify with that," I agree. "Marco had no tolerance for mistakes, unless they were his own. He didn't care if someone else was around. If he felt that he needed to punish me for something, he would do it in front of people, even if we were out. I hated that, and I would feel embarrassed when he would yank my arm to walk out of a store, or he grabbed my private parts in front of other people, allegedly joking."

"He did that? Even my father wasn't that bad."

"Oh, yes! We went to a dinner one night, and he had a couple of drinks too many. He walked by me, and he smacked my bottom. I didn't say anything to trigger his anger, but one of the other women in the room must have stared him down with a disapproving look, because he locked eyes with her, defiantly put a hand between my legs, and told her that he owned me and he could grab me if he wanted to. I was so embarrassed that it took every bit of self-control I could muster to not burst into tears, and I was glad when those friends didn't invite us back."

"Wow..." Stefano says. "I am so sorry you had to put up with such a bastard, Iliana. No woman ever should."

"I agree. As I continue on my journey of healing from the past, I would like to become active in helping other women who are dealing with abuse."

"It's a great idea," Stefano concedes. "I wouldn't mind volunteering with you. My father passed away a few years ago, and my mother stood by him to the end. I thought that, once my brothers and I were adults, she would leave him, but her excuse was that she couldn't abandon him. According to my mother, he had a rough childhood, and she always nurtured him. I honestly believe that he brainwashed her, made her feel...not so much guilty as ashamed."

"Where is your mom now?"

"She is still around. I think her mind has blocked many of the bad memories, so she can hold onto the good ones and not feel like she wasted her entire life. I think I always felt it was my fault, for not being able to protect her. Maybe helping other women who are struggling will help me, too."

"I would like to meet her, sometime," I say softly.

"I think she would like you a lot."

My cell phone rings, but the number is not a familiar one, and I almost don't answer. "Hello?"

"Mrs. Landini?" The voice on the other side of the line is as unfamiliar as the number.

"Yes?"

"This is Officer Pastella. I have Assistant Prosecutor Toglietti on the line for you."

"Okay, put him on, please."

The prosecutor takes the line and clears his throat. "Iliana, I am calling you to notify you of an accident at the jail."

"An accident? What sort of accident?"

"There is no good way to say this...Marco Landini was involved in a fight with another inmate, and..."

"Is he okay?" I ask, not sure how to feel. A part of me would be happy if my abuser was injured or dead, but Matteo would be sad if he lost his father.

"Unfortunately not, Iliana. It was a serious fight, and Marco was killed."

I gasp. There were many times when I had fervently wished Marco dead, and now I can't believe it has happened. I bury my face in my hands.

"Iliana," Stefano asks, concern etched on his face, "what is it? Who's on the phone?"

"It is Assistant Prosecutor Toglietti."

"Is everything okay?

I shake my head lightly from side to side, still in shock. "Marco is dead."

Stefano takes the phone gently from my hand, and talks to the prosecutor. Apparently, Marco and the other inmate started arguing, and the fight escalated quickly. Two other men jumped in and, although security officers intervened immediately, Marco suffered a blow to the side of his head that proved fatal.

Stefano hangs up and comes to sit by me. "Are you okay?"

"I'm not sure. On the one hand, I have hated Marco — and been terrified of him — for so long, that knowing he will never again be a threat to me gives me a sense of liberation. On the other hand, Matteo has lost a parent, and no matter how I look at it, it is one more trauma he must deal with."

"He will be all right, Iliana. My brother's wife is a therapist, and I am fairly sure she works with children. I can talk to her, if you want; even if Matteo is not ready to go see her, she might offer some input on how to help him."

"Poor Matteo! First, he almost lost his mother, and now his father is gone," I murmur, still stunned by the news.

Stefano lifts my chin. "I am here for you and Matteo. I am not his father, and I will never replace Marco in his life, but I can be a big brother figure for him, and make sure he has another man in his world, aside from your dad."

I nod softly, still numb. Stefano pays for our coffee, and we leave the café.

"You are still Marco's spouse, Iliana. Toglietti said that you need to sign some documents, for the body to be released to a funeral home. He also said that Marco's parents had not been notified yet, but because of the nature of his incarceration, he will call them, so you don't have to."

"I should still call his mother..." I whisper. "I can't even imagine how she will feel when she gets the news."

"She will be devastated, but life will go on. Her son was responsible for his own incarceration and — even though we don't know what the argument was about — given his temperament, it is likely he said the wrong thing to the wrong person. Marco was accustomed to preying on people he felt he could dominate, but he had no experience when it came to dealing with thugs."

"You know, Marco shared a secret with me, in the beginning of our relationship…I don't even know why I didn't think of this before."

"Yeah? What did he say?"

"He said that a male teacher molested him during a summer camp. He didn't share details of the abuse, but I suspect it was a traumatizing experience that scarred him for life. It didn't occur to me that Marco could have issues when it came to his sexuality, but when I asked Francesca if he had ever forced her into sexual acts she did not feel comfortable with, she said that, in her opinion, Marco had some problems. Her words got me thinking, but just now I am wondering if his anger toward women also stemmed from that incident."

"His actions were unjustifiable, Iliana. No matter what happened to him, he could have gotten help, instead of lashing out," Stefano says gently.

"I agree, Stefano, but maybe he didn't realize he had a problem. Anger was a part of him for so long that it became *him*. I think it was someone at *Transitions* who told me that we are often victims of victims, and that happy people don't lash out, or take pleasure in hurting others. Marco was a broken child who grew up into a broken adult, and he tried to destroy everything else around himself, in order to feel whole. For the first time since I can remember, I feel sorry for him, and I am ready to forgive."

Stefano looks at me, awe suffusing his eyes. "Are you sure you feel that way? You are one heck of a strong woman, Iliana."

"It's not that at all. Forgiving someone doesn't mean you condone their hurtful actions; it simply means that you no longer allow their actions to affect you. The dark side of Marco has lived in my head for a long time. It has frightened me, crippled me, and rendered me helpless, and I am ready to let it go. Marco is dead, and no amount of hatred I can cling to will change the past."

Stefano smiles. "I am falling deeper and deeper in love with you each passing day, Iliana. You have a beautiful soul, and a heart that could lift the entire world, and I don't care how long I have to wait, I will be here when you are ready. For now, I am honored to be your friend."

He takes my face into his hands, and kisses me lightly on the lips. Someday I will be whole again, and Stefano and I will be together as one.

EPILOGUE

It is a beautiful day in March. The sky is as blue as the eyes of an angel, with just a few fluffy clouds that make me think of cosmic cotton candy, and tree branches busy sprouting new life. Matteo woke up early this morning, ready to go to school, and I spent the morning hours running errands, and finalizing the details of Marco's funeral. His parents are struggling to come to terms with his death, so I offered to help, against the advice of my own parents — who feel I should just let his family deal with the arrangements. I no longer hate Marco. Realizing that he was a broken soul who was blinded by hatred helped me release him from my life. I will never forget the pain he has inflicted on me, but hanging onto the bitterness is not going to help anyone, especially Matteo. There aren't many good memories of Marco and Matteo together that I can recall, but I will do my best to tell my son about those moments, because believing that his father was a good man under the surface will help him grow into a better adult.

Matteo bursts out of the bus before the doors are completely open. "I am ready to go to the park, Mommy!"

I hold his hand walking back to Stefano's apartment. "Stefano has made a picnic for us. We can go as soon as we bring the backpack upstairs."

As promised, Stefano has two bags full of sandwiches ready for us on the table, along with three bottles of soda. The drive to the park takes about ten minutes, and I am a little apprehensive as I cross through the gate, my mind racing back to the day I came with Olivia. We hear children squealing with delight in the distance, and Matteo springs toward the sound, like a sailor pulled by a siren song. He is so excited to play that we can barely hold him at the bench long enough to gobble a sandwich before charging the swings.

How different it is, being here with my son and Stefano, this time! I think back to the little boy who came running toward Olivia and me that day, and how his babysitter ignored us when she came to retrieve the boy. I assumed she was simply rude — or merely absorbed in her own thoughts — when she didn't acknowledge us, but now I wonder if she just couldn't see us. The little boy did, of that I am sure, and he locked eyes with us and smiled when he approached the bench. I have heard that young children see spirits, but lose that ability as they get older, because they begin questioning what is real and what is not. I look around the park, wondering how many lost souls are here right now. Maybe some of them reside at *Transitions*.

"Are you ready to go, champ?" Stefano calls out to Matteo, after the little girl with whom he has been playing has gone. "I was thinking we should go for ice cream. I know of a place not too far from here that has the best ice cream. Are you in?"

Matteo runs to us, his cheeks pink and his forehead moist from playing hard. "Did you say ice cream?" he asks, more excited than anyone should be about a cone of ice cream.

Stefano leads us out of the park, and we take an immediate left, before continuing across the town square.

"We are almost there. This place has the best pastries and ice cream I have ever had. I haven't been in a while, since my business relocated, but I used to eat lunch there a lot." Stefano says, and we follow behind.

I cannot believe my eyes when we arrive in front of the same café Olivia and I visited the day we came to San Gabriele, and to my surprise, the "Closed" sign is still on the door.

"Oh, no!" Stefano says as he peeks through the glass and sees that all the equipment is gone. "What happened? I can't believe this place closed down..."

A tiny black cat comes trotting out of the narrow alleyway, and rubs against our legs.

"Buddha!" I exclaim, amazed that the cat exists in this dimension.

"The man who owned the café fed him, and he never left." A woman's voice filters through, causing me to turn my head.

"What happened to the owner of the café? Did he sell the business?" I ask, curious.

"No," the woman replies, looking at the little cat with sadness in her eyes. "He died of a stroke about two months ago. I don't know what will happen to this little guy; unfortunately, he can't come home with me, because my landlord does not accept pets."

I stroke Buddha's fur, and he arches his back toward my hand, purring.

"Claudio really cared about you, Buddha, and he was nice to me," I say to the cat. "I hate to leave you here, fending for yourself."

"Well..." Stefano interrupts, "I could use a cat. I hear they are great at catching flies, and I hate flies."

I glance at Stefano, first, and then at Matteo, who's holding his breath waiting for me to voice my decision. When I finally lay eyes on the old shopkeeper, I can't help smiling at her, amused by the puzzled look on her face. This poor woman doesn't know the back story...she doesn't know Buddha and I have met before, in another time and a different reality, and Buddha is my earthly link to *Transitions*.

To Matteo's delight, I pick up Buddha in my arms, and kiss his tiny head. Sardines, Claudio said — Buddha loves sardines. "We will need to go to the grocery store later, and pick up some sardines for Buddha."

Matteo and Stefano are both surprised that I already have a name for the cat, but neither questions my choice. Buddha relaxes in my arms and purrs contentedly into my ear. I started this journey alone, and Buddha's owner took care of me; now that Buddha is alone, it is time for me to return the favor. "Don't worry about Buddha, Claudio, I've got him…and thank you for lunch," I whisper, blowing a kiss to the sky.

www.ingramcontent.com/pod-product-compliance
Lightning Source LLC
Chambersburg PA
CBHW030917120626
46554CB00001B/182